The Waves Break Gray

by Sibella Giorello

Published by Running Girl Productions
Contact the author at sibella@sibellagiorello.com

Print Edition

Printed in the United States of America or the country of purchase.

This book is dedicated to my husband, Joe, for bringing so much love and laughter into my life. And for always finding time to dream out loud.

And freedom, oh freedom, well, that's just some people talkin'
Your prison is walking through this world all alone

~ "Desperado"

CHAPTER ONE

ALL MY LIFE I've run from love.

"Harmon!"

Fifteen yards ahead, FBI Special Agent Jack Stephanson sprinted down the mountain trail. I could catch him. Easy.

"Better kick into gear!" he yelled.

I could pass him. Win this race.

But at this very moment, liquid gold sunshine poured over the silver-granite mountains that surrounded us like a metal bowl. It was bittersweet October light, the kind that balanced summer's fading ease and winter's coming darkness—always whispering the warning.

Savor this moment.

"Loser!" Jack glanced over his shoulder.

I picked up speed as he leaped for the boulders that formed a disjointed path above the trail. The large rocks led to a cave. Crouching like a cat, I vaulted over the rocks, right hand raised, so ready to tag that cave.

"And the winner—" Jack lunged, "—is—"

The cave was inches from my hand. But a stench hit me.

Jack slapped the cave's mouth. "—me!"

One split second behind him, I brushed my hand against the stone wall. It felt cold. Damp.

"Thought you—" Jack doubled over, hands on his knees,

panting. "Wanted to race."

"I did." My nose wrinkled. I glanced into the cave's gaping black mouth. The odor was rank. Mildewy, and stomach-churning. "So catch your breath."

He looked up. Jack's eyes were blue-green, a color that could shift like sharkskin. The colors always made my heart trip.

"What?" he asked.

"We're only halfway." I smiled. "So catch your breath. You still have to run back."

"Wait, what—" Sweat dripped from his angular face. "You're saying the race is round-trip?"

"And the winner buys lunch. That was the deal." I opened my arms, taking in this dusty mountain trail, the towering North Cascade peaks, the Icicle River flowing fast below us. "Do you see a burger joint around here?" I pretended to search the area. "Nope. Not here. That means we have to run back into town."

"Harmon."

"Yes?"

He lifted the edge of his white T-shirt, wiping the sweat from his square chin. He had a good face.

No.

A great face.

The kind of face that said way back in his DNA some warring Viking bred with a high-born Anglican, and ever since, that domineering masculinity had kept marrying intellectual ability.

I could've stared at that face all day. Or stared at the holstered Glock under his T-shirt. Instead my gaze was pulled to his flat stomach. Twelve-pack of abs with a V-pattern of brown hair peeking above the waistband of his shorts. The hair grew in a twinning pattern, like the crystal named orthoclase.

Like feathers. Like—my mind grasped for any example of when two symmetrical sides are joined at the middle—*elm leaves?*—pleading with my mind to convince me those washboard abs were nothing special.

"Harmon."

It didn't work.

"What?" I looked up.

"You don't play fair."

"Gee, I wonder who taught me *that* trick?"

He laughed.

Weightless laughter. Free as sunlight. It moved around us as effortlessly as the water paddling down the river below. A musical sound with nothing cynical attached. Real laughter. The sound that said nothing bad could touch it. And it sounded so good that I started to laugh with him. But as soon as my throat opened, I felt myself pulling back. My feet hadn't moved one inch from this stinking cave yet my mind was already leaving, separating me from Jack, from his laughter, from the sunlight that brushed his russet hair. From … life.

"Okay, that's it." I pivoted. "Let's go."

Jumping down the rocks, I landed on the flat trail and was about to take off when he grabbed me. In one controlled move, he spun me around and hooked his elbow around my neck. The rear naked choke hold—I knew this move—Quantico taught it to us.

Quantico also taught us how to break the hold.

I grabbed his bicep. The hard muscles rippled under my fingertips.

He whispered, hot in my ear. "Surrender."

"Never."

"Never's long time."

"Exactly." I shifted my hips, bent at the waist. One more pivot and … I looked up.

My oxygen should be gone by now.

"That cave stinks," he said.

"It's a cave." I shrugged. "Caves stink."

"And yet you still want to check it out?" His eyes were the color of the mineral azurite.

"Of course." I shifted my gaze. The expression in those eyes. I found myself staring at his throat. Whiskers. Same color as that hair on his stomach.... *Stop or you'll—*

"Harmon."

"What."

"I want to ask you something." His voice was close, and hoarse. Raw. "You need to answer honestly."

"Okay."

"*Really* honest."

"Jack, I'm always—"

The dog barked.

The sound fractured the autumn air. I spun out of the choke hold and looked down the trail. It was empty. Stone. Gravel. Falling aspen leaves. No dog. I glanced at the river. White water flowed out of the mountains, breaking gray on the rocks. No dog.

She barked again.

"Madame?" I lifted my hand, blocking the morning sun, and scanned the steep hillside. Granite. Pine trees. Blue sky. "Madame, where are you?"

She barked again. *Urgent.* Only this time the bark sounded like an echo. Distant, retreating. *Hurry.*

Panic bolted through my heart. "Where is she?"

Jack sighed. "I told you that dog would be trouble."

I moved toward the sound of her bark. It seemed to be coming from above. But how did she get up there? She was running behind me. I'd taken off her leash as soon as we came off the main road. She hates leashes. And she never runs off unless …

"Something's wrong."

"I'll say." Jack pointed wearily toward the rock face. "It sounds like she's up there."

I grabbed the bristly limbs of the pine trees and pulled myself up over the dry loose soil. Sap clung to my fingers and the soil slipped under my shoes. About fifteen yards above the cave, I found a narrow trail.

"Madame!"

She barked. I was closer. But she sounded even more insistent.

I ran up the trail, heading into the morning sun. My shoes kicked up dust, the drought-stricken grains skittering down the mountainside and falling on the trail below, plunking into the river.

"Madame—where are you?"

I wanted to sprint, but the trail was too narrow and too steep. My right hand stayed on the rock face as I balanced my way down the path that was no more than eighteen inches wide. The mountainside plunged on my left.

"Madame!"

She barked. Twice.

I sped up. A hundred feet later, the mountain split apart and I came to a meadow. A breeze swayed wheat grass and pale wild flowers, revealing the small black dog that sat waiting.

She barked and stood up.

"Alright," I ran to her. "Alright. I'm here."

But she didn't run to me. She stayed fixed to her position, to the grass, to whatever she'd trapped there.

I moved slowly, carefully. Here on the eastern side of the Cascade Mountains, the high desert climate was perfect for rattlesnakes and poisonous spiders. "Madame, don't move."

She didn't move.

But when I reached her, it was no rattlesnake. No spider.

It was human—or part of one—sticking up out of the ground. The fingers had turned deep purple, that sickening jewel-toned hue I'd seen only one other place. The morgue.

Behind me, I heard Jack say, "What did I tell you?"

I turned. He was coming up the trail, head down, panting slightly from the climb.

"I told you that dog would be a problem," he continued. "But, no, you *had* to bring her."

I watched the sun light up his great face, all his annoyance mixed with his amusement. And right then, right there, I knew it. Things would never be the same again.

I stepped back.

"What'd she find, a snake?" he asked.

"I wish."

His gaze drifted down to the ground, then locked on the hand. The wrist was torqued, like someone had been waving from the ground.

When Jack looked back at me, his green eyes were changing to blue.

Police blue.

CHAPTER TWO

SEVENTEEN MINUTES LATER, standing with Jack in the high mountainside meadow, I watched as two vehicles raced down the road.

One car was a blue state trooper cruiser. The other was a white wagon. Both turned into the gravel parking area for the Icicle Creek Trail.

"That's right," Jack was saying into his cell phone, standing beside me. "And I need a list of all missing persons for this area." There was a pause. He glanced over his shoulder, staring at the hand. What was left of it. "Can't tell. But it's small enough that I want to say female."

Madame quivered in my arms. Her black fur felt warm from the sun beating down on us. I watched the parking lot below. An officer got out of each vehicle. One wore a blue uniform—the trooper. The officer driving the white wagon wore brown. A local deputy, I figured. He started running. The trooper in blue followed, but struggled down the trail.

I lifted Madame and whispered in her ear. "Good girl."

"Gotta go." Jack disconnected the call and moved down this higher trail to meet the new arrivals.

As he walked away, I reached into my fanny pack and took out my cell phone. Turning toward the site I never wanted to see again, I snapped several dozen photos. Panoramics that showed the setting. Close-ups that identified the hand. And the soil. Dry soil. Uncompacted. A pale beige color, it was soil that geologists call *loess*. German for "loose." Soil that gets carried by wind or water or gravity, and deposited somewhere other than where it originated. With the granite peaks above us, the crests stabbing the clear autumn sky like knives, my best guess was that winter ice and snow had deposited this loess.

"Thanks for coming so quickly," Jack was saying.

I glanced over my shoulder. He was leading both officers up the trail. Quickly, I selected the photos and sent them to Peter Rosser, a forensic geologist. I put the phone back in my fanny pack.

"We took a run on the lower trail," Jack said, pointing.

The officers squinted in that direction. They were surprisingly young, maybe mid-twenties. Beefy, like farm boys who had played high school football. I was zipping my pack as Jack introduced them. Deputy Seiler, the officer in brown. And the state trooper, Officer Wilcove. Both had blond buzz cuts and pale eyes. If it wasn't for the uniforms, I'd have trouble telling them apart.

"And this is Raleigh Harmon," Jack said. "She's …"

I could almost hear his mind searching for what to call me. Raleigh Harmon, *former FBI agent?* Raleigh Harmon, *persona non grata with the federal government?*

"Raleigh Harmon." I held out my hand. "Forensic geologist."

Deputy Seiler had narrow gray eyes. He squinted them at me. "Forensic—"

"Whoa!" Officer Wilcove pointed. "That's a—that's a—"

"Dispatch didn't tell you?" Jack studied him. "I said there was a body."

Seiler's gray eyes filled with horror. But he had more self-control. Swallowing hard, he looked away and said, "Dispatch told us some hikers with a dog found a body."

He glanced once more at the purple hand with the torqued wrist, then he looked at me. He squinted again. "Your dog needs to be on a leash. That's the law."

All three men stared at Madame. She replied with an uncertain wag, then looked up at me. The fur between her shoulders spiked. I ran my hand over it. "The dog didn't touch the body."

"Good," Seiler said. "You got a leash for her?"

I pulled her leash from my pack. Seiler lifted his radio and confirmed that a body had been found, that the dog had been loose, and that somebody needed to contact Evidence Recovery. I glanced at Wilcove. As the state trooper, he should be taking the lead here. State patrol ran the top evidence recovery team. But all Wilcove was doing was licking his thin lips, like a man on the verge of vomiting. I didn't blame him. In my ten years with the Bureau, I saw plenty of sickening things, both in the lab as a forensic geologist and in the field as an agent. But this hand—waving for help or clawing for life or pleading for mercy—ranked near the top.

Seiler holstered his radio. "They're coming."

Wilcove licked his lips, wiped sweat from his forehead. "You think it's her?"

Seiler's gaze flicked at him, a warning to be quiet.

"Her, who?" Jack asked.

"Nobod—" Seiler started to say.

"Annicka Engels." Wilcove cut him off. "She's been missing since last week."

"What happened?" Jack glanced at Seiler.

Seiler said nothing.

"Troubled teen?" Jack asked.

Seiler stayed quite.

"Oh, Annicka wasn't in trouble." Wilcove said. He was an eruption of nerves. "She wasn't in any kind of trouble. She was perfect."

"Perfect," Jack said.

"Well, I mean ..." Wilcove's sweating face reddened even more. "She got a full athletic scholarship to U-dub."

U-dub. UW. Otherwise known as the University of Washington. A Pac-10 school. If she had a full athletic scholarship, she was a serious athlete. I glanced back at the hand. My eyes burned.

"Any suspects?" Jack asked.

"Her boyfriend," Wilcove said. "Everyone around here suspects the boyfriend."

Seiler lifted a hand, halting the discussion. "Do you two have some ID?"

"Good call, deputy." Jack reached under his shirt, exposing the hip-holstered Glock, and removed the small leather case clipped next to the gun. When he held out his credentials, sunlight stuck the FBI's gold seal. The stars glinted.

"Thanks." Seiler looked at me, waiting.

"I didn't bring my cards." I lifted Madame. "Just thought we were running in the mountains."

"And it would've been if you'd obeyed the law," Seiler said. "You expect me to believe you didn't see that big sign at the entrance, the one that says all dogs have to be on leashes?"

"I missed it." But I was getting a good look at the embroidered patch on his shoulder. *Chelan County Animal Control.* I glanced at Jack. Maybe there was a fine. "We were running pretty fast. But you're right, officer."

I gave the leash I'd clipped to her collar a slight tug, showing him my new lawful obedience. Madame gave me a look. In her mind, leashes were punishment. I stroked her back and resisted the urge to blurt out: *If I'd leashed my dog, nobody would've found this body—which might be the girl who's already been missing an entire week.*

But I kept my mouth shut. I was learning.

"Ma'am," Seiler was taking charge. The Animal Control Nazi. "Please step away from the scene. Deputy Wilcove will take your statement."

I glanced at Jack again. But what could he say? I was banished, no longer part of the law enforcement clan. And maybe I imagined it, but some of the blue in Jack's eyes was turning green again.

Holding Madame in my arms, I followed Deputy Wilcove down the trail. She kept lifting her nose, sniffing something. I took a deep breath. *No.* I took another sniff. *Couldn't be.* Wilcove kept walking. The wind blew his scent toward us. *French fries?* He moved further and further away, until we were almost back to the cave. Far away from the waving hand.

"That's better," he said, turning around.

"Excuse me?"

"That hand." He wiped his sweating face with the back of his wrist. "Oh, man."

"What about it."

"I don't want to be anywhere near it," he said.

I nodded.

But I was thinking, *That makes one of us.*

CHAPTER THREE

THREE HOURS LATER, sitting in Jack's float plane with Madame on my lap, I couldn't decide if the fluttery feeling inside my chest was from the turbulent updrafts bumping his plane over the Cascade Mountains, or that the pilot was admonishing me.

"Harmon." Jack raised his voice to be heard over the plane's engine. "You can't keep telling people how to do their job."

I pet Madame.

"What were you thinking?" he asked.

"I was thinking that soil samples are crucial, and they're not taking any soil samples. That's what I was thinking."

"Terrific. But you kept lecturing them on how to do it."

"Because—"

"And that's why they kept questioning you. But as soon as they started that, you demanded we leave."

"So …"

"So it looked suspicious."

"Did not."

"Did."

"Not."

"Also," he continued, "they're going to do a background check on you and see that you used to be with the FBI. Then they'll wonder why you left. Or if you got fired—"

"I *resigned.* And the real point is soil samples."

"Those guys are not geologists."

"And I was being honest. I really did have to leave."

"But they don't know that!" He looked away, glancing out the plane's side window.

I stared at his profile, that face as strong and solid as the peaks around us. When he finally looked back at me, his mirrored aviator sunglasses reflected my face. Sunburned nose. Forehead wrinkled with worry. Brown hair and ponytail messy from running. *Lovely.*

"Harmon, all those guys see is a witness at a crime scene who knew way too much about evidence collection. Who somehow, magically, found the body—"

"Madame." I pointed to the dog in my lap. "Madame found the body."

"That's even worse."

I stroked the dog's fur, fluffed with anxiety. Every stroke felt like an attempt to wipe away this whole awful day. At dawn, we'd flown out of Seattle for a day in the town of Leavenworth. Neither Jack nor I dared to call this outing a "date." Our relationship—or whatever it was—tottered on new ground. Former colleagues in the Bureau. Former avowed enemies. Former friends? And now we were …what?

Today was supposed to provide answers.

Instead I got a dead body.

And yes, I had explained the soil collection procedures to Wilcove and Seiler. When a tech from evidence collection finally arrived, I repeated the procedures and looked at my watch. It was time to go. Wilcove took my statement three times before driving us into town. His cruiser smelled like French fries.

"Harmon, just admit it. You really want to be the one doing the collection."

"No. I've got obligations."

"Yeah." Jack took a deep breath. I couldn't hear his sigh over the engine noise but his chest rose and fell. Twice. "But why do you have to make yourself look like a suspect?"

"Okay, let's take a probability quiz," I said. "Some woman from Seattle goes all the way over to Leavenworth—which, by the way, would take three hours by car. She kills somebody. For whatever reason. And somehow she manages to carry the dead weight up a steep mountain. She also carries some kind of tool so she can dig a hole and bury the body. Then, she goes home. A week or so later, she returns to the scene of the crime—with an FBI agent and her dog—only to 'discover' the body. Give me the probability, Jack."

He looked over.

"Right," I said. "Start with point one percent."

"We've both seen weirder things," he said.

He was right. And I hated it. But would I admit it? Never. I looked out my side window. Mountains upon mountains. Plateaus. Ice-milk glaciers that persisted through summer. Washington state was one of the most beautiful places I'd ever seen. It was fantastic geology.

"Your statement," Jack said.

I kept my gaze on the window. Charcoal clouds gathered on the western side of the mountain pass, like hordes of barbarian raindrops waiting to invade the drought-stricken eastern side. "Can we change the subject?"

"Your statement sounded resentful."

"Did not."

"Did."

"Not."

"Just like you sound right now."

"I'm fine." I stared at the dark clouds, their grays marbling.

"Imagine what would've happened if you'd taken that gun with you," Jack said. "You'd be in real trouble, Harmon. Which reminds me, have you even applied for a concealed carry permit?"

"I don't have time." The clouds were the same gunmetal gray as the Sig Sauer that Jack gave me after I left the Bureau. Protection I couldn't afford to buy. "Look, all I was doing was making sure the geology evidence got collected the right way. So it could offer clues. And stand up in court. That's all I wanted."

"And you could've done it yourself. Just take the job."

"I can't take the job so quit bugging me!"

I wanted back the words as soon as I blurted them. *Resentment?* It dripped from every syllable. Jack was right. I wanted to stay at that crime scene. Investigate all day, all night, fueled by the passion to nail the creep who caused such a tragedy.

But I couldn't.

I stroked the dog and controlled my voice. "If I didn't have to be at the—"

"You don't have to explain. Really. I understand."

I glanced over. Those russet whiskers were even thicker than this morning. So thick this day might be two days pressed together. So much *time.* I glanced at my watch. Already noon.

"You'll make it," Jack said.

I looked out the window and saw the town of Snoqualmie. Tidy houses spread from a wide river and climbed hills golden with autumn trees. But the clouds overhead promised rain.

Jack reached out. Madame lifted her head.

"When will that dog trust me?" he asked, his hand hovering.

"When you're safe."

He nodded. “Harmon?”

I waited.

“I understand,” he said. “Really.”

There was no teasing in his voice. No playfulness. Not even one drop of sarcasm.

And somehow, it only made me feel even worse.

CHAPTER FOUR

THE CRAZY PEOPLE closed in.

Lady Anne.

Bad Knight.

Father Brother, dipping his filthy fingers into the paper cup and flinging "holy water" into the mental asylum air at Western State Hospital. I prayed that water didn't come from a toilet.

And yet, Father Brother wasn't even the worst of the patients living side-by-side on this ward with my mother.

The worst patient was Sir Post-it. The ringleader. An insane bully, he ran this small wing like his fellow patients were nothing but serfs in his feudal kingdom. I didn't know his real name. But he wore yellow sticky notes on the first of his three chins. And right now, as I stood beside my mom with her dog, Sir Post-it proclaimed the afternoon's new ridiculous decree.

"By order of decree," he said, the yellow paper flapping up and down like hinged chin on a ventriloquist's dummy, "all vermin are banished from my kingdom."

My mother cradled the dog in her arms. "But Madame isn't vermin."

"Vermin have fur." Sir Post-it pointed his fat index finger. "That dog has fur. *Ergo didacto—*"

"Ergo *didacto*?" I glanced around, hoping someone understood that no such Latin phrase existed. But all that came back were glassy-eyed stares.

"Ergo didcato, et cetera and et cetera," Sir Post-it continued. "That dog is vermin."

On the other side of this recreation room—a disinfected rectangle of shiny white vinyl and windows embedded with chicken wire and guarded by iron bars—a red-headed nurse stood behind a high counter. She was depositing pills into paper muffin cups. "Yeah, man," said Father Brother, dipping his dirty fingers into the paper cup, "that dog has fleas."

"And fleas carry the plague," said Bad Knight.

"I don't want the plague," said Lady Anne.

"Okay, stop." I held up my hand. "Madame does not have fleas."

"You!" Bad Knight stepped forward and pointed his "sword." A limp oblong of aluminum, he'd cobbled the sword together from all the foil that covered their hot meals. "Peasants are not allowed to speak to his highness directly. If you have something to say, you must tell me first. Then I might pass it along to his highness. And I might not."

The saddest part of this whole situation?

These lunatics were an improvement from the people my mom used to be housed with. Several months ago, she'd suffered a psychotic break—triggered by me, her daughter, the peasant—which led to an involuntarily commitment to Western State. For most of the months, she'd refused to see me. Finally, I got permission to bring her dog. Then I got permission to stay during the visits. Day by day, I was earning back her trust. I vowed never to lose it again.

"Banish the vermin!" Sir Post-it bellowed.

"Oh, my lands!" My mom's southern accent pitched higher. "Please don't do that. It's not right. *Please.*"

The troubled look in her hazel eyes punched my gut. I held

up both hands, once more signaling Stop. The same way you communicate with preschoolers.

"My mom's dog is not vermin," I said, trying to restrain my tone. "And the dog isn't leaving. Period."

His highness of office products stepped toward me. Standing toe-to-toe, he opened his mouth and the flapping yellow paper wafted his putrid breath toward me. "How dare you defy me, you peasant."

My eyes watered from the stench. I forced myself not to blink. "The. Dog. Stays. Period. End of discussion."

"Vermin!" he cried.

He was loud enough that the nurse behind the counter looked up. I leaned to the side, getting some fresh air while I tried to signal her attention. She went right back to the pills. This particular ward was supposed to work out its conflicts. On their own. That was a big part of their "improvement."

"Guess what my husband's name is?" Lady Anne said.

She waited for us to make some connection. Nobody did.

"Virgil!"

Oh, no. My mother got it. "Isn't that strange," she said. "Virgil *sounds* like vermin."

"Virgil knows everything." Lady Anne wore a crown of red pipe cleaners in her curly gray hair—another improvement, since pipe cleaners were otherwise dangerous craft products. "Virgil builds rockets for Boeing."

"Who cares?" Bad Knight waved his foil sword. "Nobody wants to hear about your stupid husband."

"Virgil isn't stupid."

"He married you."

Lady Anne tilted her head, wondering.

"And only a dummy would marry you, dummy." Bad Knight glanced at Sir Post-it for affirmation. "Correct, your highness?"

"Verily."

"Yes." Lady Anne stared down at her worn green slippers. The red pipe cleaners slipped forward. "I guess that's true."

"That's not true." My mom moved to her side. "Lady Anne, I'm sure Virgil loves you very much. Just like my David loved me."

Lady Anne shook her head, the crown slipping further. "Nobody loves me."

"How about I forgive you?" Father Brother dipped his dirty fingers. When the water hit her, Lady Anne didn't so much as flinch.

Madame growled.

"Vermin!" Father Brother flung more water.

Madame barked.

"Rabid vermin!"

My mom clutched Madame so tightly she almost choked her. The dog shot me a desperate glance. I reached out, resting my hand on her small head, hoping to calm her. My heart pounded. Fear. Anger. Resentment. *Why doesn't that nurse come over—*

"Your highness, banish this vermin!" Bad Knight lifted his foil sword. "I plead your permission, your lease!"

"Lease?" My mother was suddenly distracted by the word. "Lease … lease. *Lease*?"

"He means *liege*." I took her elbow as gently as possible and led her away. "Let's go to your room."

She was still holding the dog like a drowning baby but turned to look at the group. Her once-glossy black hair fell flat, hanging in ragged strips turning gray.

"Lease!" Bad Knight came trailing behind us. "The word is *lease*."

I glanced over my shoulder. Everyone was following. *Crud.* I tried to pick up our pace but my mom wasn't strong and the fifteen-foot hallway suddenly seemed longer than a football field.

"I know I'm right," he persisted. "And if you weren't so dumb you would know his highness owns everything. See? We're just *leasing*. Get it now?"

"Lease ..." My mom. One word can hook her troubled mind and yank her right out of reality. "Lease, least, east . . ."

"Virgil would know the word," Lady Anne said. "Virgil knows everything."

I sped up.

"But we can't ask Virgil because he never comes to see you."

I tried to walk even faster but a keening sound filled the air. My mom halted and Madame gave a howl, harmonizing with the sound of crying.

"Lady Anne?" My mom asked. "Are you alright?"

Bad Knight swung his foil sword like a conductor's baton. Father Brother—finally out of water—flung dry dirty fingers. And Sir Post-it stared at the broken-hearted woman with such contempt the sticky note on his fat chin trembled.

"Mom," I said, "I think we should go to your—"

They were talking. All of them at once. Crazy chatter so loud it took me several moments to identify the other sound. *Trumpets.* Blaring trumpets. I dug my hand into my pocket and tried to silence the Tijuana Brass ringtone before anyone noticed it was coming from my cell phone.

Too late.

"That song." Bad Knight's foil sword switched tempos, now conducting the horns. "Yes, I know that song!"

"So do I." Lady Anne looked up, her wet eyes bright with distraction.

"Yes, uh huh—" Father Brother pronounced, "—that song is Burt Bacharach."

"Wrong!" Bad Knight aimed the sword at my hand holding the phone. "That's Frank Sinatra and I should know. We played poker together in Vegas. Ol' Blue Eyes borrowed ten dollars from me. And he never paid me back."

"Impossible," said Sir Post-it. "I banished Sinatra to the dungeon."

I stared at the Caller ID. I normally shut off my cell phone before coming in here. My mother's been diagnosed as paranoid schizophrenic. Cell phones are suspicious. But I was rushing today, frantic from the morning's events with Jack. I looked up. My mom was the only person paying attention. Too much attention. Her hazel eyes flinty as jasper, filled with suspicion. I smiled, slid my finger over the screen, and said, "Hi, Peter, how are you?"

"Bacharach!" cried Lady Anne. "Virgil's mother gave us that glass for our wedding."

There was a pause on the phone. "Raleigh?" said Peter Rosser.

I kept my gaze on my mom. And kept smiling. *Yeah, this is what I get for lying to her.* I smiled even harder. "Yes, Peter, it's me."

"And then," Lady Anne raised her voice, "I smashed all that glass in her driveway. Take that, Mommy Dearest!"

The phone was silent.

I waited.

Peter's voice had a cowboy twang. Right now it sounded extra twangy. "Where're in the world are you hanging out?"

"Just visiting my mom." I smiled. *See? Nothing to hide.* "How are you?"

"Dandy." He paused. "You want me to call you back?"

Absolutely.

"No." Ending the call right now would make her even more suspicious. "Go right ahead, Peter."

"I ran a check on missing persons in that area."

I pressed phone against my ear so tightly it hurt. I didn't want her to overhear any of this information. "That's great."

"There's a recent report on one Annicka Engels. Is that the one they mentioned?"

"I believe so."

"She went home for the weekend, from college. Took a run. Serious runner, apparently. Dog went with her. The dog came home. She didn't."

They were staring at me, all of them suddenly diverted from their bizarre discussion of my ringtone.

"Isn't that interesting." I reached out, gently guiding my mom toward her room. The single. The single room that had taken weeks for me to negotiate. My next step was getting her out of this place.

"You are totally wrong!" Bad Knight shouted. "Totally!"

"Raleigh?" Peter asked.

"Still here."

"The state police are gonna need some help with this case," he said. "The new guy, one who took over for me?"

"Yes."

"He isn't a geologist. How about you drive up there tomorrow?"

I said nothing. The chief shrink here had already warned me. If I missed one day of visiting hours, I'd lose every inch I'd gained with her. Paranoia was a wily enemy. It sprung to life on the tiniest changes. It would probably come alive just from my phone ringing.

"I know," Peter drawled. "You got some obligations. But my case load's filled the barn or I'd wrangle up there myself. Plus you got that mighty quick car of yours …"

We stepped into my mom's room. She held Madame and sat down on her bed. The mattress had no sheets. Sheets were dangerous. Instead, plastic covered the mattress. Plastic the color of skim milk. She placed Madame beside her. The plastic crinkled. The crowd stood at the door.

"Burt Bacharach is not made of glass!"

"What about Sinatra!"

"Raleigh?"

"Still here." I stared into her hazel eyes, dark with cloudy thoughts. All that medication. The suspicion. Me. "It's great to hear from you, Peter."

"You want me to call back later?"

"Yes. Thank you."

I disconnected the call, slid the phone into my pocket, and smiled so hard my eyes hurt.

"I say, Smash all the glass!"

I pushed the door shut. It slammed.

My mom jumped.

"Sorry." I leaned against the door. "Didn't realize it was so light."

She stared at me. After a moment she turned toward the putty-colored wall above her bed. With a finger, she traced invisible letters on wall. "Lease." She spelled it on the wall. "Least. East." Her fingernails were ragged.

"Mom—"

"Once upon a time, once upon a time. Once upon a time, he was nice."

My hands went numb. "Who's that?"

"You don't know him."

The door pushed against my back. I stepped away, ready for the assault, but it was the nurse. She held a small tray, topped with the muffin cups of pills. And small paper cups of water. The kind Father Brother used.

"Raleigh," she said. "These doors must stay open. You know the rules."

"Right. Sorry."

She walked over to my mom. Her name was Sarah. She had red hair that was the color of autumn maples. "Nadine, are you feeling alright?"

"Henry said Madame was vermin."

Henry, that was his name. Maybe.

Sarah glanced back at me. The expression in her blue eyes made me swear to never to complain about any job ever again. "Was he acting up?"

"Uh, yeah."

"Madame isn't vermin," my mom said.

Madame wagged her tail.

Sarah offered a muffin cup of pills. My mother looked inside. Then looked at Sarah.

"You know me, Nadine." The nurse smiled. "I was here yesterday. And I'll be here tomorrow. And the next day. I'm here to help you."

I held my breath as my mom lifted each pill slowly, as if she expected them to explode.

"You're doing great, Nadine." The nurse took the muffin cup and water cup, and passed me on her way out.

"Four minutes," she whispered.

I sat down on the bed. Madame, symbolically, sat between us. My mom scooped her into her arms.

"Will you be here tomorrow?"

I couldn't tell who she was asking. So I said, "We will."

Twenty-two hours until the next visit. And each goodbye felt worse than the one before, like some Greek curse—say goodbye again and again and again. Say goodbye today, say goodbye tomorrow. Say goodbye forever.

"Will you be going out tonight?" She wouldn't look at me.

"Not tonight." My throat ached with every word. "But earlier today I went on a date."

She looked up. I saw a familiar light in her eyes. Hopeful. Good light. "What did you do?"

"Hiked." My eyes stung. "In the mountains."

"Was it with DeMott?"

DeMott. My former fiancé. From Virginia. The man my mother spent years praying I'd marry. I opened my mouth, wondering how to explain—*Mom, we are not in Virginia, and DeMott is gone*—the electronic bell rang.

Visiting hours were over.

I stood. My legs felt made of ice.

My mom leaned into the dog, and whispered in her ear. "I can't wait to see you tomorrow."

CHAPTER FIVE

THIRTY-TWO MINUTES LATER, I opened the back door of a historic Victorian in Tacoma's North End and leapt from the fire into the frying pan.

"You're late," said Eleanor Anderson.

I held the door for Madame who was relieving herself on the back lawn. "Traffic messed with my time."

"Time?" Eleanor was eighty-four, tiny as a teacup, yet had a bellowing voice that could reach the cheap seats. The projection was left over from her days acting in a Tennessee Williams troupe. To this day, the playwright's lines still fell from her lipsticked mouth. "Time rushes toward us with its hospital of infinitely varied narcotics."

Like that.

I closed the door.

"Who said that?" she asked.

"You did."

Madame trotted across the large kitchen to her water bowl.

"Tennessee himself uttered those words." Eleanor stabbed four stuffed green olives with a long toothpick and dropped them into her martini glass. Every night, at precisely five o'clock, she enjoyed a dirty martini with a splash of lecture.

"Never forget those words, Raleigh."

I opened the fridge, found a can of Coca-Cola, and followed Eleanor into the living room. She wore yellow ballet slippers that somehow matched her violet trousers. They helped her sashay over the oriental rugs. Even by my historic Virginia standards, this old house was impressive. But it was jammed with ten million knickknacks from Eleanor's world travels with her late husband, Harry, a wealthy businessman.

"We could toast your health," she said, gracefully depositing herself into her favorite plush green chair. "But you're ingesting poison."

Just for that, I opened the Coke can slowly, savoring its singular sigh of carbonated splendor—*ffffffftt*. Raising the can to Eleanor's martini, we sipped. Her keen brown eyes peered through rhinestone eyeglasses.

She set the martini on an Italian coaster that protected the French walnut side table. "Do I dare ask what that brute Stanley made you do today?"

"His name's Jack."

"A prosaic name."

"Why don't you like him?"

"I liked DeMott."

Just like my mother.

"I liked DeMott too," I said. But last month, while I was still employed by the FBI, DeMott flew out here from our home state of Virginia. Two days later, he flew back. Our engagement was over. "But DeMott's gone so let's fast-forward."

"Alright. Tell me what that knuckle-dragger made you do today."

"We went to Leavenworth."

"You drove?"

"He flew his plane."

"What a showoff." She sipped again. "And once you got there, what did you do?"

"We went running."

"How utterly awful."

"And there was a dead body."

"You're *much* too patient." She waved her toothpick of olives. "I would've killed that man *weeks* ago."

"Jack's still alive."

"Pity." She bit the olive.

"Madame found the body."

"Raleigh, this is totally improper cocktail chatter. *Please,* continue."

I described our morning above the Icicle River, how the police interviewed me three times, how Jack thought I made myself look suspicious by instructing the evidence recovery crew, and how Peter asked me to take the job. I was explaining why I turned down the job when my cell phone went off again.

"That ring!" She rolled her eyes. "The man's a troglodyte."

Just for that, I let the ring go on. Herb Alpert and his Tijuana Brass. A ringtone programmed by Jack, after he gave me a cellphone that the Bureau was going to throw out. I let the ring go on. And on.

"Answer it!"

I looked at the Caller ID and swiped my finger over the screen. "Hi, Peter."

"They want us."

"Excuse me?"

"The family. I just called 'em. They wanna hire us."

"What family?"

"State police just identified the body. It's that girl who went missing. The runner."

Eleanor's gaze was glittering rhinestones.

"I'm sure they'll be glad for your help."

"Not my help—*yours*."

After I resigned from the FBI—before they could fire me—Peter offered me a position. After decades of working for the state, he was opening a private forensic lab. It was located in Spokane, on the far eastern side of Washington. Peter needed a geologist around the Seattle area. And I certainly needed a job but I didn't take his offer. "That drive to Leavenworth would—"

"—would go really fast in your sports car."

I glanced at Eleanor. My last assignment with the Bureau was undercover. Eleanor posed as my rich aunt and had me drive her classic 1972 Ghibli. It was fast and white and gone before you saw it. I nicknamed it The Ghost.

"I can't do it, Peter."

"But the state lab doesn't have a geologist."

"I'm sorry."

"We both know how many answers are hunkered in that soil. Government's gonna take *weeks* getting to that evidence."

"I don't have the time—"

"Time!" Eleanor bellowed.

"What'd you say?" Peter asked.

"Nothing."

"Time!" Eleanor repeated. "The longest distance between two places. Who said that?"

"Where are you?" Peter asked.

"Not where I was before. But there are similarities."

"Fine," Eleanor said. "I'll tell you. *The Glass Menagerie*."

"Raleigh …"

"Still here."

"This girl was really young."

"I'm sorry."

"The family's hurting. Badly."

"And I'm sorry for their loss."

"They *really* want to hire us."

I grit my teeth.

"Her daddy was practically begging me."

"Peter, if I could, I would. But my afternoons are non-negotiable."

"But you got to Leavenworth and back today."

"Because somebody flew me in their plane."

"Aw, man." He sighed. "I hate saying *No* to these people."

"So do I. But that drive's six hours round trip. I can't—"

"I know, I know." He sighed, like a cowboy whose horse was dying. "You change your mind…"

"You'll be my first call."

I disconnected. The dark silicon screen showed my reflection. Forehead even more tortured by worry.

"I'll pay for it," Eleanor said.

I looked up. "Pay … for what?"

"The speeding ticket you'll get doing real work."

"I'm not taking the job, Eleanor."

"So you're turning down a job?"

"Yes." *For once in my life.* "I'm choosing my family over my work."

"And that dead person just stays there, in the dirt?"

"She's not in the dirt, Eleanor."

"So it's a woman?"

"A girl." I sighed. "The state police collected her body."

Eleanor lifted the hand not holding the martini and laid it across her forehead. The rings glittered. Diamonds and rubies and emeralds in carat sizes that defied even my calculation. I braced myself. Her chin was rising, Tennessee was coming.

"Nothing human disgusts me unless it is unkind."

"Eleanor—"

"Who said that?"

"I don't know, I don't care." I shoved the phone in my pocket, picked up my can of Coke. "Because I'm not taking this case. End of discussion."

CHAPTER SIX

But it wasn't the end of the discussion.

Of course.

Eleanor was on the war path.

For dinner, she served lentil soup with too many do-gooding vegetables and more lecturing. Normally, after these healthy dinners and attempts at pounding good sense into my head, I took Madame for a walk—straight down the hill to the local McDonald's.

But tonight, the dog and I both crashed.

And yet, the discussion continued.

I was at the ocean. A deserted beach. Those same dark gray clouds, the ones weighted with rain, hovered overhead. Wind gusted and whirled the sand. I turned my back to keep the sand out of my eyes and saw a black house on the dunes. On the widow's walk balcony, my mother paced—back and forth, back and forth—clutching a black shawl to her shoulders, muttering to herself. On the porch below, my sister Helen slashed a charcoal pencil across an artist's canvas. I could see her pictures from where I stood. They were pictures of women, screaming.

I turned away, knowing I shouldn't go to that house. In the sand, footprints led down the beach. They seemed like the only safe path. But safe only if my bare feet stepped inside the impressions. I followed them down the sand until a foul stench filled the air. It was the smell of that cave that Jack and I ran to, the cave above the trail.

When I looked up, fish covered the sand. All of them were trying to reach the water but it was too far away. They twisted their bodies, mouths opening and closing, choking on air. Scales fell from bodies and littered the sand. The air smelled like ammonia. Like death.

I started running. I wanted to get away. But my dad suddenly appeared. I stopped. He wore his usual Saturday outfit, old chinos and a T-shirt from the University of Virginia.

"Dad?" My words drifted down the beach. The surf muffled my voice.

"Dad!"

He picked up one of the dying fish and walked toward the water. Waves crashed at his knees, soaking his pants. But he waded deeper, then leaned down and held the squirming fish in the water until the waves swept it out to sea.

"Dad?" My throat ached.

He walked back to the fish on the beach.

I waved my arms. He didn't see me.

But now thousands of fish smothered the sand. A dying silver sea. My dad picked up another one, carrying it into the surf, and releasing it into the ocean. Then walked back for another.

I ran. I ran and ran and ran until I stood beside him. But he still didn't see me. As he reached down for another fish, I tugged at his shirt. The material tore in my hand.

"Dad?" I felt like sobbing. Here he was, right here. Alive. But he couldn't see me. "Dad it's me. Raleigh. Say something!"

"Help me." His blue eyes glowed.

"Help you—what?"

He swept his arm through the wind, taking in the ocean and the dying fish that now covered almost every inch of sand. “We have to save them.”

“But there’s too many,” I said. “We can’t—”

He reached down for another fish, carrying it into the water. This time, when he walked back, I stepped into his path.

“Dad, what’s going on?”

“Please?” He picked up another fish. It struggled in his hands, twisting, the silver scales falling from its body like shards of mercury.

He carried it to the water.

“Dad!” I yelled at his back. “You can’t save them all!”

He set the fish in the water but turned to look at me. His deep blue gaze pierced my soul.

“I know we can’t save them all.” He released the fish, and watched it swim away. “But I was saving that one. And to that one, it matters.”

CHAPTER SEVEN

At 4:55 A.M., The Ghost was cresting Blewitt Pass when I called the last incoming number. I put the cell phone on Speaker. The ringing went on for a long time.

Peter Rosser answered with a grunt.

"Did I wake you?" I asked.

He took a moment. "Raleigh?"

"I'm heading for the crime scene in Leavenworth."

"Raleigh?"

"I need to stop for coffee, but I'll be at the Icicle River in about an hour."

The phone crackled. It sounded like Peter had rolled over in bed. Maybe checking the clock.

"I know it's early," I said. "But could you do me a favor?"

"Anything."

"Contact the family. See if someone can meet me there. It'll save me some time."

"Diggity do." His twang was happy. "And here I went to bed thinking this case was a bag o' nails."

"Yeah. How about that." I regretted my next words even more. "I need to tell you, I can only do the preliminary work. The early exam, a couple interviews. After that you or the state police or whoever will have to take it."

The Ghost blew past an abandoned mining town. The

sagging wooden shacks were dove gray in the dawn light. Somebody took all the gold, then left.

"Peter, you there?"

"She getting any better?" he asked.

When he offered me this position, I didn't say much about my mom. Mostly because my throat ached with suppressed sobs. But Peter had spent thirty years investigating crime, interviewing victims, three decades of wondering why people do the things they do. He figured it out.

"Kind of," I said. "I'm sorry I didn't explain it better."

"Happens," he twanged. "Everybody's holding something back. It's how we're built."

Alongside the winding road, autumn leaves fluttered in the breeze as if torn by the wind of my car. Their colors shimmered like fish scales.

"Thanks," I said.

"For what?"

"Understanding."

He paused. "Just outta curiosity, what changed your mind?"

I glanced at the rearview mirror. The golden leaves blew across the road.

"I realized it matters," I said. "It matters to this one."

CHAPTER EIGHT

When I pulled into the parking lot for the Icicle River trail, the sky was that tender baby pink, as if this day was born with its own life, full of promises.

Beside the trailhead, a dark blue van waited. The driver's side door opened before I'd even cut The Ghost's engine. A tall man got out. He had a white beard and walked across the gravel to stand beside my car.

"Raleigh Harmon?" he asked.

I nodded. His cheekbones protruded above the white beard like a man resigned to starving, suffering.

"I am Johann Engels. My daughter …"

His daughter. Annicka Engels.

"I'm sorry for your loss," I said. "Thank you for meeting me here."

He nodded and for one brief moment his haggard face looked almost relieved. Like this tragedy might change, even a little bit. I knew that feeling. It'd been seven years since my dad died and I still unconsciously held out for some kind of hope. Some other signs were recognizable. His eyes jumped, connected to a mind that probably couldn't complete its thoughts. Curved posture, weighted with grief, bent forward like a wilting plant.

I handed him one of the cards that Peter had made when I

tentatively accepted this position. Johann Engels read the information carefully while I opened The Ghost's back end and took out my rock kit. I checked the contents, having thrown things inside this morning at 2:30 a.m., right after waking from the dream about my dad and the dying fish. I hoisted the pack to my shoulders, and considered which questions to ask first.

But Johann Engels was already walking down the trail beside the river.

It matters to this one.

I yanked the zipper on my fleece pullover and jogged after him. It seemed impossible that I'd run this same trail with Jack yesterday. The river was still white and gray with silt, but now dew dripped on my shoulders, falling from the red birch leaves.

Johann was moving fast. I picked up my pace. He wasn't slowing, even after the first quarter mile of brush and loose rocks. After a half mile, I pulled up close behind him. "Mind if I ask you some questions?"

"Everything." He didn't slow down, didn't turn around. He was a locomotive of agony. "Ask. Everything. Who—why—why my girl."

The fractured sentences were another sign. He wasn't sleeping. After my dad's murder, my best night's sleep was two hours, tops.

"I heard she went running."

"Runner, a good runner."

"Was this a regular route for her, this trail?"

His head sunk so low between his rounded shoulders that his nod was almost undetectable.

"And the dog, did it always go with her, or just this time?"

He had reached the rocks below the cave and turned to face me. The cave exhaled its foul odor, ruining the pink morning air.

"Day before her birthday," he said.

I stared at his features. The man was in so much obvious pain, yet also numb. Not feeling the effects of this hurried walk, ignorant of the cold autumn air. He wasn't feeling anything, really.

"How old?" I asked.

"Eighteen. Would've been."

He turned and climbed the boulders like a goat.

I scrabbled up the rocks behind him, my heavy pack bouncing against my spine. I was eye level with his hiking boots. The soles been repaired—badly. Thick glue leaked from between the rubber and leather, like muddy tree sap. We bypassed the cave and turned, east, toward the rising sun. I considered my next question. Ten years in the Bureau had taught me many things, but among the saddest was that families were capable of doing the worst things to the people they supposedly loved. As much as I hated trick questions, I also didn't know this man. Or the dynamics of the Engels family.

"When did you realize she was dead?"

He stopped. He turned to face me, one hiking boot dug into the steep hillside to anchor his position. Behind him, Ponderosa pines stretched out their drought-stricken limbs, looking like arms raised in some plea for rain.

"Gone with the archangel," he said.

"Pardon?"

"Feast of St. Michael."

I squinted into the rising sun. "Do you have a date?"

"Twenty-ninth. Sunday."

"Twenty-ninth of September," I clarified.

"Home. From Church."

In the growing light, I could better see his weary blue eyes.

The color was jewel-toned. He seemed to gaze at something—or nothing—under the pine trees.

"I drove," he said. "From church. Busy. Hotel. We have a hotel. But holidays, church, we go. I saw her dog. By the door. Leash chewed." His gaze shifted to me. His eyes were an ocean of blue misery. "Children?"

"Me?" I shook my head.

"You will know things. Parenting. You can't always explain. I never liked it." The skin quivered over his cheekbones. "That leash …"

He didn't go on.

"You saw the dog, and its leash was chewed off," I kept clarifying. "And that told you something was wrong?"

"You can't understand. No children."

"I might."

"My wife, talking. On and on. Careless Annika. Leaving Kaffee outside. How could she?" He wiped a long hand over the white beard. "Kaffee is her dog."

I nodded, encouraging him to keep going.

"All the way to the door, my wife complained. The dog. Dying of thirst. Hot weather. No rain." He took a deep breath and the next words burst in a dry sob. "I knew, I knew."

He started hiking again.

I lunged up the mountain, trying to put his words in order while also keeping up with him. Sweat rolled down my back. Suspicions pricked my brain. Either this man was totally innocent, or he was among the top-tier of liars. Still possible.

"You notified the police?" I asked.

"Right. Away." His voice sounded different. "Too soon. They said."

Bitterness, that's what I heard. And yet, unless there were signs of foul play, nobody was officially missing—particularly a teenager—until twenty-four hours had passed. And one chewed-off dog leash didn't necessarily qualify as foul play. I stared at his back.

We hiked the narrow trail. Once more I kept my right hand in touch with the granite wall and tried not to look down. According to Peter, this family had asked us to work the case. It was rare for the guilty to hire specialists, and Peter's services weren't cheap. But as we cut across the gray batholiths—molten granite cooled in place eons ago—I noticed Johann didn't hesitate. He'd been here.

When—that Sunday of St. Michael the archangel?

I listened to the falling loess, all those dry grains skittering down the mountainside.

"After she was declared missing, what was the police response?"

"Too late. Futile. No answers."

More bitterness.

The mountain opened its stony fist. I saw the tall grass where Madame had stood barking. Yellow crime ribbon circled the perimeter and the grass was trampled by the many people collecting her body and the evidence. But to the far right, there was now an army-green sleeping bag on the ground.

I slid the backpack off my shoulders. Nausea washed up my throat. I blamed drinking coffee on an empty stomach. But I knew the real cause. Her hand. I kept thinking about her hand. Was she buried alive, clawing her way out? Waving for help?

"What can I do?" her father said.

I wanted him to leave. But he'd already camped beside her open grave.

"Stand here, don't move. I'm going to collect some samples. But I have more questions for you."

"Please."

I unzipped the pack. "When you saw the dog and the chewed-off leash, what time was it?"

"12:22."

I looked at him. "You're sure, exactly?"

"Checkout is 12:30."

"Checkout?"

"Hotel. We run a hotel."

"Right." He told me that. They didn't make it to church regularly because they ran a hotel. They went to church for holy days, like the Feast of St. Michael.

"Did you look at a clock?"

He tapped his wristwatch. The crystal was so scratched it looked fogged. He said it was his habit to check the time all morning long, to gauge how close they were to checkout.

"Okay," I said. "12:22 you saw the dog."

"Thirteen days, eighteen hours …" He looked at the clear morning sky. "…and twenty-four minutes ago."

I removed the supplies from my pack. Soil collection bags, Nikon camera, GPS. Rock hammer, ruler, notebook. Garden spade. Not exactly high-tech equipment. And Johann Engels seemed to notice. He frowned, yet said nothing. I crossed under the police ribbon, and was tempted to explain it to him. Forensic geology sometimes used very simple procedures in the field. But since nobody had come up with a solid suspect in thirteen days, eighteen hours, and twenty-four minutes, my telling him that wasn't going to make him feel better. Right now, it seemed highly possible that Annicka Engel's murder was a random killing. An impulse murder. Killed, hurriedly buried. The kind of horrendous death that leaves behind traces of evidence, but most of it depended on the killer making mistakes, or already having his DNA in the criminal records system.

But I reminded myself that part wasn't going to be my

issue.

Collect evidence. Send it to Peter. Do what you can. And be done.

I laid on my stomach at the edge of her grave. Annicka Engels was buried in a shallow depression, probably due to geology. I lowered the ruler into the hole. The first seventeen inches of soil was mostly loess. Light enough that someone of average strength with a standard shovel could dig right through it. Beneath that, the stubborn granite stopped them. Only a jackhammer or dynamite would—

"You found her."

I looked up.

Johann Engels stared at the ruler.

I lifted it from the grave and wrote the dimensions in my notebook. I wanted to clarify the facts—*my dog found her*—but that sounded so wrong. Like his daughter was nothing but discarded bones. I took a deep breath. It tasted of the soil. Did anyone tell him about her hand? *Peter's problem.*

"Someone told you I found her?"

"Sheriff."

A cold sensation climbed up my spine. "What else did they tell you?"

"The dog. Ran away. From you."

His tone sounded afraid, yet still indignant. I gazed into the grave. The rising sun was casting my shadow into the opening. If not for Madame, his daughter might've stayed buried here for seasons. Years. Long enough for rain and snow to wash away every bit of evidence.

I laid on my stomach again and took several dozen photographs, zooming in on the grave's walls. The camera highlighted the stratigraphy—the alternating bands of pale and dark soil—that looked like Mother Nature's barcode. The dark bands, I presumed, were deposited by forces capable of carrying heavier material—snow and ice picking up metals and denser grains. The golden bands probably came from gentle rains of spring and summer winds. Altogether I counted eighteen layers of deposition—roughly, nine years—with two seasons when the pale soils left behind extremely narrow bands. Droughts, I suspected. Like the current drought. I set down the camera and closed my eyes. The barcode played on my eyelids.

"What's wrong?" Johann asked.

"Nothing."

Just like that leash told Johann something bad happened to his daughter, crime scenes had their own atmospheric delivery system. Things beyond the facts. Above the details. Things sensed, absorbed, perceived. I kept my eyes closed until the bar code disappeared and my mind could see this grave for the first time.

Now the banded soil layers looked ragged. Like rough-cut pages in a vintage book. I squinted. The layers bled into taupe wall, a flat, two-dimensional background.

With one dark vertical line.

I shifted my gaze and squinted again. The vertical line cut into another section of soil. And another. Like a string bookmark laid across the ragged edge of the pages. I picked up the ruler and measured the horizontal distance between the vertical marks. It was almost evenly made at ten inches. I wrote that in my notebook, and took a photo.

"Was your daughter tall?" I asked.

"You."

I looked up. "Five-eight?"

He nodded.

The grave was just under five feet in length. So either her legs were folded, or broken. Were they broken before she was buried, to keep her from getting away, or after, so her body fit this hasty grave? Another wave of nausea swam up. I refocused on that vertical line. I was fairly certain the mark was made by a tool, something that scraped down the soil. At the grave's northern end, the line was smudged. Probably where the police had removed her body, dragging it over the soil.

"Something?" Johann asked.

I laid the ruler between the gouges and took more photographs. The gouge could've come from the tool itself, a defect of some kind. Or a pebble that got lodged inside the tool. I prayed it was the tool itself. A pebble could disappear, never to be found. Never to be connected with this gruesome burial.

"We know." He stepped back, standing beside the sleeping bag. "Her boyfriend. Did this."

I kneeled at my pack and opened the collection bags. "Who is 'we'?"

"My family."

"The police claimed there are no suspects."

"They don't believe."

Using the sterile garden spade, I took eight soil samples and placed each inside separate Ziploc baggies. I marked their location with a Sharpie and tried not to think about the expensive and amazing cotton mesh bags I used to have, courtesy of the federal government. Now, it was Ziploc.

I opened my notebook, bracing myself for these even more uncomfortable questions.

"Tell me what she was wearing."

In a flat voice, he described her purple-and-gold shorts, her purple running shoes, and a purple T-shirt with a Husky dog's face on it—the mascot for the University of Washington. "Scholarship," he said. "Paid everything."

I remembered Officer Wilcove saying she had a full athletic ride to UW. "She came home for the weekend?"

"Michaelmas."

"Michael . . .?"

The family was Catholic, he explained, and celebrated all the German Catholic holidays. Michaelmas, the feast of St. Michael. It was why he and his wife went to church that morning instead of working at their hotel, and why Annicka came home from college, to celebrate with them.

"But she didn't go to church that morning?" I clarified.

He reached down, tapping his shin bone. "Fracture."

"Stress fracture?"

He nodded.

That cold sensation climbed my back again. "She went running with a stress fracture?"

He shrugged.

Something wasn't adding up. Stress fractures were usually caused by too much running. When I got them, even walking hurt, never mind running. The remedy was rest. "Why would she run here if her legs hurt?"

"Sabbath." He gave another sobbing burst of breath. "This trail. Every Sunday. Even just to walk."

"But the stress fracture must've affected her college running."

He blinked into the sun. It had crested over the mountains, turning silver granite to gold crowns. "She didn't like it."

"What?"

"College. Seattle. Big city."

I was writing everything down in my notes, but glanced over them a second and third time. Annicka Engels got a full ride to a Pac-10 school, but she didn't like the place. She had stress fractures, but hiked this mountain. Maybe she didn't like the team, or college competition. Maybe she didn't have stress fractures but was only looking for an excuse to drop out of practices, come home on the weekends, but keep her scholarship funding. I glanced down the trail. Waking down this mountain with stress fractures would've felt like hot knives stabbing into the bone.

Asking these kinds of questions was only going to wound this man further. Especially as we stood here by her grave, the depression like an open hand, waiting for someone to drop answers into it.

I packed up my gear. Johann followed me down the mountain, leaving his sleeping bag behind. We moved in silence. I could hear the river, that white-noise wash like steady wind. When we reached the parking lot, I shook his hand. It felt as rough as a rusted spade. But his eyes held tender questions.

"Peter Rosser will be in touch," I said. "Soon," I added. "He'll be in touch soon."

That dry sob came back.

"God bless you," he said.

CHAPTER NINE

FROM THE TRAILHEAD I drove into the town of Leavenworth. The road was choked with traffic, and it wasn't even nine o'clock. Oktoberfest traffic—deluxe motor coaches from Seattle, flocks of touring motorcycles, RVs from God knows where. I took the first available parking spot and followed the scent of warm bread down the crowded sidewalk. It led me to Kris Kringle's Kreme Kastle.

Aka, a bakery.

Although its Kansas namesake was known for its prison, Leavenworth, Washington was renowned for tourism. The area was settled by German farmers in the early 1800s. But their local fortunes plunged when the trains stopped running through here. By the 1970s recession, it looked like the bitter end for these people. But the town fathers—German descendants, all—got the crazy idea to make the town into a perfect replica of Bavaria. The town's surrounding mountains resembled the European Alps, and many of the small downtown businesses already looked like chalets. Soon plaster-and-lathe architecture stood on every block, and yodelers performed on every corner. These days, more than a million tourists came through town annually, eager to see "little Bavaria." And Octoberfest was almost on a par with Christmas.

In the German bakery, I ordered what sounded like my beloved Egg McMuffin gone Bavarian—bratwurst, egg, and cheese on a pretzel roll. I ate it while strolling down the sidewalk and checking my phone. People were shopping for lederhosen, Christmas ornaments, everything German. I was searching for directions to the local Sheriff's office.

I found a police annex at the edge of town. Another chalet-style building. But inside, it was the typical American cop shop. Acoustic tile ceilings, indoor-outdoor carpeting, and the acrid scent of cheap coffee. Behind the reception counter, a young woman with long brown braids and a Bavarian beer-maid's costume was making more coffee.

"Can I help you?" she asked.

"I was looking for the sheriff. Is he around?"

Her face tensed. She set the coffee grounds next to the machine and wiped her hands on her costume's white apron. "Are you reporting a crime?"

"No."

"Something related to Oktoberfest?"

I shook my head. "I'm looking into the murder of Annicka Engels."

Her gaze shifted. She glanced over my shoulder. I turned, but nothing was there.

"The Engels family hired me," I added. "I'd really like to speak to the Sheriff."

Her face didn't relax. "I'll go see if he's available."

SEVEN MINUTES LATER, I was seated in a vinyl-and-chrome chair in Sheriff Felix Grubman's small office. He was one of those small men who looked powerful—compact as a coiled spring—with steel gray eyes middle age hadn't filed down.

I explained why I was there, that I'd just come from the

burial site, that Peter and I would appreciate his help.

I handed him my card.

Grubman read it. More than once. “You say the family hired you?”

“Yes, sir.”

“How much you gouging those people for?”

“Pardon?”

“You find the body *and* you get those poor people to pay for your—” he raised his hands making air quotes around the next word, “investigation. How convenient. For you.”

“Actually this is completely *in*convenient.”

“That so.”

“I don’t consider a six-hour drive convenient.”

“State police took your statement, according to my deputy.”

“Deputy Seiler? Yes, he and Officer Wilcove got there within minutes of our finding the body.” I was feeling extra cautious. If he hoped to get anywhere on this case, Peter would need the sheriff’s cooperation. And already, the sheriff wasn’t cooperating. “Would you like me to give my statement again?”

“We’re a small town.” He leaned back in his large chair, as if in relaxed command. But in truth, Sheriff Grubman looked more like an aging elf in Santa’s workshop. “Everyone knows about you. And you oughta be ashamed, taking money from those people.”

“The Engels *hired* us.”

“Us?”

“Peter Rosser.” I nodded at the card. “Former head of the crime lab in Spokane. I’m sure he’s helped your department on several cases. We’re colleagues.”

He dropped the shame tactic but kept asking what, exactly, we planned to do. I was getting tired of repeating myself—

we're forensic geologists, not magicians. But I wasn't in a position of power these days, I wasn't backed by the Feds anymore. Instead I was like a character from Eleanor's plays, relying on the kindness of strangers. I explained, ad nauseam, how forensic geology worked, how I'd collected soil samples from the burial site, how Peter would be examining them to find trace evidence. "Our hope is to help y'all with your investigation."

He smiled. It looked a lot like my FBI smile. "Your *plan*, is it."

"Sheriff, I don't see why—"

"A case like this can go on for years. What're you gonna do, keep charging the Engels?"

I bit my tongue. Pride wanted to rear its head, snarling about how many murder investigations I'd already worked, how these cases didn't go on for years—sometimes they stretched out for *decades*—which was why small departments like this one should be thankful for any extra help.

But I was learning to shut up.

I dispatched my own law enforcement smile and said, "Sheriff, I want this case closed as soon as possible. And if we work together, we can hold down costs for the family."

"Work together. How?"

"Bring me up to speed. Mr. Engels seems convinced Annicka's boyfriend was involved in her death."

He leaned forward. "Johann told you that?"

"And he sounded certain."

The sheriff thought about it. "We checked out the boyfriend. We don't think he was involved in her disappearance."

"What about her murder?"

He gave me a cold look. "Same thing."

"You have no doubts whatsoever about the boyfriend?"

"I got doubts about everybody."

I smiled. "We have a lot in common."

The sheriff's steely eyes ground into me. "Geologist." He made it sound like *undertaker*. "You just look at the dirt, what's that about?"

"Mineralogy. Trace evidence. I worked for the FBI's Materials Analysis unit in D.C." I didn't want to brag, and didn't want to mention my time as an agent. Local enforcement didn't have warm feelings toward FBI agents, often for good reason. "Now I'm an independent contractor."

He picked up my card. He looked at it like it just came off the Xerox machine at Kinkos. "Still mighty convenient you found that body."

Dear God. I got to my feet. *Let Peter deal with him.*

"If you think of anything else," I said, "please give me a call."

I BROKE THE speed limit driving over the mountain pass, then swung by a post office to overnight the soil samples to Peter in Spokane.

I bombed into Tacoma.

Eleanor wasn't home—spending the day with her thoroughbreds at the local racetrack—so I left her a note, gathered Madame, and broke another speed limit to reach Western State Hospital on time. Back when my dad was alive—instead of showing up in fevered dreams—we decided my mom shouldn't know that I worked for the FBI.

"You're a geologist," he said. "Tell her that. It's not a lie."

David Harmon never lied.

We both figured that someday, we would tell her the truth. Someday. The day she got well. The day when everything went back to normal. But that day evaporated the night David Harmon was killed. Soon after, I left the FBI mineralogy lab, applied to Quantico, and graduated to special agent.

I still told my mom I was a geologist. Not a lie.

Not totally.

But Shakespeare once said, *The truth will out.* And the truth outed me during our summer cruise to Alaska. And when a paranoid schizophrenic realizes they've been lied to—by the people they're closest to—it's like throwing kerosene on that strange fire already smoldering inside their head. When the ship docked in Seattle, those proverbial "men in white coats" were waiting. They brought my mom to Western State.

I vowed to never again lie to her.

I was keeping that promise. Barely.

Holding Madame in one hand, I signed the visitor's sheet and waited for the buzzing locks to release the heavy steel doors. I gave the dog one last pat, and climbed the stairs.

Sir Post-it was waiting.

CHAPTER TEN

AFTER MY DAILY dose of crazy land, I drove Madame back to Eleanor's, changed clothes, and climbed back into The Ghost. Alone.

I was just in time for Seattle's rush hour traffic. The crawl up I-5 gave me time to watch dusk paint Puget Sound with a brush made of violet-gray dove feathers. Across the water the mountains cupped the setting sun, as if rock alone could hold back time.

Beside Lake Union, I parked in a small lot and walked down a wooden dock toward a cluster of houseboats that hugged the lakeshore. Each houseboat looked different. One was painted orange, like a squared-off pumpkin. Another had window boxes spilling herbs. Another hoisted three rainbow windsocks from its sod-like roof.

At the end of the dock sat a tidy cedar-shingled saltbox. It faced the lake water and across the water, the Space Needle positioned at the bottom of Queen Anne hill. A now-familiar float plane was tied to the dock, which also held a two-seat rowing shell. For several moments, I watched the sky melt into the water. Somewhere behind me, piano was playing in one of the houseboats, a soft riff that sounded less like someone reading sheet music and more like someone coaxing emotion from the keyboard.

"Nice shorts, Harmon."

Jack stood at the door. He wore a white rowing singlet and black lycra shorts, just like mine.

"It's getting dark," I said.

"Is it really?" He gazed at the gloaming sky, then back at me. He raised his eyebrows. "Was there something you want to do with me in the dark?"

"Row." I ignored his grin. "You said we could row."

"Oh," he said, as if just remembering. "Right. No dog with you?"

"I didn't realize you were so attached to her." Madame deserved a break after the asylum. And I didn't think she'd enjoy riding in a rowing shell. "You want me to go get her?"

He stepped out, closed the door, and picked up the fiberglass shell from the dock. He held it canoe-style, under one arm. His bicep knotted. Shoulder muscles striated.

I gave my heart a swift kick. *Quit fluttering.*

"Something wrong?" he asked.

"No." *You sound defensive.* "I've got a lot on my mind."

"Amazing that unemployment can do that." He set the shell on the water. Liquid amethyst ripples rolled across the surface, disappearing in the dark.

"How are we going to row in the dark?"

"Be patient." He reached for the pointed prow of the shell and clicked a button. A light beam gleamed forward, bright as any high-powered flashlight. He clicked a second light on the shell's back end. The shell seemed to elongate. "And since you're such a tough girl, you can be anchor. But try not to capsize us."

I stepped into the shell. It wobbled. During two fall seasons at Mount Holyoke College, I'd stroked an eight on the Connecticut River. I liked rowing, it gave me a peace I'd only found in running. But I quit when the long practices took me away from the geology lab. That was eleven years ago. Now, as the shell bobbled, I threw out my arms and prayed to keep my balance while Jack, naturally, did nothing to help. I crouched, lowering my center of gravity, and managed to position myself on the rear slide board.

Jack climbed in front, whistling.

I yanked the straps, tightening my feet into the slanted platform, and shoved at the bad question in my head. *Mr. Alpha Male has a two-person shell? Who's his rowing partner?* I tested the cleats. Made sure my oars were locked in place.

"You done putting on your lipstick?" he asked.

"Are you?"

He pushed us from the dock.

I grabbed my oars.

When we cleared the dock, we slid forward on the roller seats, dipping the oars. As soon as he started back, I pressed my feet into the platform and muscled the oars against the water. My shoulders felt stiff. Another slide forward. I let out my breath. Slid back. *Better.*

A motorboat chugged past our port side, green lights blinking on the rippled water. I kept my oars timed to Jack's movements. The motorboat's wake splashed cold water on my arms. I shivered. We slid back, pulling.

Oars up, slide forward. Back, pulling. Forward, back, forward, back—we hit a rhythm—the movement as timed as a weaver's baffle and loom.

Jack slid back, turning his head. "Good day?"

Forward. "Long."

His oar feathered over the darkening water. I slid with him, dipping in tandem. The shell shot forward. His shoulders flexed, grew wider.

I glanced away. "How's your day?"

"Paperwork." His elbows kicked out. "Almost envied unemployment."

"I'm employed."

His oar thunked, missing the catch. The shell bobbled, recovered. We slid forward and back.

"Sorry," he muttered.

"What a novice."

In four strokes, he had us back in sync. But now his rhythm was faster, our seats shuttling top speed, the rollers making a *whisk-whisk-whisk* sound. My shoulders burned.

He slid back. "Employed … how?"

Cool night air seared my throat, torched my lungs. I blinked. His back glistened with sweat, his muscles as solid as river rock. I shifted my gaze, begging the blue-black sky. *Please. Show me something other than his muscles.* The breeze blew across the water. My pony tail flipped. His scent came with the wind.

Male. Musk. Delicious.

Thanks a lot.

"Harmon?"

"What."

"Can't you row any faster?"

My legs were on fire. I pushed with my quads, pulled with my shoulders and back. The boat shot like an arrow across the water, the light slicing through the darkness like a sword. I counted out the rhythms, the split-seconds, and soon a trance fell. I surrendered to the pain, stared at his back, and felt that euphoria of exertion. We were leaning so far back at the end of each kick that Jack's head nearly touched my legs. I gazed up at the sky, pleading with the night. *Blot out all my feelings.*

What did that get me? An image, that last moment before Madame barked. Jack's lips were on my ear. He was about to ask a question—

"Curious."

"What," I panted.

"Work?"

"Leavenworth."

"Cops called?"

"Family."

His oar snagged the water, the shell sank on the right. I shoved both of my hands down, raising my oars from the water before they flipped me out of the boat. But Jack's oars were stuck underwater. The shell spun. I gasped, closed my eyes, dizzy. The shell tottered. When the movement slowed, I opened my eyes. He was gripping the oars like a man trying to choke someone to death. My heart pounded. Adrenaline. Ache. The water so cold, so black, so—

"I got it," Jack said.

"Famous last words."

We bobbled and took in some water. I waited for Newton's laws to teach us all about force and momentum. But Jack lifted one oar from the water, then the other. We coasted under the Ballard Bridge. Car tires thrummed over the drawbridge's metal grooves. He let the right oar drift, raising his right hand, signaling me to turn the shell around. We were heading back.

My arms felt like mushy linguine.

Raggedly, we made it back to the houseboat. But my solar plexus was spasming under my rib cage, that horrible sensation that comes right before vomiting. When Jack let go of his oars, letting the shell coast for the dock, I leaned forward and kept my head between my knees, sucking in air until I stopped hyperventilating and my head stopped spinning.

"Sorry about that," Jack said. "Just surprised me."

"How?" I managed.

"You said the drive up there was too far."

"Only prelim work." I willed my voice to steady itself.

Stop panting. "And already done."

"That's too bad," he said. "The Bureau needs a consultant up there."

I raised my head. The front light beamed onto the house-boat's cedar shingles.

"Did you hear me?" he asked.

"Yeah." I wasn't about to get pulled in. "So get a consult-ant."

"Harmon, I flew you over there for that reason. But that mutt ruined the whole agenda."

A brick dropped on my heart. "So it was a work trip?"

"I've got a hate crime case up there." He turned, trying to glance back at me. "And hate crimes are your specialty. Right?"

"Uh-huh."

He lifted the white singlet, wiping his face. "But when that body turned up and you had to get back here, I decided not to bring it up. But we could use a consultant on this case."

So it wasn't a date.

What was I thinking?

"Harmon."

"What."

"Someday you're going to realize we're two of a kind."

I lifted my oars from the locks. *This is how DeMott felt.* He assumed we had a relationship. But I was just adding him to my work schedule. My heart ached. For DeMott. For me. For life.

"Well, it's too late now," I said. "I just went to make sure the soil evidence got collected. Get the case rolling. That's all."

"Wait a minute." He grabbed the dock, steadying the shell. "You finally get offered a real job and you *still* turned it down?"

"I can't—"

"Forget it." He lifted his other hand, signaling me to stop. "Don't say a word. It makes perfect sense—for you."

He climbed out of the shell. I followed on wobbly legs, carrying the oars as Jack clicked off the shell's lights and picked up the boat. I lowered myself into one of the deck's Adirondack chairs. He went inside, clicked on a lamp in the front window, and returned with two towels. He tossed one to me. I wiped down my face. The amber light from the lamp spread over the dock's weathered wood. My heart pounded.

Jack whistled. Wiped down the oars and the shell, put them away, then he sat down in the Adirondack chair next to mine. I kept my gaze on the houseboats that gathered on the opposite shore. Their lighted windows sparkled on the dark water, as if sparks were falling off the Space needle.

"I've got another case up there," he said. "It's what you might call agricultural."

"Marijuana, grown in the federal forest."

"Harmon, I can't tell you. And since you *know* I can't tell you, your question is even more egregious."

I turned toward him. "Egregious."

"Yes. And I know what the word means."

"You're sure?"

"Yes." The light from the window lit half his face, outlining that powerful bone structure. "It means you're a very, very stubborn girl."

"You better check *Merriam-Webster*."

"I did." He grinned. "Your photo is right next to the word *stubborn*."

I looked away.

"So this hate crime," he continued, "falls under civil rights. Which you're practically an expert in."

I squinted at the inky water. During my time in the Richmond, Virginia field office, I worked several high-profile civil rights cases. “How can there be racial crimes in Leavenworth? Everybody’s white.”

“Religious persecution.”

My face flipped to his. “In little Bavaria? Who doesn’t like the German Catholics?”

“Somebody who set fire to church property.” He waited. “This case is like a double for you, you being a Christian and all.”

“Nice try. But I can’t work over there.”

“You could, if I flew us up there.”

The light from the window wasn’t enough to read his full expression. Or see the color of his eyes. Green?

Or police blue?

“I can fly us there in thirty minutes,” he said. “That means total travel time of one hour. Which leaves you plenty of time to get … where you need to go.”

I looked out at the lake.

“And I’m flying up there tomorrow.” He waited. “You want a ride?”

Across the water, across the city, across the sky, the faintest hint of a sunset showed as a thin red line lingering above the Olympic Mountains. Like God traced the range in blood.

“Harmon?”

“And what if I need to leave and you’re not ready to go?”

“Well …”

The water lapped against the dock, soft as that piano music I’d heard earlier. One, two, three… I counted it. Four, five, six …. Jack always had this sense of space. Never crowding words. Never crowding me. I loved it, and hated it. Because it also meant he didn’t need me for anything.

“I promise to leave whenever you need to go.”

“You can’t promise that.”

"Harmon, I've got to get someone on this case who understands hate crimes. And arson. That's all I can tell you."

A marching band was trapped inside my chest.

"And I promise, I will get you back here in time."

"I don't know …"

"I *promise,*" he said. "Okay?"

The word rang in my ear. Again and again. Returning and returning and returning like the water lapping against this dock. But a familiar voice joined the chorus, the voice that meant more to me than any other voice on earth.

It matters to this one.

"Okay?" Jack asked softly.

I looked over.

"Okay," I said.

CHAPTER ELEVEN

THE NEXT MORNING, Jack's float plane touched down on Lake Wenatchee. Under dawn light, the water was liquid silver. Madame sat up in my lap as the plane's pontoons sent ripples across the water, rolling like liquid mercury toward the emerald green forest that cradled this mountain basin.

"Welcome back to Shangri-La," Jack said.

He nosed the plane toward a log cabin on the lakeshore. His family cabin. Last time we were here, he didn't take me inside. I didn't expect he would now.

"Your family comes out here a lot?" I asked.

"Not anymore." He hesitated, thinking of something. Then said, "Just me."

The truck was still parked next to the cabin's screened-in porch. He'd used it to drive us into town. But now a familiar blue passenger van was here, too. Johann Engels got out. I watched him lope down to the gravelly beach. I tried to sound casual.

"So you come here by yourself?" I asked.

"No. I always bring someone."

I looked over. He was grinning.

"You're here. And the mutt."

I ran my hand down Madame's warm fur and felt something clutch my heart. Not that long ago, Jack had said things that made me believe he wanted us to be more than friends. But I was still working for the Bureau then. People change. And maybe I'd been reading too much into things. And maybe …

I looked away again, staring out the window.

Johann looked even thinner than yesterday, elongated like some cold-water eel pulled from this mountain lake. Reality, I decided. It was sinking in. When Annicka was missing, hope stayed alive. Now he knew his daughter was dead. Gone, forever. And he knew her last moments on earth were terrifying.

Johann lifted his hand. A stiff-armed greeting.

Jack cut the engine and opened his door. As the plane coasted toward the beach, he threw a rope to Johann, who caught the line like someone learning how to clap. The pontoons scraped against the gravelly sand, and Jack jumped out.

I opened my door, Madame leaped out. I grabbed my backpack from behind my seat and stepped on the pontoon. Jack stood beside Johann on the beach, one hand clasping the grieving man's shoulder.

"I'm so sorry," Jack said. "She was a wonderful girl."

"Thank you, my friend." Johann patted his hand. "And you? How is—"

"I don't know."

"Perhaps she will—"

"Maybe." Jack said abruptly. He turned toward me. "You okay?"

I nodded, and tried to read his expression. It seemed studiously blank. *She*? I wondered. *Perhaps she will*—what? Come back to Jack? Rekindle their romance? I'd heard Johann's tone of voice. It was intimate, even pained.

Jack turned back to Johann. "Thanks for taking Raleigh

into town. We'll meet up later at your place."

Johann nodded, then walked up the sloping beach, leading me to the blue van. Madame ran ahead of us. Jack stayed behind. I didn't look back, and kept my gaze focused on the van's passenger door. The sign read:

Das Waterhaus.
Your mountain hideaway.

JOHANN DROVE WITH his bony hands gripping the steering wheel at precisely ten-and-two. The twisting two-lane route snaked through the mountains for several miles. Neither of us spoke. I held Madame in my lap, listened to the van's bloviating muffler, and then built up the courage to ask.

"So you already know Jack?"

"Everybody knows everybody." Johann shrugged. "Small town."

I stared out the window and hated myself. What was wrong with me that I cared about Jack's personal life? Especially when this poor man just lost his daughter. I took a deep breath, closed my eyes, and said Annicka's name over and over in my mind, like a prayer. *Annicka Engels.* She was my sole focus.

I opened my eyes. "Did you hear anything more from the state police?"

"Sheriff. Autopsy report." He glanced over at me. His blue eyes were paler than yesterday, as if loneliness had leaked in. "I didn't want to know."

I nodded.

"Is that the dog?" he asked.

"Oh, yes. I'm sorry—"

"Annicka was like that."

"Like … what?"

"Took her dog everywhere." He started to smile, but reality smothered the good memory. "Sometimes it seemed Annicka came home to see the dog. Not us."

Last night, as I drove home from that hard row, I decided Madame should come with me to Leavenworth. Just in case we were late getting back. I planned to explain it to Johann. Right away. *I have an appointment in Seattle later, with the dog*. I wanted to explain because otherwise bringing Madame seemed callous, even cruel.

But I hadn't considered how awkward it would feel. This empty van felt crowded with pain. Violent death was throwing down all its layers of grief. Shock, denial. Anger. Depression. Shards of it poking up without warning, like cut glass riding on a river of despair, slicing open veins only to deposit more pain. It had been seven years since my dad's murder, and that river was still coming at me, even as well-intentioned people said things like, *time heals all wounds*. It was a lie. With violent death—unjustified death, sudden death—time turned into a delta. Time laid down pain upon pain, until all of it hardened into bedrock, into the foundational knowledge that the world was fallen, fallen, fallen.

"Veterinarian," he said.

"Pardon?"

"Annicka. She wanted to be a vet."

"That's admirable."

"I gave her away."

"Excuse me?"

"The dog." He glanced at Madame. The sorrow in his long face stabbed me. "Kaffee."

"Kathy?"

"Kaffee." He spelled it out for me. "Her dog. I couldn't take it. Kaffee whimpered all night outside her bedroom. All night. I gave the dog away."

"I understand." I ran my clammy palms down Madame's fur. "Sometimes it feels like the pain might kill you, too."

He looked over again. And nodded. Then looked back at the road.

I left him to his silence.

And was grateful for it.

DAS WATERHAUS SAT at the east end of town. A rambling Bavarian-style inn, the entrance faced the main drag. Johann parked the van in front so that the passenger door sign could be seen by all the traffic already rumbling down the road. Hordes of Oktoberfest tourists.

I hoisted my pack and walked with Madame to the imposing carved-wood doors. With the timber-frame casement, the place looked like quintessential Bavarian architecture. Strong, heavy, German.

"My wife doesn't like dogs in the main building," he said.

"Of course." I pointed at her. "Madame, stay."

Her black eyes had a dubious look.

"I mean it, Madame. Stay here."

She circled a worn boot scraper, sniffed the landscaping by the door, then settled herself on the smooth concrete pad. And sighed.

"Kaffee did that for Annicka."

Another wave of guilt filled my heart. I started to explain but he'd already pulled the wrought iron door handle, gesturing for me to step inside.

More Germanic atmosphere. Dark wooden walls. Antler chandeliers. Stuffed cougars roaring silently. And at the front desk, a well-dressed man with a suitcase raging at the help.

"None of this showed up on the Internet," he said.

The woman behind the counter wore one of those Bavarian beer-maid outfits. But the puffy white sleeves and tight bodice clashed with her wrinkled face and gray hair braided in a coil around her head.

"I'm sorry, sir," she said. "We make every effort to ensure that our guests—"

"The sink doesn't drain. The carpet isn't vacuumed. My towels are—"

Johann moved toward them. But I took a sharp right and walked to the big window by the front doors. Madame was facing the busy road like a little black sphinx.

"—and your swimming pool is *green*," the man continued. "I want a refund."

"Sir." Johann stood at the counter. "What about a free night."

"*Free night?*" He spun on Johann. "You couldn't *pay* me to stay here."

A volcanic temptation was bubbling up inside me. I wanted to tell this guy the sheriff was just here—with their daughter's autopsy. But that would only embarrass them more. So I moved across the lobby to the other side. Gray river rocks climbed the wall for two stories, its center carved into a fireplace. Up on the mezzanine, more stuffed creatures waited. Hawks. Rainbow trout. A standing bear. Brown bear or black, I couldn't tell because the fur was covered with dust.

"Our refund policy is clearly printed on your receipt," the woman said.

"No refunds." Johann's voice sounded like a bucket scraping a dry well. "But exchanges. We do exchanges."

"Are you kidding me?" the man said.

I stared out the window beside the river rock. A small courtyard surrounded a swimming pool. The guy was right—the water was peridot green.

"Our best suite," Johann said. "You can have it."

The man said nothing.

He was glaring, first at Johann, then at the woman. She had deep dark eyes, almost black. They smoldered under her gray braid.

"Fireplace," Johann added. "Balcony."

I looked out the window again. A youngish guy was coming across the courtyard. He opened a wooden shed beside the pool and removed a long metal pole with a net attached to the end. He dragged the net over the surface of the water, slowly. He looked around, checking out the wooden balconies above him. He was barely paying attention to the green water.

"Christmas," Johann said. "Nothing like Christmas in Leavenworth. Lights. Carols. Drinks."

"Fine." The guest sighed. "But I want that suite. For Christmas."

The woman behind the counter hesitated.

"Good," Johann said.

"Yes, wonderful," said the woman, in a tone that said anything but. "I'll make your reservation right now."

Johann picked up the man's suitcase and followed him outside. When he returned, the woman narrowed her dark eyes.

"Great," she said. "Just. Great."

"No worries," Johann said.

"*No worries?* Johann, he'll probably post a review on the Internet."

Johann was motioning to me with his long hand. "Raleigh, come meet my wife, Helen."

I walked over, a polite smile fixed on my face. I considered telling her that my sister's name was Helen. But both of these Helens shared a similar personality, so I didn't say it.

"Raleigh's that geologist I told you about," he said.

"*What?*"

"Geologist. I told you. Yesterday."

Helen Engels' dark eyes had the long-burning quality of anthracite. "And what's *she* charging us?"

"Nothing," Johann said.

My head swiveled.

"Johann, how can she charge us nothing?"

Good question. My head swiveled back to Johann.

"It's a trade," he said. "Barter."

"A trade." She arched one dark eyebrow. Pinpricks of perspiration dotted her forehead. "You're giving away more rooms?"

"Yes. Free rooms."

"For how long?"

"For life."

"*Life?* Are you *crazy?*"

"Raleigh found Annicka."

Her mouth tightened. But her brown eyes glistened. That was just like my sister, too. She could never show any vulnerability.

"Johann, you just gave away our king suite for Christmas. Our best week! How am I supposed to pay the bills with *bartering*?"

Another good question. But now I had some questions of my own—like, why didn't Peter tell me this crucial detail about payment?

"I appreciate your offer," I said. "It's very generous. But I won't be able to stay overnight."

They stared at me. I could read the uncertainty in their eyes. *She's not staying because of what that guest just said?*

"I have an obligation in Seattle," I added. "I need to get back by afternoon. Every day."

Helen Engels drew a deep breath. Or tried to. That Bavarian bodice seemed tight, constricting her lungs. She was a handsome woman. Not pretty—her dark features were too powerful for pretty—but the strong features almost hid the agony in her brown eyes. Only I recognized it. Because it was like staring into a mirror.

She seemed about to say something else, but the phone rang behind the desk.

"We'll discuss this later," she told her husband. Then, lifting the receiver, she gave a hearty greeting. "Willkommen to Das Waterhaus!"

Johann turned to me, melting with sadness.

"Get your dog," he whispered.

CHAPTER TWELVE

FROM THE LOBBY with its hunting theme, we walked down a wing of hotel rooms. I was carrying Madame, and moved around a maid's cart that stood in the hallway by an open door. Johann turned right at the next corner, leading us down yet another wing. The hotel's walls were made of white plaster, with hairline fractures under the aluminum-frame windows. The floors were thin carpeting.

"Watch your step," he said, turning left.

He walked down a flight of stone stairs, and ducked under an archway. The air turned chilly, dank. Like our basement cellar back in Virginia. Madame shivered in my arms.

Johann opened a brown steel door where a sign read: NO GUESTS ALLOWED. PRIVATE RESIDENCE.

Closing the door behind me, he walked down still another hallway. This one was so dimly lit with stone walls that it had all the charm of an abandoned mine shaft. Up ahead, light leaked from an open door. Johann stepped into that room.

"Fritz," he said. "This is the geologist. Raleigh Harmon."

Fritz was the same guy who'd "cleaned" the pool. He sat at a small desk with a computer monitor, the machine's back facing the door. Behind him, metal shelving held rolls of toilet paper and wrapped bars of soap. Fritz clicked his mouse before standing and extending his hand over the monitor.

"I'm Fritz Engels," he said.

He had his mother's dark eyes. His father's height. And, judging by the doughy hand in mine, none of his sister's athleticism.

"How do you do," I said.

"I'm not happy," he said, letting go of my hand. "But I'll be ecstatic if you nail the bastard who killed my sister."

Oh boy. I gave him the same smile I offered his mother. "That's the goal."

"Great. How are you going to do it?"

"Well …" I set Madame on the stone floor. "I'll be looking into what happened. And I could use your help."

"I can tell you right now who did it," he said. "Annicka was killed by her boyfriend."

I took a notebook from my pack. "You sound certain."

"My sister went for a run just like she always did, and he knew exactly where she went running." Fritz glared at his father. "And her boyfriend also knew her dog, so it wouldn't attack him. The bastard."

I wrote down his statement. Some thoughts nudged the back of my mind. I'd wondered over these same details—how somebody caught a champion runner, killed her, and convinced her loyal dog to leave. "What's the boyfriend's name?"

"Mason Leming." He said the name with a sneer.

"He's a runner?"

"Yes."

"A runner like your sister?"

"No. Mason wasn't in Annicka's league. In anything."

"Can you think of anyone else who might've wanted to harm your sister?"

"No." His dark eyes filled with hate. It made him resemble his mother. "You should also know that Mason asked Annicka to marry him. She turned him down. And she broke up with him."

"When was that?"

"Two weeks before she went missing."

I kept the surprise out of my face. "You told this to the police?"

"The police." Fritz gave a hard laugh. He picked up a pen from the desk, scratching it several times on a small pad to get the ink to flow. He handed the note to me. "Mason Leming lives with his mother on an *herb farm*." He made air quotes. "Total mama's boy."

"This is very helpful, thank you."

"It's the truth. But you should know the cops believe Mason's alibi. So good luck with it."

I pocketed the note, and resisted the urge to tell him luck didn't exist.

This family already knew that.

CHAPTER THIRTEEN

FROM THE BASEMENT office, Johann led us further down the chilly hall. Most of the light came from high transom windows set inside the stone walls. The window sills were deep, ten inches at least. The basement was built like a German bunker.

At the last door, Johann stopped. He didn't open it.

"I'll be upstairs," he said in that bucket-scraping voice.

I opened the door. "Thank you."

Annicka Engel's bedroom was a narrow space. One single bed pushed up against the back wall. One transom window showing the grass outside, sunlight slashing through the individual blades making them look like green hash marks. The light slipped into the room and fell on the trophies standing on a shelf behind her bed. The gold glittered like pyrite. I walked over. First place, first, first … A female figure stood on each one, frozen in mid-stride.

"She was a very good runner."

Johann stood in the doorway.

But as soon as I turned, he closed the door—quickly—as if something might jump out. Numbered running bibs were thumbtacked on the back of the door, swaying in the breeze. Madame, standing beside me, continued to stare at the door, waiting for it to open again, like some game of peek-a-boo.

"Stay," I told her.

She lay down where the column of sunlight struck the chilly floor. I opened my pack, took out a pair of latex gloves, and snapped them on.

Her computer sat on a shelf inside a small closet, with clothes hanging on either side. I turned it on. Her desktop wallpaper was a series of shifting photographs. Blond girl. A black-and-white dog—Kaffee, I guessed. One lanky guy with brown hair and a narrow face, smiling into the camera. The boyfriend? The next photo showed her racing. She wore a cross country uniform for Cascade High School. Two competitors struggled behind her, looking desperate. Annicka's quad muscles stretched like rubber bands, blond ponytail flying behind her like a flag for the perfect Aryan specimen. Except her eyes. In next photo, which was a close-up of her face, I saw her brown eyes. Like her mother. Annika was smiling and biting down on a gold medal, as if testing its authenticity. Those eyes. They looked even darker against the bright blond hair. Although Hitler would disagree, the brown eyes made her even more beautiful.

When the photo loop restarted, I watched it again. Something else caught my attention. She was so much younger than her brother, Fritz. He seemed close to thirty. But Johann said Annicka died right before her eighteenth birthday. That was a huge age span between two children. I watched the girl on the computer. She was happy. Confident. Untroubled. And I remembered what Officer Wilcove said that first day. *She was perfect.*

I shifted the mouse. The system asked for a password. I broke it on the first try. KAFFEE. Her dog.

I found English class essays. History assignments. One running log. I clicked on that and found she ran about fifty miles weekly, sometimes sixty. Each day was a different route, but the rotation stayed the same. *Ski Hill Road, Farm Road, School Trails*. And every Sunday: *Icicle River trail.*

Every Sunday.

Anybody who had that information could've waited for her. With a weapon. And a shovel.

I glanced at my watch. I still wanted to get to the sheriff's office today and check on that autopsy. I clicked through her other files, but found nothing very interesting. The same password opened her Internet browser. Her favorite sites were bookmarked and included YouTube videos of famous runners—Joan Benoit winning the Olympic gold—and animal pages, veterinarian advice columns, how to get into veterinarian school.

Her Trash folder was empty.

I combed through her emails. Notices for team runs at UW. Practice details. Freshman orientation. Travel uniforms. I also found a series of emails back and forth with the team's captain. Annicka had missed two Saturday meets. The captain wanted to know if Annicka was alright. Annicka had replied: "Lots going on at home."

She said nothing about stress fractures.

Which meant either she lied to her father, or lied to her team captain.

But other than that, I saw nothing else suspicious, or dangerous. I also found no emails from Mason Leming. And none sent to him. That seemed odd. Did she delete them all and empty the Trash folder? But there were no threats. No harsh words. Nothing to indicate her life was in danger.

Another series of emails came from an account labelled *Apple Orchard.* I didn't understand what they were about, some kind of work schedule. But one email came in the Saturday morning before she died.

The subject line read: "See you tomorrow?"

Annicka replied: "Right after my run. Kiss Buster for me."

I wrote the name *Buster* in my notebook, and turned on the printer. While some of the emails printed, I knelt in her closet.

There were only three pairs of shoes. Green flip flops. Black dress shoes, barely worn. And beat-up white tennis shoes. I found some soil in the tennis shoes' soles, but it was mere microns. The drought alone would keep soil from sticking to shoes. I opened one baggie, scraped the microns in, and pinched the bag shut.

Madame blinked in the sunlight.

"Good girl," I said, taking out a Sharpie and writing *white tennis shoes* on the bag. I put it in my pack, then looked around the small space again.

Something bothered me here. But I couldn't put my finger on it. I searched the rest of the room. Lifted her single mattress. Opened each drawer and every book on the narrow shelf by her bed. I moved all her clothes in the closet, searched the back wall, checked under the computer, the printer, inside each shoe.

There was nothing.

No notes.

No scrapbooks.

Nothing.

Standing in the middle of the room, a sadness gripped my heart. The bare walls. The plain bed shoved up against stone. One small window allowing one narrow column of light inside. The room felt as soulless as a boarding house. Some place to sleep. Some place to dream about better things to come.

And now they never would.

CHAPTER FOURTEEN

I WAS WALKING down that dimly lit hall in search of a bathroom when Tijuana Brass erupted on my cell phone. Madame cocked her head, listening until I slid my finger over Peter's number.

"I'm at their hotel," I said.

"What?"

"The Engels' hotel, in Leavenworth. That's where I am."

"But you said—"

I explained the new situation, how Jack promised to fly me in and out. "Plus the Bureau needs a consult on a hate crime here. Arson on a church. So it's two jobs up here."

"Howdy-do!" Peter said.

"I'm glad you're excited because we need to talk about the Engels."

"How's the dad doing?"

"Oh, never better."

"Just so you know," he said, sighing, "I get to ask one dumb question every single day."

"I'll be counting." I glanced down the stone hallway. Still empty, but I lowered my voice even further. "What's this about trading our fee for hotel rooms?"

"Oh. Yeah. That."

"Yeah, *that*."

"Raleigh, you get free hotel rooms—for life. Hitch your wagon to that deal."

"And what if I don't want to visit little Bavaria all the time?"

"Beer-n-brats, it ain't bad."

"We'll discuss it later. Did you get the soil samples?"

"Right here," he said. "My conclusive technical analysis is this is weirdsly beardsly."

"Why?"

"That soil's got hair in it. And it ain't human hair."

"Probably from her dog. It was running with her."

"Nope. Not dog hair."

"You're sure?"

"You also get one dumb question a day."

"Sorry."

Peter was head of the state's crime lab in eastern Washington for decades. Being based in rural territory, his cases saw a lot wildlife—poaching, trespassing, ranch thefts. He would know dog hair from another animal's hair. I recalled her burial site. That hand rising from the soil. "Cougar hair?" I asked.

"Nope."

"Raccoon?"

"Not."

"Field mice?"

"You can keep guessing," he drawled. "Or you can take it into a specialist."

"*You're* a specialist."

"But not one of my wildlife hair samples matches this here strand. But I got a connection with a gal who lives over in your neck of the woods. Works with U-dub."

"Okay." I glanced around the grim basement. If this was where the family got away from irate guests, I felt even sorrier for them. "Send the soil back."

"Be there when you get back."

"You already sent it."

"Specialist's number is in the package," he added.

"How did you know I'd take—"

"I got a feeling about you, Raleigh. Why I hired you."

Madame was wandering down the hall, sniffing the stone floor. I followed but found a bathroom on my left. I patted my leg for her to come and flicked on the bathroom light. More stone walls. And a strong odor of mildew. In one corner, beside the stand-up corner shower, a pair of hiking boots waited. I walked over to them. "Where did you send the soil?"

"Your aunt's house."

"Which aunt?" I checked the boot's tag. Women's size 8. "Charlotte Harmon?"

"Isn't her name Eleanor?"

"Oh, *that* aunt." Eleanor had played my "aunt" when I was undercover for the FBI at the racetrack. My real aunt—my dad's sister, Charlotte Harmon—lived in Seattle. I explained it all to Peter.

"Clear as kaolinite," he said. Kaolinite was clay, thickest mud around. "You might want to handle the box kinda careful. I packed some equipment in there. Just to get you started. Nothing fancy."

"Peter, you didn't have to. I'll find some equipment." *Somehow. Somewhere.*

"Know what she told me?"

"Who?"

"Your make-believe aunt."

"Eleanor." I lifted one of the hiking boots. A dark brown soil was buried in the deep treads. Lots of it. I reached for my pack. "What'd Eleanor say?"

"She said, 'Funerals are pretty compared to death.' "

I pulled out a baggie, shook it open. "Did she also tell you that she thinks that phrase should be your lab's motto?"

"It ain't bad …"

I knocked the soil loose, deposited it into the baggie, and pinched the top closed. "Unfortunately," I reached for the Sharpie, "that line belongs to a southern playwright."

"Maybe he'll let us use it."

"He's dead."

"Even better!"

I opened the Sharpie and wrote *boots in bathroom* on the clear plastic. Madame moved toward the open door, her fur raised between her shoulders. I looked up.

Fritz Engels stood there, his dark eyes like deep caves. "What do you think you're doing?"

"I'm just collecting—"

"Raleigh?" Peter's voice drawled through the phone.

"I'll call you back."

"And see if you can get her autopsy," Peter added.

"I'm on it." I disconnected the call.

Fritz stood rooted to the floor, hands in his front pockets. "I asked you a question," he said. "What are you doing."

Now not a question. "I'm collecting evidence."

"In our bathroom?"

I pointed the Sharpie at the muddy boots. "Are those her boots?"

He nodded.

"When did she last wear them?"

"When she was alive."

Such a funny guy.

"I'm curious where the mud in the soles came from," I said, "since it hasn't rained here in months."

"How would I know that."

"You have absolutely no idea where she could've worn those boots?"

"They're her boots." His hands jingled something in his pocket. Keys, coins, a cold metallic music that rattled in the mildewed air, each note sending a shiver down my spine. "Are you done?"

I still needed to use the facilities. But not here. "Yes, I'm done. For now."

Fritz stepped aside. Madame followed me into the hall, her fur still up between her shoulders. Fritz closed the bathroom door. "My mom doesn't allow dogs in the main hotel," he said.

"Right, thanks." I pulled out my notebook, as if writing myself a reminder. But it wasn't about dogs in the hotel.

The reminder said:

Run background check on Fritz Engels.

CHAPTER FIFTEEN

I CARRIED MADAME up the stone steps, searching for Johann. The hotel's many additions created a maze of hallways and alcoves and somehow, I ended up right back in the taxidermied lobby.

Helen Engels glanced up from the front desk, scowling at the dog under my arm. But she said nothing. Probably because a young couple was checking in with three children.

"Is your pool heated?" asked the mother.

"No," Helen said.

"Is there a lifeguard?"

"We don't have a lifeguard."

I passed under the antler chandelier, almost jogging for the heavy front door. When I pushed it open, Madame leaped from my arms. I circled the outside searching for Johann, but soon decided he didn't want to be found. Who could blame him. And I didn't really want to quiz him about his son before I did my own background search. Pulling out my cell phone, walking back to the Front Street, I called Jack and got his voice mail. All it said was: "Leave a message."

No identification, no way for somebody to trace it to an FBI agent.

I held the speaker to my mouth. "It's about ten o'clock. I've got some time to check on your church burning. Call me back."

Traffic down the main drag was a steady stream of white noise from wheels, motors, radios, all of it periodically interrupted by a burp of a loud truck. But I could see why people were coming. In the autumn sunshine, this Bavarian village looked as quaint and cozy as a town inside a snow globe. Not one piece of litter on the street. Everyone smiling. Every single building a perfect Bavarian replica.

Perfect.

Except for a killer.

A killer, I decided, who must live here. It was unlikely a stranger knew the Sunday running routine for Annicka Engels. She was supposed to be at college. But what about those stress fractures, which she didn't mention in her emails with teammates?

I was still walking down the sidewalk, making a second call to the sheriff, when the scent hit me. Madame was already tracking it, nose up, sniffing the air, glancing back at me.

"Good girl!"

Led by our noses, we followed the lusciousness, down the sidewalk, past a hair place named Gustave's and a music store named Mozart, and when we reached the corner, plumes of gray smoke curled from the short roof. Amber grease coated the small windows. And a plastic sign closed the deal.

Das Burgermeister.

"Now we're getting somewhere."

Madame picked up her pace, I started jogging. But my excitement soon surpassed greasy food. I knew bait when I saw it.

That smell.

Fries.

I lifted the phone to my mouth and asked the magical technology for the phone number for the Washington State Patrol.

CHAPTER SIXTEEN

"NEVER TOO EARLY," said Officer Wilcove.

His patrol cruiser still reeked of French fries, but now the smell was fresh from *Das Burgermeister*. Sitting in the back seat behind the steel cage, because Madame was at my feet enjoying her own breakfast of champions, I said silent grace—two words, *thank you*—and dipped one hot crispy fry in mayonnaise. When I bit down, my throat hummed. God bless the potato, the mineral salt, and the inventor of mayonnaise.

"How is that?" Wilcove turned his large head, speaking through the cage. "The mayo, I mean?"

"Check it out." I dipped a fry and offered it to him.

He chewed slowly like a true connoisseur of American great, savoring the pleasure of fast food. "Hey, that's pretty darn good."

He lifted his Styrofoam milkshake cup and tapped it against the cage.

Oh, the warm glow of evangelism. I slipped him a foil travel packet of mayo and watched my cult of fries-with-mayo gain another member.

"I would've invited that deputy, too—the Animal Control guy, what's his name, Seiler?"

Wilcove dipped his fries. "Tom Seiler."

"Right. But he doesn't seem like he'd enjoy this kind of thing."

"Well ..." Wilcove's forehead tightened. "Seiler's kind of..."

"Suspicious?"

He shrugged.

"Definitely seems serious about his job." I thought of him nagging me about the leash when there was a dead body right behind me. "He probably wouldn't like my dog unleashed in here, either."

"He's a good guy," Seiler said. "He's helped me a lot."

"I'm glad." I dipped a fry. "I was just searching Annicka Engels' bedroom."

He said nothing.

"But you guys already searched her bedroom, right?"

He sipped his shake.

"She didn't deserve to die like that."

He looked up, into the rearview mirror. "I can't stop thinking about it."

"Me, neither."

He held my gaze. "I heard you worked for the FBI."

I bit, chewed. *Small town,* Johann told me, *everybody knows everybody.* The sheriff probably told every lawman within a fifty-mile radius that I used to work for the FBI.

"How long were you with them?" Wilcove asked.

The French fry waited, poised for enjoyment. But Wilcove was staring at me, expecting something. Two days ago—could it have been just two days ago?—it was hard for me to tell him and Seiler apart. Both beefy farm guys with shaved blonde hair. But where Seiler's eyes were narrow with suspicion, Wilcove's eyes slanted down at the outer corners. A wistful boyish expression. And right now, his gaze in the mirror looked like a six-year-old meeting a fireman.

"I was with the Bureau about ten years."

"Wow." His eyes widened. Six-year-old learns the fireman once saved a baby from a burning building. "But you don't work with them anymore?"

"It was mutual."

His forehead tightened. Boy learns fireman dropped baby. "And now you're a … *geologist*?"

Fireman turned fry cook.

"I've always been a geologist." I explained the forensic mineralogy lab at the Bureau. And I would've explained how minerals show up in everything from cosmetics to car bombs, but Wilcove had another question.

"Did you ever work as an agent?" He really wanted to know *what happened.*

"Yes." I looked down at the wax paper where my cheeseburger was waiting. "I became an agent after my dad was murdered."

"Oh." He stared out the windshield. "I'm sorry."

He'd backed his cruiser into the parking lot of the burger joint, well-trained to keep an eye on things. At 10:14 a.m., the cruiser was the only customer vehicle here—which is why we received the freshest grease of the day. Beyond us, traffic kept its steady stream down the Front Street. Problems probably started after lunch, when the German lager kicked in.

"Was it hard to leave that, after ten years?" he asked.

"Yes."

"Why'd you leave?"

"I tended to ignore the rules."

He looked up. "What kinda rules?"

"Well." I glanced out the back window. *Did I really want to have this discussion?* Behind us, a pluton of granite loomed like a cliff. Half my brain was noting the chemistry, how tiny garnets were embedded in the quartz veins, stones as red as drops of blood. The other half of my brain wondered why my heart was suddenly accelerating. I set my fries on the vinyl floor mat. Madame wagged and dove in.

"The FBI has a rule that agents have to be armed at all times. But I didn't take my weapon with me all the time. I got attacked by some guys. And I was rescued by a civilian." Named DeMott Fielding. The same civilian who asked me to marry him, then asked me not to.

"Everyone makes mistakes," Wilcove said, sounding just like that six-year-old boy.

"True." Madame's tongue rasped, licking all the salt on the wax paper. "But I kept bending the rules."

His dashboard radio crackled. I heard something about a wolf. Or a coyote. It had wandered into someone's front yard. Chickens were at stake. Another unit was responding. Maybe even Seiler. Wilcove's pale eyes came back to the mirror. Another question.

I beat him to it.

"You're wondering if I'm buying you breakfast to get something out of you."

"I'm not dumb, I know why you called."

"I really did want to eat." I reached into my pocket and found Fritz's note. "But I'm also curious about this guy Mason Leming."

He bit down on a fry. "I can't talk about it."

"The Engels believe he killed Annicka."

"I know."

"You know they think that—or you know he could've killed her?"

"Mason's got an alibi."

"Do you believe it?"

He placed his shake in the dashboard cup holder.

I could feel my opportunity closing. "I'm just trying to

find out what happened to Annicka. We both want to know. Let's help her rest in peace."

He looked down. In the rearview mirror, all I could see was his buzz-cut hair.

"I promise," I said. "Despite all my rule bending, I never once compromised a source's identity. And I never will. This conversation is confidential. I just need to know if Mason Leming *could* be guilty, and there just wasn't enough evidence to hold him."

"You don't understand." His kept his attention on the traffic. "Leavenworth needs tourists. Every job here is tied to tourism. Even mine."

"Bad publicity, I get it." I watched him. "You knew her, right?"

"Everyone knew her. Annicka was, like, famous. She was a star. But she never snubbed anybody. She was always nice."

"What about Mason Leming, is he a nice guy?"

"I really don't know him." He sounded bitter.

"You think he killed her."

"There you go again." He snatched the shake from the cup holder. "I *knew* I shouldn't have come here."

"Look, I'm not asking you to convict the guy. Just tell me why he *might've* killed her."

"Because he was in love with her."

Love. Only in this broken-down fallen world can *love* be a motive for murder.

"But his alibi—"

Wilcove sat up as a black 4-by-4 truck roared into the parking lot. As soon as the driver saw the patrol cruiser, he swung left and crossed to the lot's far side. For at least a minute, nobody got out of the truck. Wilcove's attention didn't shift, even when my cell phone went off. I checked the screen. *Unidentified Caller.* Jack. I let the call go to voice mail and looked up to see two white guys getting out of the truck. One had dirty-blonde dreadlocks. The other wore a T-shirt with a huge cannabis leaf on the front. They studiously ignored Wilcove's car. I wondered about Jack's *agricultural* case. Wilcove tracked them into *Das Burgermeister*.

"About Mason," I said, as the diner's door closed.

"I don't know…" His voice still had wonder, but now it was the bad kind. "I'm starting to believe anybody can do anything. Like, all they need is the right circumstances." He looked up into the mirror. "You know what I'm saying?"

Yes. The weight of it suffocated my heart. "It's the price of admission."

"What?"

"This work changes you." My voice was heavy, remembering.

He turned in his seat to look at me.

"My first case in the lab was a pair of lungs. They were so small." I held up one cupped hand to show him. "I found soil inside the air sacs, lodged deep in the tissue. Do you know what that means?"

He shook his head.

"It means somebody buried that child when she was still alive. She breathed the soil into her lungs."

"Oh, man," he said softly.

"And *that* was my first assignment for the Bureau." I stared down at Madame. She lay at my feet, content with a full belly. "I went home that weekend and told my dad I wanted to quit."

"But you didn't."

"No." I paused, recalling that moment burned in my soul. "My dad said, 'Raleigh, I don't always like being a judge, because some cases never let you forget. But we're called to live beyond our fears. And we can't pretend evil doesn't exist.

The stones cry out. They cry out for justice. And the only way to get justice is to listen to those cries."

"Geology." He blinked, then nodded. "You stayed with it."

"And that's the price of admission. We're here to get the truth. For the dead."

Wilcove looked away. "There's another girl."

I held still.

"Another girl …" He turned all the way around, looking at me directly through the cage. "Another girl was bled out."

"Sorry—what?"

"Bled out." He said it fast, like he didn't want the words in his mouth. "Annicka was bled out."

My mind flashed to the burial site. The soil. Her body. The hand waving. "Bled—"

"You can't tell *anyone* how you heard this."

"You have my word. I promise."

He faced forward. "Six years ago, there was another girl who died the same way. Somebody slit her throat and bled her dry."

I felt sick, my stomach churning. *That's* how Annicka died? No wonder her father didn't want to see the autopsy. I swallowed. "How old is Mason Leming?"

"Nineteen."

So six years ago, he would've been thirteen. Too young to kill the other girl? "Is that why he was dropped as a suspect, because of this connection?"

The agriculturalists stepped out of *Das Burgermeister*. They carried a dozen white bags. Munchies, no doubt. Wilcove tracked them to their black truck, and watched closely as they backed up, ever so slowly, and flicked on a blinker to indicate a left turn onto the road. They weren't giving the cops any excuse to pull them over. Wilcove's face was almost pressed to his side window, his breath clouding the glass. “They didn’t tell us about the link to the other girl until yesterday. One of the detectives is working the case, in the sheriff’s office. Nobody wants any reporters to find out.” He looked up. “You know?’

I nodded. “Can you tell me the other girl’s name?”

“Esther Heller.” He sighed, more breath condensing on the glass. “I always heard that Esther was murdered. You know, small town talk. But nobody said how—the tourism, you know.” He looked up in the mirror. “You sure you understand?”

“Yes.”

“Her parents run a hotel, just like the Engels. So now we’re trying to go over both the guest list. See who might’ve stayed in both places.”

“Over a six-year span? That’s a long list.”

He turned around again, pleading. “This can’t get out. Do you hear me?”

“Loud and clear.”

“I should get going,” he said. “Thanks. For breakfast.”

“My pleasure.” I grabbed my backpack, slung it over my shoulders, and gathered up my food wrappers. Madame stood.

Wilcove started to get out—the back seat of cop cars don’t have handles—for obvious reasons.

“Just one more question,” I said.

He groaned. “What?”

“Where would I find the Hellers?”

CHAPTER SEVENTEEN

OFFICER WILCOVE DROVE away. Madame inspected the pine trees at the back of the parking lot. And I listened to Jack's voice mail.

"I'll pick you up at the Waterhaus, eleven-thirty."

I checked my watch. Ten-forty.

"And you can stop checking your watch," Jack said. "I'll get you back to Seattle in time."

I disconnected the call, feeling an odd resentment. I check my watch that much? And so what, I'm concerned. Big deal.

Madame trotted back to me.

"Ready?" I asked her.

We jogged—a slow, full-belly jog—down the main drag. Despite sun shining high above the snow-capped peaks, the air still felt crisp with autumn. Sweater weather. With sweater-wearing tourists strolling past the shops full of German knickknacks and roasting bratwurst and nutcrackers. In the city park, an oompah band was setting up. The sunshine's alchemy turned the brass tuba into gold.

Even if Wilcove didn't tell me where to find it, I couldn't miss the Eiderdown Inn. The hotel swallowed an entire block smack-dab in the middle of town. White stucco walls criss-crossed with dark wooden lathes. Painted scenes played on the stucco. Lederhosen farmers steered Clydesdale horses through wheat fields. Or maybe it was hops, for the German beer.

Madame took a shady spot near the four huge planters of mums at the entrance. Inside, the air smelled of cinnamon and apples. Three pretty blonde girls worked the front desk, each swaddled in those Bavarian outfits, taking care of the long line of cheerful guests. Accordion music floated from ceiling speakers. I looked around for someone like a manager, but another clump of guests walked in. They carried tiny white dogs and chattered in French.

I walked back outside. Madame was still waiting in her sphinx-like pose. "Good girl."

We circled the block and found an alley that cut behind the main building. A Tyrolean-style sky bridge linked the main hotel to another building. Madame investigated the green dumpsters—cleanest dumpsters I'd ever seen—while I gazed up at the five stories of rooms. Windows opened to the fresh mountain air, their white lace curtains billowing in the morning breeze. Further down the alley, I found what I was looking for. Just like that sign at the Waterhaus:

Private Entrance. No Guests Allowed.

A tarnished brass doorbell stuck out from the white plaster. Nobody answered my first, so my second press lasted longer, vibrating like a wasp's nest.

A voice called from the other side of the door. "Deliveries go to the Front Street entrance."

"I'm looking for the Hellers." I yelled back.

There was no reply.

"It's about their daughter, Esther. I'm working with the Engels. They hired me to—"

The door gapped four inches, just enough to see a woman's face. It was as pale as the building's stucco.

"What d'you want?" she asked.

"I'm sorry to disturb you." I held out my card. "I'm working for the Engels family and—"

The door opened further. Her pale hand snatched my card. "This about Annicka?"

"Yes, ma'am."

She glanced furtively down the alley, then motioned for me to come inside. "Hurry up!"

I patted my leg to call Madame and scooped her up. "Sorry, she's—"

"Just get in here."

The door closed so fast wind blew my hair.

"Martha Heller," she said, in some kind of introduction, lifting the reading glasses that hung round her neck. She peered at the card. The knuckles of her hand were knotted from arthritis. Her hair was short and platinum blonde. When she looked up at me, her brown eyes seemed impossibly dark against the pale skin and hair. "How do you pronounce your name?" she asked.

"Raleigh. Like the city."

"Tea?"

She didn't wait for a response.

I followed her quick steps through another bunker-basement. But that's where the comparisons stopped. These walls had been troweled smooth with plaster, and displayed painted scenes like the ones outside. No farmers though. And no plough horses. Only small woodland creatures. Rabbits hiding in grass. Birds swooping through blue skies. Leafy trees arching over ponds and meadows.

"Take a seat."

The kitchen wasn't much bigger than Annicka's bedroom. And it was cluttered. Thin paint brushes stood in milky water glasses by the sink. I took a seat at the small wooden table with two chairs and set Madame on the floor next to my backpack. Martha Heller filled a kettle and clanked it onto an electric stove. The burner looked dirty.

"Cream? Sugar?"

"If that's no trouble."

She didn't reply.

I heard voices above us. The accordion music, too. Footsteps marched back and forth, back and forth. I imagined the girls behind the front desk. Or the guests streaming into the lobby.

"Serve yourself." She plunked a chipped china cup and saucer in front of me, followed by mismatched cream and sugar containers. All chipped. The tea came black as coffee. I loaded up the cream and sugar while Martha Heller sank into the chair opposite mine. She gripped her own chipped tea cup.

"Engels hired you?" She leaned forward, eyes black as obsidian.

"Johann." I stirred the tea. "I just came from their place."

"Somebody told you about my daughter?"

"Yes."

"Now you're wondering if her murder's connected to Annicka's."

I watched her carefully. The pale skin, pale hair. But those eyes, black as forged iron. They anchored her face. "My understanding is there are some similarities. But also a long period of time between their deaths. I know it's difficult, but if you could tell me—"

"What're you going to do with the information?"

I held her gaze. Somehow she reminded me of a bank vault, where the steel door is open but might slam shut at any moment, locking me out. "My father was murdered."

I saw something flicker in her intense gaze.

"We still don't know who killed him. So I understand your

reluctance. I'm trying to find out who killed Annicka. Maybe the same person killed your daughter Esther. I don't know. But I'd like to find out."

She rubbed a knobby index finger over the chip in her china cup. "Got something to write with? I'm not gonna say this twice."

I opened my pack, took out my notebook and pen. Madame lay under the table, and, sensing something, she placed her head on my right foot. When I looked up again, Martha Heller's dark gaze focused somewhere over my right shoulder.

"My husband didn't want our kids to get spoiled," she said. "We make money here. A lot of money. So when they were old enough to carry a towel, he put them to work. In the hotel."

"How many children?"

"Four. Three boys. Esther."

A dog barked. Then another. And another. It was coming from upstairs but Madame lifted her head, growling. I glanced at the small window above the sink. Were the dogs in the alley, rioting?

"Upstairs," Martha said. "We allow pets. You get used to the barking."

She shifted right back into talking about Esther. She described a quiet, diligent, artistic girl. An only daughter who never gave her parents one moment of trouble. When I asked if Esther had a boyfriend, the arthritic finger tapped the teacup.

"No. Esther liked solitude. And work. At least, she enjoyed making money. She saved every penny to pay for college. But then she got a full scholarship to an art school in Seattle." The finger tapped. "She didn't go."

"Because—?"

She stared at me, a molten suffering breaking through her

forged iron eyes.

"I'm so sorry."

She nodded. We belonged to a club, a club we never wanted to join. A club we could never leave.

"The maids always work in pairs. But Esther worked alone. Because she liked to be alone. And because she came in later, after school. My husband gave her all the deep-cleaning jobs, when a room isn't being turned over right away for another guest. Esther was thorough. My husband used to say she was his best worker."

"She sounds unusual for a teenager."

"*Highly* unusual." Martha Keller sighed. "But that was true from the moment she was conceived. Three boys, I really didn't want another kid. But …" She shrugged. "So I started praying this last kid would be a girl. Prayer answered. And a star was born." Her gnarled hand wrapped around the entire cup. "After she cleaned the rooms, Esther would go straight for the kitchen. More work, more pay. We serve our guests a German breakfast every morning. Sweet rolls from scratch. They take all afternoon to make and have to rise overnight." She shook her head. "Those stupid sweet rolls. Esther would work on them because they're such a pain. She was patient."

Mrs. Heller's eyes glowed, remembering. I waited.

"The other maids didn't see her cleaning cart in the hall. But they didn't think twice about it. They punched in their time cards and went home. Esther didn't show up at dinner that night either." She set the cup in the dish. It rattled. "She was found in Room 412. The room she was cleaning. The bathtub was red."

Words scraped up my throat. "Who found her?"

She stared at me. The molten grief spilled over.

My heart clenched.

"Hey!"

It was a voice upstairs. It jolted me.

"Hey, you!"

Madame raised her head, growling again.

"They cut her throat," Martha continued. "They drained all her blood."

I gave her a moment. "Did someone tell you how Annicka—"

"Sheriff's deputy was here yesterday. Asking me questions. Told me not to say anything." She leaned forward. "The last time, I obeyed their instructions about keeping quiet. Now I want answers."

"No suspects in Esther's death?"

"None." Her gnarled hands turned into fists. "Somebody literally drained the life out of my baby girl and got away with it."

Every footstep above us felt like a kick to the heart.

"You need anything else?" she asked.

"Not at the moment." I stared blindly at my notebook. I needed the autopsy report, the evidence files. "But if I have more questions—"

She pushed back her chair. "You know where to find me."

I hoisted my pack and tapped my leg. We followed her down the grotto-like hallway. All those cloudless painted skies, the pristine scenes in pastel. Only now I saw something else in the scenery. A girl. She stood in the far corner of each panel, her back to the viewer. She was a small figure with dark hair. She seemed to be looking at the scenery. The flowers, meadows, bunnies. The skies that never clouded.

Martha Heller waited by the door.

"Thank you." I held out my hand.

Her swollen knuckles felt like pebbles. I thought of the paint brushes by the sink.

"You painted the walls?" I asked.

She almost smiled. "You like them?"

I hated pastels. And most landscape paintings bored me. But it was that dark-haired girl in them. And the twisted knuckles of the mother who found her in Room 412. She recreated Esther, gazing into eternity.

"I think they're beautiful," I told her.

CHAPTER EIGHTEEN

HEADING BACK TO the Waterhaus, Madame trotting beside me, we shifted around the tourists like a stream bypassing boulders. It all seemed unreal—all the sunshine and schnitzel, chatty guests and cheery accordion music, going on right above Martha Heller's grotto of grief.

And the reality of it all … a killer walked among them.

A tourist?

I stopped at one of the beer gardens. Inside the cordoned area, a red-faced man wearing a Seattle Mariner's cap hoisted a blue stein and grinned. Would somebody come here and kill, then wait six years before killing again? And blood-letting? That required knowledge, planning. Expertise. Especially for a killer to leave almost no clues.

I started walking again. Half a block from the Waterhaus, I saw Jack. He was standing outside the inn talking to Johann, and before I could stop it, something tripped inside. My heart. So full of grief, sadness, even a little scared … and there stood Jack. Solid and strong and sure of things. Sunlight fell on his broad back and shoulders. His hiking shorts were dusty. He didn't see me approaching, and as I moved closer, the breeze brushed over him. I smelled pine and trail dust and man. *Rugged man.* My heart flipped again. I wanted to lean into him, feel his muscular arms curl around me. A safe harbor in a wicked storm.

"—relationship was fine," he was saying, "until she decided to—"

Johann's gaze shifted.

Jack spun. "How long've you been standing there?"

"Not long."

I couldn't read his eyes. He wore those mirrored shades.

"Everything okay?" I asked.

"Yes." He smiled but it seemed uncertain. "You okay?"

"Fine."

Back to business.

I turned to Johann, to ask some questions about Esther. But he was already walking toward a tour bus that had just pulled into the parking lot. He walked stiffly, his posture curved forward, like a man shielding his own broken heart.

WE RODE IN the pickup, Madame sitting between us on the torn passenger seat. It was lunchtime and the Oktoberfest traffic had thickened. More crowds filled the streets. The truck crept forward at about five miles an hour.

"Sure you're okay?" Jack asked.

"How long does it take for a body to bleed out?"

"*That's* what you were thinking about?"

"Another girl was murdered."

"When?"

"Six years ago."

He stared straight ahead, but he wasn't even blinking.

"You must've known about the other murder," I said.

"Are you talking about the Heller girl?"

"Annicka's death might be tied to hers."

"How?"

"They were both bled out."

He slowed at the corner of Ski Hill Drive and turned right. "Esther Heller was Leavenworth's first murder in decades. It never got much publicity."

"Thanks to tourism."

"Don't judge them, Harmon. Without tourism, this whole place dies."

I turned away, gazing out the side window. We passed a farm, brown horses standing in fields of cut hay. "My source says law enforcement isn't releasing the blood-letting information. But that's how Annicka died, too."

"They're also withholding that detail for a good reason."

"You have local connections here. You're an FBI agent." I turned to him. "Nobody told you about this blood-letting six years ago?"

"Harmon, you see things differently because of what your family's been through."

"Mrs. Heller looks like a ghost. I don't think she's seen daylight in years."

Jack glanced at the road, then me. Then the road. Then me. Those mirrored shades reflected my sunburned face, tense with concern.

"And Johann," I said. "The man's literally dying inside. If the person who killed Esther hadn't come back and killed again, his daughter might still be alive. *If* that person came back."

"What's that supposed to mean?"

"How well do you know the Engels?"

"Family acquaintances. Why?"

"Her brother …"

"*Fritz*?" He looked over at me. "You suspect Fritz?"

"He's, what, ten years older than his sister?"

"So?"

"So whoever killed Annicka knew her running routine.

And they knew her dog so well it ran home." I pointed to Madame, sitting between us like a chaperone. "If I got attacked, would this dog run home?"

"Don't even ask that."

"Fritz also works in a hotel." I described the storage shelves of housekeeping supplies, all that wrapped soap and paper products. "The person who killed Esther Heller knew housekeeping routines. They picked a time when the Hellers were too busy to check on her. And knew enough to hide Esther's maid cart from the other maids. Who knows that kind of thing?"

"But ... *Fritz*?" He shook his head. "He seems so..."

"Seems. That's the key word." I described Fritz's reaction to my search of the basement bathroom. "Your sister gets killed, and you get mad at the investigator for doing a thorough job?"

He was quiet, and spoke softly. "No, you don't."

"And finally, Fritz made sure to tell me all about Annicka turning down a marriage proposal from her boyfriend. But my source says the boyfriend's alibi holds. Plus, the boyfriend would've been in seventh grade when Esther was killed."

"Who's your source?"

"Remind me, what's the definition of *egregious*?" I tilted my head.

"We're two of a kind." He looked over. "I keep telling you, Harmon—two of a kind."

CHAPTER NINETEEN

JACK PARKED OUTSIDE a church.

I read the large wooden sign. "They can't be serious," I said.

"Why not?"

I read the church's name aloud: "Our Lady of Snows"?

"Harmon, it's an alpine tourist town." He got out of the truck, then looked directly back at Madame, who waited expectantly on the bench seat. "The mutt can come, too."

She jumped out the door.

Our Lady of Snows looked like the architect wanted to design a nun's head-covering. Two long white stucco wings projected from a dark centerpiece. Positioned below the granite peaks, I fully expected Julie Andrews to burst out and remind me that the hills were alive.

Instead, a chubby priest stepped out. He wore jeans, tennis shoes, and a navy sweater with the white divinity collar. "Jack!" he called out.

They shook hands like old friends.

"Father Anthony, this is Raleigh Harmon. She's the person with the hate-crime experience."

I held out my hand, but Father Anthony squatted next to Madame. "Nice to meet you, Raleigh. Who's this?"

"Madame."

"What a tremendous name!"

She wagged. The priest scratched her back.

"Her full name is Madame Chiang Kai-Shek."

"How wonderful!" Father Anthony's chubby face lit up, and the dog moved closer for a really good rub. "Smart, is she?"

"Very."

"Sorry to interrupt that mutt's fan club," Jack said, "but we need to get back to Seattle soon."

"My apologies." The priest stood. "Right this way."

Madame stuck close behind him. He led us to the left, around one of the long white wings where a grassy slope tilted toward Ski Hill Drive. The grass was green. Which was remarkable considering the drought. Even more remarkable was the crime scene in black, beneath three flag poles.

"It scared a lot of people," said Father Anthony.

The burn marks formed a six-pointed star. A huge star, at least ten feet in radius.

I told Madame to stay, then stepped on the grass and set down my pack. The fire had melted irrigation tubes that snaked through the soil. I took out a pair of fresh latex gloves, my camera, and a tape measure. I handed Jack one end of the tape and walked backwards along the black lines. "When did this happen?"

"The night before the Feast of St. Michael."

I stopped. Father Anthony was kneeling down, petting Madame again. "September twenty-ninth?" I asked.

"Was it the twenty-ninth?" His hand paused. Madame lifted her face, urging him to keep scratching. "By George, you're right. The twenty-ninth!" He glanced at Jack. "Do we have another German Catholic among us?"

"No, sir," I said. "I know the date because Annicka Engels went missing the day after the feast."

"Oh, dear God." He looked at Jack. "Could—could these things be connected?"

"I doubt it," Jack said. "Do *you* see any connection?"

"The Engels are members of the church."

"Just about everybody in this town's a member," Jack said.

The priest seemed lost in thought. I wrote down the burned star's measurements, took photos, and wiped down my trowel with a sterile alcohol pad, soberly removing the soil from Annicka's grave.

"Did you see it burning?" I asked.

"No." The priest shook his head, hard, as if dislodging a thought. "I was home, preparing for the long weekend. We have three services on holy days, plus the feast. The sheriff's office called." He pointed to the road. "Someone drove up the hill and saw the flames."

"What time?"

"Oh, it was past midnight."

I pinched the ground, lifting the soil to my nose. It smelled foul, bitter. Just like the motivations behind it. "Did the local fire department investigate?"

"Yes, but …" He seemed to consider how to say it. "They're a volunteer company."

"Good enough to save lives," Jack said. "But not trained for arson investigations. Or hate crimes."

I dug a chunk of soil out of the ground and placed it in a plastic bag, sealing the top and writing the location on it with the Sharpie. "Anything about this feast of Saint Michael that might cause someone to threaten your church?"

"That's just it." The priest stared at the burnt grass. "I could see this coming from the Oktoberfest crowd, some drunken prank. But Saint Michael—the angel of God? *That's* what we're celebrating."

"And no threats leading up to it?"

"Well." He glanced at Jack again. "You know about those."

Jack nodded and looked at me. I was close enough that I could see my reflection in his shades. Three flags behind me flapped in the wind. And there I stood, one solitary woman, at the foot of a burned-out star. *My life in one picture.*

Jack said, "Father Anthony isn't exactly the most traditional Catholic."

"How so?"

"Oh." The priest chuckled, a little nervously. "People never like it when their church changes. I keep telling them, the church's best days come when we break with man-made traditions."

"No kidding," Jack muttered.

I snapped off my gloves, a sound that echoed the flapping flags. "What kind of traditions did you break?"

Father Anthony, the passionate type, went into a long discursive about the church's beginnings. I took photographs of the charred star while he talked about the late 1800s, when a German priest invited local native tribes to worship here. And, in the early 1900s, women were given positions of authority. During World War II, Our Lady of Snows helped bring orphans from Nazi Germany to America. During the 1960s, parishioners flew to the South and marched for civil rights.

I laid my wooden ruler next to one of the sooty streaks. I zoomed in the camera's focus. "And what did *you* do to upset people, Father Anthony?"

"Oh, nothing like that."

I lowered the camera.

"Really." He pinched his sweater, then the jeans. "I got rid of formal dress codes."

"And," Jack nodded at Madame.

"Yes, twice a year I bless the animals. In the name of St. Francis of Assisi."

"Patron saint of mutts," Jack muttered.

"What would it take, Jack." Father Anthony smiled. "To get you back in church?"

Jack said nothing.

"Father, has anyone threatened you personally?" I asked.

"You mean, threatened my life?"

I nodded.

"No, but." He glanced at Jack. "Our numbers are dropping. When I proposed casual dress, I lost about ten percent of the congregation. No matter how many sermons I preach about God looking at the *inside*, not the outside. Or how we want people to be comfortable in church. I've even pointed out that Jesus didn't wear formal robes like the religious leaders."

"We'll be classifying this arson as a federal hate crime," Jack said.

"Yes." The priest sighed. "And I've already forgiven whoever did it."

"Good for you," Jack said gruffly. "You do your job, we'll do ours."

I packed up my equipment and gave the priest my card. "If you think of anything else," I said, "call me."

"Certainly." Father Anthony gazed at the charred grass. His cheerful demeanor was gone. He seemed cloaked by something heavy, painful.

"Is something wrong?" I asked.

"Yes. It's a terrible thing when I can think of *too* many people who might do such a thing to my church."

Human nature. It taught such hard lessons to everyone. But people working in law enforcement had nothing on the clergy.

CHAPTER TWENTY

IT TOOK ALL of three minutes.

"Harmon."

"What."

Jack's plane lifted off Lake Wenatchee, sunlight sparkling on the water like we'd tossed glitter out the windows.

"What's going on with you?" Jack asked.

"I'm fine."

An updraft hit the wings. The plane bumped higher. My stomach lurched. Madame circled my lap, and quivered.

"Anything you want to talk about?" he asked.

I shook my head. There was too much to talk about. Annicka and Esther and ruthless killers of innocent girls. Hate crimes. And why Jack froze as soon as he realized I was standing behind him at the Waterhaus. But I was too tired for all of it. We'd left Seattle at dawn, and now I was heading into another visit to the insane asylum.

I wanted to sleep.

But the question wouldn't leave me alone.

A girlfriend? I looked over at Jack. He'd told Johann, *the relationship was fine until she decided to ...* Then stopped. Who was *she?* Was *she* why he still hadn't kissed me? Because he was still attached to somebody else. *Terrific.*

My mind wandered in circles until we reached the city.

Jack was speaking through his headset to the Lake Union marina. I glanced at his profile. It'd been a year since we met—or collided—in the Seattle field office. I despised him back then. Typical male Alpha agent, barreling over everyone else to close his cases. And he was especially tough on me, the only female in the Violent Crimes unit. But then, on that fateful cruise to Alaska, I'd seen another side of him. Or did I?

He looked over, sensing my stare. "What?"

"Fatty acids."

"*That's* what you're thinking about?"

"I need to check the soil in Annicka's grave for fatty acids." Every decomposing body excretes fatty acids, compounds that pathologists used to calculate the time of death.

"How are you going to check for that—with a microscope?"

I glanced out the side window.

"Harmon, you do have a microscope. Don't you?"

Sailboats glided across the lake like toys in a bathtub.

"Do you even have a computer?" he asked. "Please tell me you at least have a computer."

"I'm fine." But I was really thinking, *Free hotel rooms for life*. Which meant waiting even longer for decent equipment.

Jack radioed the marina once more, confirming landing. I closed my eyes, wishing for a nap. I sighed.

Madame sighed.

Jack sighed.

I started to laugh, but stopped as soon as I opened my eyes. Jack was rotating his head back and forth, stretching his neck like someone desperately trying to release tension. He even rolled his shoulders forward and back. And sighed again. "Okay," he blurted. "I'll do it."

"Do what?"

"See if the Bureau is tossing out any computers."

I gazed at his flexing jaw—more tensions—and pondered the male species. They were such a strange animal. Especially this one male. This one who I once hated with my whole heart and who now made my heart pound so hard it hurt. I reached out, touching his arm, and my heart hurt even more.

"Yeah, yeah." He smiled ruefully. "You're welcome."

But it wasn't that I'd forgotten to say thank you—no true southern girl would—it was that I could find no words. Even after we landed on the water and climbed out of the plane and walked across the wooden dock to his houseboat. Even as our footsteps made hollow knocking sounds on the weathered wood. Even as he keyed open his cottage and I stared at the back of his shirt, dusty and wrinkled. Even when Madame left my side, trotting toward the parking lot. Even then, I struggled to find the right thing to say. The words that would let him know just how much he meant to me.

"Harmon." He pushed open the Dutch door. "You need a nap."

"Pardon?"

"You're exhausted. Go sleep."

Later I'd never be able to say how long the moment lasted. Two seconds? Ten? Twenty? All I know is that while I stood there, a telephone rang inside the next houseboat. Someone answered it. Their voice slipped through one of the open windows. *Hello?*

"Don't think too much." Jack looked back at me. "I just don't want you to crash that beautiful car."

"The car." I woke up. "You're worried about the car."

"Absolutely." He stepped inside, glanced over his shoulder. Oh, those eyes. Blue-green. "Get over yourself. I'm going to the office. You have time—catch some Zs on my couch."

I stood on the door's threshold. Madame walked back to

me, slowly. I watched Jack go into the small kitchen and splash water on his face. He dried off with a paper towel, then walked down the hall and disappeared into a room on the right.

Madame stood next to me. I looked down at her. "Hey, you got to sleep on the plane."

Jack stepped out of the back room, wearing jeans and buttoning a clean shirt. "So I'll see you tomorrow morning."

"Why?"

"You need another ride to Leavenworth. Right?"

"Right."

"Lock the door before you leave."

He walked out the door, trailing a scent of pine, and disappeared down the dock to the parking lot.

I hadn't moved an inch. My body felt as divided as the Dutch door. Top half wanted sleep. Bottom half wanted to leave. *Run. Far, far away.*

The dog barked.

"I need a nap," I said, irritably. Because there's nothing quite like having a canine as your conscience. "One quick nap and we'll go."

I closed the door and kicked off my shoes. His couch was positioned beneath the picture window that framed Lake Union. I laid down, closed my eyes. But couldn't sleep. I stared at the couch's fabric. Green. Green as malachite. I rolled over. Then flipped on my back. One mountain bike hung on the wall. But there were two bike hooks. *Where was the other bike?*

Next to the bike, a small fireplace. It had a burled wood mantel. Framed photos were displayed on the mantel. I glanced at Madame. She had stayed just inside the door, her dark eyes fixed on me.

"It's not a big deal." I got up and walked to the mantle.

The photos were faded from all the sunlight that reflected off the water. Some of them were also quite old, probably from around the turn of the nineteenth century. In palest sepia, lumberjacks worked enormous two-man saws. The cedar trees were as wide as this houseboat. One of the men looked directly at the photographer. He had Jack's eyes. In another sepia photo, three women wore white bustle dresses, their hair rolled back, standing on the porch of a Craftsman-style house. The other photos leaped forward in time. I recognized the cabin at Lake Wenatchee. And a picture of four blond kids sitting in a red wagon. They were pulled by a muscular man grinning down on them. Same grin as Jack.

I turned around. Madame stared at me.

"See? No big deal."

She twitched her nose, as if sniffing the air for mendacity.

"And if you don't mind, I need to use the restroom."

She followed me down the hallway. There were two rooms in back, doors closed. But one of the rooms must be his bedroom because he went in there to change clothes. I congratulated myself on not opening either door—then realized something was *really* wrong with me if I was patting myself on the back for not trespassing.

The bathroom was larger than expected, given the houseboat's size. An antique claw-footed tub, painted forest green, matched the shower's tumbled-glass wall tile. Pedestal sink. Retro light fixtures from the 1930s … *Wow.*

I looked back at the tub.

Clue number one.

Jack was a guy who splashed his face at the kitchen sink and used paper towels as washcloths. Not the kind who takes bubble baths. And the tub's tasteful green color? For a testosterone-saturated agent who …

Clue number two.

The color. *That* green. That green of Jack's eyes, when he's being playful or loving or—

I washed my hands in the pedestal sink, and tried to avoid my reflection in the antique mirror above it.

I failed.

My hair needed combing. Auburn wisps curled around my face. My brown eyes stared back at me, filled with painful questions. What was wrong with me—why was I so obsessed with Jack? I stared at myself. My eyes burned. The realization hit like a punch to the gut.

Jack didn't decorate this bathroom. Some woman did. And then what happened—they broke up?

Got divorced?

Or worse.

Separated, not even divorced. Jack was totally unavailable.

You know who.

The *relationship.* Which was *going fine until—*

Madame watched me from the threshold. I stepped over her. "Don't hound me," I said.

Face on fire, eyes burning, throat dry, I found a clean glass in the kitchen and turned on the faucet. I held my hand under the water, waiting for it to get cold. But it didn't. *Ice,* I needed ice.

I turned and grabbed the freezer's handle.

The fridge had one magnet holding one photograph. The photo showed a woman with honey-blonde hair, her bangs tousled by the wind. Sunshine glinted from her white smile. She wore mirrored sunglasses. I leaned in. The lenses showed the man taking her photograph. No mistaking his grin.

At the bottom of the photo, in flowing feminine handwriting, someone had written:

Love you with all my heart, Jackson.

—M.

I set the glass back in the cupboard.

"Madame?" I whispered.

She waited by the door.

"You were right," I whispered. "Let's go."

CHAPTER TWENTY-ONE

HOLDING MADAME UNDER one arm, I scrawled my name on the sign-in sheet at Western State. My mind was so distracted, thinking about what just happened and what might be awaiting us upstairs, that I almost missed the signature on the line above mine.

Charlotte Harmon.

My aunt. She was already here.

When the door lock vibrated, I yanked it open and raced up the stairs. Madame raised her nose, sniffing. The air carried that oily scent of chicken soup. Dinner in an hour. I reached the next door, and pulled it open when it buzzed. I expected to see Sir Post-it waiting for us as usual. But the hallway was empty. So was my mom's room.

Everyone was gathered in the recreation room. Including my aunt.

"Back off," she was telling them, pivoting so fast her batiked silk tunic wafted around her plump figure like the gossamer wings on an enormous bird. "I'm holding some serious power here."

What she waved at them was a long necklace of dark stones. The crystals glimmered under the fluorescent lights. My best geologist's guess was black tourmaline. Onyx. Or possibly a smoky quartz. My aunt believed certain rocks produced life-altering energies. Improved health. Mental clarity. Protection. Whatever she expected from these particular crystals, they were doing a lousy job at repelling weird personalities.

I turned a full circle, searching the room. Across the room, the red-haired nurse named Sarah worked behind her counter, setting out afternoon meds. Around my aunt, the feudal gang clustered. I finally found my mom when her face peeked from behind the bulwark of her busty sister-in-law. My heart bucked at my ribcage.

"You must obey the laws of my kingdom," Sir Post-it was telling Aunt Charlotte. "Or you will be thrown in the dungeon."

"Bullcrap." She waved the black necklace. "Get away from us."

The nurse continued to dole out the meds, as if this was all playing on television instead of flesh and blood and who knows what principalities. I wanted to shout, wave my arms, yank Sir Post-It away from my family. But I'd already been told the rules around here. Hospital staff wasn't allowed to touch any patient—even if that patient was attacking them. That was the state law. More informally, the hospital believed these "encounters" between patients helped then learn the art of negotiation. And look how well that was working—a demented despot ran this ward.

"Hi, Mom."

Her once-beautiful face looked vague and uncertain. Whatever the medication was—and nobody would tell me, more state laws—the drugs had a flattening effect. Gone was the woman with shimmer and southern sparkle. The woman who broke into hymns at random times.

I lifted my hand, like a peace offering.

She came toward me with her arms open wide.

"Hi, Mom," I tried again.

"Oh, Madame." She took the dog from my arms and buried her face in the black fur. "I missed you so much."

The knife slid into my heart. And twisted. Madame glanced at me, questioning, and I held her gaze, forcing myself to smile. Mental illness was one rotten deal after another. You trade one aspect for another, always hoping you made the right choice. Here I'd traded my paranoid schizophrenic mother for this vague woman no longer haunted by voices, but she was like a stranger to me.

Meanwhile, my aunt sounded a little panicked. "Raleigh, get over here."

Another trade.

I blinked away the burn in my eyes and raised my voice. "Aunt Charlotte, is that black tourmaline?"

"Yes!" She smiled. "*Lots* of black tourmaline."

"Oh, no." I tried to sound shocked. "You shouldn't bring that in here."

Bad Knight spun toward me, his foil sword flashing. "How come?"

"Don't you know?" I asked.

"No." He turned to Sir Post-it. "Should I know?"

"I grant you permission to order the peasant to explain," Sir Post-it replied. "Speak!"

I aimed for an ominous tone. "Black tourmaline has secret powers."

"Secret?" Bad Knight asked.

"That's right." My aunt waved the necklace. "So you better get away from me."

"Nay." Sir Post-it raised one flabby arm. "Seize the jewels!"

"Seizing!" Bad Knight swung his foil sword. "Hand over the jewels. They are property of the king!"

My aunt began waving the necklace like it was some spiritual air freshener. Father Brother flung that water. And Lady Anne whimpered. I turned to find my mother. Her nail-bitten fingernails were digging into Madame's fur.

"Nurse." I wasn't playing any more games. "Nurse!"

"Uh-oh." Father Brother dipped his fingers in the paper cup. "Now look what this fat one's done."

"I'm not fat!" Aunt Charlotte said. "And if that water so much as touches me—"

"*Nurse!*"

Sarah lifted the counter partition, taking the tray of meds with her.

"Aunt Charlotte." I moved to my aunt's side, whispering. "Please, stop."

"I didn't start this," she said.

"But you can end it."

"Raleigh, my chakras are launching into outer space. These people are invading my boundaries. I can't stop any of this."

"You can. Apologize."

"What—I will not!"

"Haircut, remember?" I shifted my gaze toward my mom. "Our mission was to get her out of here for a haircut. Remember that part?"

My aunt, my beloved aunt. For all her New Age nonsense, all the tiki-torch kooky ideas that flamed her passions, she loved her family more than anything else. She took one glance at her bedraggled sister-in-law, and swallowed, hard.

The nurse stood here now, just outside the circle, holding the tray of pills and water.

"Your royal …" Aunt Charlotte pushed the next word out. "Highness."

"Ye-es-ss." Sir Post-it gave a ghoulish smile. "I give you

permission to address the king."

"I … I …" Aunt Charlotte swallowed once more. "I—I—"

"Aye, aye!" said Lady Anne.

"Oh, shut up," said Bad Knight. "We're not pirates."

My aunt gripped the black necklace so tightly her knuckles turned white.

"Haircut," I whispered.

"I'm sorry." Her voice sounded as wooden as a drawbridge. "I didn't mean to offend you."

"Isn't this wonderful?" Sarah the nurse smiled at them, including Aunt Charlotte. Like my aunt was one of the patients. "I'm so very proud. You just showed such great self-control." She raised the tray. "Ready for meds?"

They lined up in front of her like dutiful third graders. She handed each one their medicine, their water. Sir Post-it gulped his pills with one toss of the cup. My mom gave the dog back to me without a word and picked each pill out of the cup. One small blue tablet. A large pink capsule. Another as yellow as condensed sunlight. All the bright happy colors for the darkness of schizophrenia.

Sarah handed her the cup of water.

Like communion, only nothing about this process would reconnect my mom to her maker. If anything, I was sure the medicine was keeping the holy away. The holy, and the unholy. Another trade.

"There," my mom said softly, after the last pill. Then she said it again, her southern accent stretching that one word into a song. "There."

"Nadine," Sarah said, "I'm very proud of you."

My mother nodded and took Madame from my arms.

"And I guess you'll be back soon." The nurse turned to me. "Will you be getting her dinner out there?"

"Out where?" my mother asked.

"Nadine, don't you remember?" Sarah smiled like we were headed to Disneyland. "Your family's taking you for a haircut."

"Outside?"

"Of course outside," Aunt Charlotte said. "Look at the haircut you got in here."

My mother frowned, her pale forehead creasing. "Who will be cutting my hair?"

"Somebody decent." My aunt took her arm.

But my mom pulled away. "What's this person's name?"

Uh-oh.

The crease deepened on her face and I felt that far-far-away sensation sweep over me. Inside, I was pulling back, pulling away, putting distance between me and the mother who looked at me with suspicion. Her ragged gray curls shaking with fear.

"Scissors." Her mouth trembled. "You can kill people with scissors."

Aunt Charlotte tried to explain. Sarah stepped away, moving across the room to the counter. I heard my aunt say something about *there's no danger*, but I was watching Sarah. She opened a manila folder and wrote something inside.

No danger, my aunt kept saying. You're safe with us.

But I knew it was over. The opportunity was gone.

I handed Madame back to my mother. She backed away from us, chin still trembling, clutching the dog, soaking up the love.

The love she so desperately needed.

The love she wouldn't accept from me.

CHAPTER TWENTY-TWO

When I pulled into Eleanor's long driveway, I had five minutes to spare before the cocktail hour.

Madame sat up, ready to get out.

"Give me a minute." I said.

The Ghost's buttery leather seat was felt as soft and pliable as a broken-in baseball mitt. I laid my head back, closed my eyes. This day. This long, long day. Two girls bled out. Quaint Leavenworth with a killer. Hate crime against the Catholic church. My mother. Jack. The picture on his fridge. *Love you with all my heart.*

I drew a deep breath, and held it tight. *Do not cry.*

My car door swung open.

"You're late!"

"Eleanor." I blew out all that pent-up breath. "This has been the world's longest day. I really don't have energy for—"

"Move over." She threw her sequined purse into the car. "I'll drive."

"Drive—where?"

"None of your bee's wax."

She eased the Italian sports car onto I-5 north. Rush hour traffic swung around us, horns blaring. After two minutes, I realized the problem.

"Eleanor, I think it's illegal to drive on the freeway at twenty-five miles an hour."

"Go to sleep."

I glanced at Madame, perched on the backseat ledge, and closed my eyes.

The Ghost lulled me to sleep.

"WAKE UP!"

We were in Seattle, parked on the street near the waterfront. To my right was the sidewalk. To my left, cars whisked past Eleanor's window which also framed a piece of the wharf. I leaned forward, glancing up at the pieces of dusk that floated between the glassy skyscrapers like amethyst. The street sign read *2nd Avenue*.

"What're we doing?" I asked.

A man appeared at Eleanor's door. He wore a blue uniform.

"Hello, Mrs. Anderson," he said. "I'm your valet."

"Hello! Aren't you cute?" She grabbed her sparkly purse, then latched onto the guy's arm, hoisting herself from the low-slung seat. "I am certain this sports car will tempt you, young man. So here's my offer. You may take one short drive within a three-block radius. After showing off, park it. Understand?"

He nodded.

I opened my door. Madame jumped out. My backpack was still in here. I considered the guy driving around with it. If somebody stole it … I slung the pack over my shoulder and climbed out. The valet was leading Eleanor to the sidewalk.

Her chin was rising.

Uh-oh.

"When so many are lonely," she called out to Seattle, "it

would be inexcusably selfish to be lonely alone."

"Right, sure," he replied.

"I can take her from here," I said, literally taking her off his hands.

"Raleigh," she said, "who said that?"

"You did."

"*Camino Real*—and where's your dog?"

I pointed. Madame was already heading toward a gray-haired doorman who stood beside a bright brass door. The building itself was white marble, weathered by years of heavy rain. I glanced back to see The Ghost, disappearing down 2nd Avenue. "Eleanor, tell me what's going on. I *really* don't like surprises."

"But I *adore* surprises." She waved at the doorman. "Hello, you must be new."

"Yes, ma'am." He tipped his hat, opened the door. "And you must be Mrs. Anderson."

Eleanor snapped open her purse and pressed a dollar bill into his hand. He thanked her. We stepped inside.

"Oh, Raleigh, look!" she cried. "Just like old times."

"Maybe for you."

We stood in a lobby covered in marble. Walls, ceiling. But it wasn't white like the exterior. And it wasn't ordinary stone. A deep brown, the marble was veined with ochre and gold. I ran my hand over the polished surface. "What is this place?"

"The Smith Tower. Harry owned part of it."

An elderly black man stepped out from behind a guard's desk. His posture was stooped, like the brass buttons on his blue uniform weighed too much. "Miz Anderson?" He gave Eleanor the world's best smile.

"Patterson!" Eleanor's voice ricocheted off the marble. "Oh, I'm *so* glad to see you. Please, come meet my friend Raleigh."

We shook hands. His skin felt dry. His smile never faded.

"Right this way," he said.

He ushered us into an elevator. So old it still had the accordion-style door. I picked up Madame. Patterson yanked the clattering brass cage closed, swung a brass lever, and we took off. The floors swept past, inches from the cage door. *Two, three, four…*

"Patterson, tell Raleigh about the Smith Tower."

He began a speech that had the practiced rhythms of a tour guide. The Smith Tower was built in 1914. At the time, the tallest building west of Chicago.

"Tell her about that silly gun man," Eleanor said.

Seven, eight …

"What silly gun man?" I asked.

"He's the Smith," Patterson answered. "Of Smith & Wesson."

"Now I'm interested."

He talked about the building's many owners, including Harry Anderson. When he shifted the brass lever, the elevator slowed.

Ten, eleven…

"Ladies, welcome to the twelfth floor."

"Thank you, Patterson," Eleanor opened her purse and took out a twenty. "Please give my best to your family."

"Yes'm. Thank you."

Patterson pulled open the cage, winked at me, then disappeared back into the elevator.

More marble. And it glowed like moonlight. Eleanor led me past the office doors with pebble-glass panels. The business names painted on them were antique black-and-gold. I counted three lawyers. One dentist. Two architects. One psychologist…

"And here we are!"

The last door, at the end of the hall. It read: Anderson Enterprises.

Eleanor inserted a key, and raised her chin. "You can be young without money, but you can't be old without it."

I waited for the *who-said-that* question. Instead she swung open the door and tilted her head.

"Don't just stand there," she said. "Go in."

The office had three large rooms. A main area with a leather couch, two reading chairs, and a breathtaking view of Seattle's waterfront. A utility kitchen sat to the side, with another window facing north, framing a piece of the Space Needle. The bathroom was pink tile, pink sink, pink toilet...all for Eleanor, I suspected.

When I looked over, she was standing beside the leather couch, brushing her hand over the worn surface. She stared out the window. City lights sparkled along the waterfront.

"Eleanor?"

She turned. Her eyes shone like those city lights.

"Why're we here?"

"Shame on you. You haven't been listening to me. What did I just say?"

"You can be young without money. But it sucks to be old and not have it."

"That is pathetic paraphrasing."

"Come on."

"I never wanted anyone to rent his personal office." She glanced around the room, rhinestones sparkling in her glasses. "But now I've found someone he would approve of."

"Eleanor." I gasped. "I can't afford to rent this—"

"Of course not. It's free."

I blinked. "Free."

"Consider it a gift."

"I can't accept it."

"Raleigh, if you reject this gift, I will throw you and your little dog out on the street. Do you understand me?"

I opened my mouth. But her expression closed it. There was a real woman underneath the actress and she was more formidable than any character Tennessee Williams ever dreamed up.

And yet, there was also an unexpected softness in her eyes.

"*Why* do you think I keep those high-strung thoroughbreds? They cost me a fortune just to feed. But they're highly entertaining. It's the same reason I agreed to help you with all that skullduggery at the track. I hate being bored. And frankly, my dear, your unemployment is boring. I want you to start doing real work."

Madame jumped up on the leather couch.

Eleanor glared at her. "I don't suppose that creature will be told to disembark from the furnishings?"

My first smile of the day began inside my chest. It climbed up my throat and spread across my lips. *Eleanor.* That little glittering general. Out the window, neon and streetlights blurred. When I blinked, I felt something trace down my cheek. The feeling in my heart was heavier than sorrow, yet lighter than laughter. And it made me think of something my dad once said.

Did I ever tell you what Thornton Wilder said? he'd asked me. *He said we're only alive when our hearts are conscious of our treasures.*

"Raleigh?"

I looked over at her. Such a gift. *Such a treasure.* "Thank you."

"You're welcome," she said. "Now get to work."

CHAPTER TWENTY-THREE

SHE WASN'T KIDDING about getting to work. Behind Harry's desk, I found boxes. They contained even more surprises. A new computer delivered directly from Microsoft's headquarters in Redmond. Glass beakers, pipettes, brass sieves for separating soil by grain size, and a heat lamp.

But the crown jewel? One gorgeous microscope, direct from a science supply warehouse in Tacoma.

"That cowboy fellow in Spokane told me what to order," Eleanor said.

"I'm speechless."

"Excellent." She sat on the couch opposite Madame. "If your mouth is closed, you'll work faster."

I still had geologic maps in my pack, bought during my time with the Bureau's Seattle office. I found the quadrant that contained the Icicle River and traced my finger along the water line as it ran through the mountains where Annicka Engels died. The river cut through the ancient granite like a buzz saw.

"How long will this take?" Eleanor asked.

I shook my head. I needed to concentrate.

"When will you be done?" she asked.

"Science isn't like a Broadway play."

"But it's forensics."

I tried to smile. *Television.* Once again, it was ruining reality. “Forensics is really slow work. It requires extreme patience. So maybe you should go get some dinner.”

“All by myself?” She feigned horror. “You would let me wander the streets of Seattle unprotected?”

“Take my gun.”

“Heavens!”

“Take the dog.”

She eyed Madame, poised at the couch’s other end. “Will she obey?”

“Will you?”

I received one withering look—from both of them. Let the smart set believe dogs don’t have human-esque personalities. I knew differently. “Madame.”

She jumped off the couch, stretched, and wagged her tail.

“Perhaps.” Eleanor stood. “I’ll have Patterson call us a cab.”

“Order something for the dog,” I said.

Eleanor slammed the door.

WITH MY NEW equipment stationed around the office, I cut open the box Peter sent back, and took my new soil samples from my backpack.

Snapping on gloves, I divided the soil from Annicka’s boots into two parts. The first half I rinsed in a sterile beaker—*thank you, Eleanor*—in the pink bathroom which still had monogrammed towels marked *E* and *H*.

Draining the water, I placed the sample under a heat lamp—*thanks again.*

I didn’t rinse the burned soil from the church arson. I was concerned I could wash away the flame accelerant. Gasoline, propane. Lighter fluid. Alcohol. Who knows what they used?

I also didn't rinse the second section of the boot soil. Taking ChapStick from my backpack, I rubbed it over a glass slide, pinched the dry boot soil and dusted the grains on the now-sticky slide, and placed it under the sleek new scope. It was even nicer than my scope at the Bureau—*God bless Eleanor*—with eight levels of magnification.

And what did I see?

A wild mess.

The sand was shard-shaped. That meant geologically young, not rounded by eons of erosion. But the silt grains were soft-edged. And it was hard to get a good look at anything else because there was so much biological material in here. Organic matter. Grass. I adjusted the focus. No, hay. I also found two strands of something that looked so fine, it required the most powerful magnification, 2000X.

Hair.

I pushed away from the scope, rubbing my eyes, and called Peter.

"How you likin' them fancy digs?" he asked.

"And you told her what equipment to buy."

"No red-blooded American man could ever say No to that woman."

"Not to mention that this whole setup works entirely in your favor."

"Good and howdy." He chuckled. "I thought it might also keep you from being ticked off about gettin' paid in hotel rooms."

"We can discuss that later. And I don't expect the Bureau to barter with us." I explained the burned grass at Our Lady of Snows.

"KKK?"

"They usually burn a cross. This is a six-pointed star."

"Satanic?"

"Maybe. FBI's classified it as a hate crime. I come in as the freelance consultant."

"Hot dog. Let's move it fast."

"I'm on it." If I could make a quick and accurate turnaround, we might gain a foothold with Bureau's field office. That would mean more work. And less dependence on Jack. "I'm sending you the arson soil."

"What for?"

"I need you to run it through the GCMS." Gas chromatography—mass spectrometry. A mouthful of a name that was the gold standard of forensic testing. The GCMS instrument doesn't just find unknowns, it names them, and any trace elements that otherwise would be disintegrated beyond identification. I'd used it before on several mineralogy cases, including a cross burning in Virginia. "Run it through the machine, then call me. I'll take it to the Bureau."

"Can't."

"Why not?"

"Raleigh, that doo-hickey of a machine costs a small fortune. I don't got one. Unless you want to ask Granny Warbucks—"

"No." I dropped my head. "If we have to send this soil to the state…" I didn't need to finish that thought. Why should the Bureau hire us if we needed the state to identify the compounds?

"Take it to the wildlife biologist," Peter said.

"Who?"

"You missed my note. Didn't your mama teach you to read the card before you open the present?"

I shoved my hand into the Express mail box and found a folded piece of paper. His handwriting was precise, block lettering. Lab handwriting, the kind that stands up in court. I read the wildlife specialist's name. "Lani Margolis?"

"Formerly of Stanford. One really smart cookie."

"Okay."

"She's brilliant," he said. "But now nobody'll hire her full-time. Got one of them independent streaks. Like another gal I know."

I glanced at his note again. "There's no phone number."

"She refuses to use a phone. See what I'm saying?"

"Not at all."

"Get in that spiffy little car and go find her."

I looked at my watch. Past seven o'clock. "You're sure she's at this address? It's not like I can call her and find out."

"She'll be there."

"How do you know?"

"Because Lani never leaves the lab."

CHAPTER TWENTY-FOUR

THANKS TO PATTERSON, I found Eleanor and Madame at a tiki bar on First Avenue. When I parted the beaded curtains, a familiar figure was up on stage holding an unnecessary microphone to belt out the Karaoke version of *My Way*. Six people sat at the various tables, sipping umbrella drinks and listening to Eleanor talk about a few regrets. In the wings, the small black dog waited. What an animal.

I got them both into The Ghost and headed north.

"I've been meaning to tell you," she said. "Every woman needs one thing from a man."

"Good to know."

Her breath smelled like vermouth, that mix of sweet and musty. It must've been a few martinis because she didn't follow up with her usual question. So I prompted. "Who said that?"

"I did." She brushed one bejeweled hand over the cloud of white hair. "But I would like you to name that one thing. Because every woman needs that one thing from a man."

I checked my phone's GPS. We still had a ways to go.

"Well?" she demanded. "Tell me."

"Safety. Every woman needs safety."

"My dear, if that were true, you would've married the lovely Mr. Fielding."

DeMott. My ex-fiancé.

"Okay," I said. "Adventure."

"Raleigh, I said *every* woman. Not you with Stanley."

"His name's Jack. And I wasn't thinking of him."

Not entirely.

She scooted up in her seat. "You can't tell me the answer?"

"A really good kiss."

"Have you been kissing that animal?"

I glanced in the rearview mirror. Madame took no offense, although her ears did prick forward. Probably because with Eleanor's voice, everything sounded urgent.

"I have not kissed Jack."

"I suggest you keep it that way."

"I might not have a choice," I said, handing her my phone. "Check the directions, I think we're lost."

I leaned forward, peering through the sloping windshield. Pop-up headlights were definitely high on the cool factor, but at night driving downhill through hairpin turns, it felt like I was following two light sabers straight to my death.

"This says …" Eleanor glanced out her window. "Puget Sound is directly below us. So one wrong turn and we're out of this mortal coil."

"Maybe I typed in the wrong address."

Eleanor wasn't listening. She'd rolled down her window and stuck her head out, bellowing into the black night. "I don't want realism!"

I glanced in the rearview. I *swear* Madame rolled her eyes.

"I want magic!" Eleanor cried.

"Hello? I need to drive."

She pulled her head back into the car, patting the white crown. "That line's from *Streetcar.*"

"You promised," I said.

"I promised not say a word *during* your interview with this person we're going to see." She rolled up the window. "I promised to be as silent as Gloria Stuart."

Whoever that was, I didn't care. The Ghost was growling through the sharp turns like a prowling lion. When we finally reached the bottom of the hill, the road dead-ended at a beach. In my headlights, one solitary figure sat beside a fire in the sand, the embers glowing orange in the darkness.

"We should make a fire," Eleanor said.

I grabbed the phone.

The road ran parallel to the beach. I followed it for a quarter mile. We seemed to disappear into a forest of madrone trees before the road went uphill, then down, and we were back by the water. I checked my phone. Our destination was right here. End of the road.

"Airstreams!" Eleanor exclaimed, pointing. "I love Airstreams. Now we've got magic."

Three or four silver trailers waited under patio lights. I picked up Peter's note, checking the address with my phone. Eleanor was already out the door with Madame following.

I grabbed the soil samples, still clutching Peter's note, and headed for the silver trailers. I counted four, each one connected to the other by the strings of bulb lights that swooped from the surrounding trees like lightning bugs. Between the trailers, the trail was lined with conch shells. Sand dollars. Dried starfish. Seashells, seashells, seashells.

"Could this be a trailer park?" Eleanor asked. "Because they don't usually show such good taste."

"Eleanor. You promised."

"Quiet. As a mouse."

Madame sniffed the ground, trotting under the lights, gazing left and right.

"But I do think it's magic," Eleanor said.

"You promis—"

"Listen! Music. I think that's Billie Holiday."

I stood outside what appeared to be the main trailer, where the music was coming from. Loud enough that Billie Holiday's up-all-night-drinking-and-smoking voice seemed to vibrate the trailer's steel rivets. The short front stoop was made of cinder blocks that led to a door painted seafoam green. I knocked.

The music quieted. But the door didn't open.

"Yoo-hoo!" Eleanor called out. "Anybody home?"

"You prom—"

The door swung open—outward. I jumped back, just avoiding getting smacked.

A tiny Asian woman squinted at us through wire-rimmed glasses. Black hair spiked off her forehead, like some mohawked halo.

Eleanor said, "I simply adore your music."

"Thanks." The woman gave the glasses a push, getting them closer to her squinting eyes. "You need something?"

I lifted the paper in my hand but Eleanor was already talking, chin going up.

"I'm sorry to say that the Grim Reaper has set up his tent on our doorstep."

The Asian woman stared at her. Then turned to me.

I lifted Peter's note again. "Are you Lani Margolis? I work with Peter Rosser. My name's Raleigh Harmon and I need—"

"Raleigh!" The woman slapped her hand against the door, slamming it against the trailer with a *bang*. "Raleigh Harmon?"

"The name is southern," Eleanor said. "They often give girls last names as first names."

"Raleigh!" Now the woman slapped her hand to her chest, thumping it twice. "It's me—*Lanette*!"

I stared at her. "What?"

"Lanette Yee!"

How could—I looked down at Peter's note. How could—I looked up again and in an instant I saw the fifteen-year-old girl from long ago. "But … this says … Lani … Margolis."

"Guilty as charged!" She raised her left hand, fluttering her small fingers. The silver band was on the third finger. "I'm married."

"Lanette?" I tried to think of something more to say, but came up blank.

"Raleigh!" She threw her head back and laughed. "Come here!"

I leaped up the steps and grabbed her in a tight-tight-*tight* hug. Her laughter shook her body and reverberated into me, until I was laughing, too. The kind of laughter, that sudden joy that strikes hidden fault lines and cracks them wide open. It felt like every emotion trapped inside me was erupting. I held my laughing friend from years ago and wanted to cry. The voice behind us spoke to no one in particular. And yet, to everyone.

"I asked for magic," Eleanor said. "And here it is."

CHAPTER TWENTY-FIVE

WITH ITS LOW curved ceiling, the Airstream felt like the interior of a magma tube. Molten volcanic mass that hardened around an elongated bubble of air. And it seemed every surface in here was painted some watery shade of blue, from sapphire and tourmaline to opal and turquoise.

Lanette—*Lani*—walked over to the built-in shelves and lowered the sound on the stereo system. Billie Holiday went into a whisper.

"I still can't believe it," Lani said. "You were *never* going to leave the South."

"Yeah, well, work transfer." I glanced over at Eleanor. She was eyeing the Airstream like it might be her next purchase.

"What kind of work?" Lani asked.

"FBI."

"So you did it?" She smiled, the familiar dimples showing. "You always said you wanted to work for the FBI."

I nodded.

She pushed the wire-rimmed glasses up the bridge of her small nose. The gesture launched a landslide of memories. We were two fifteen-year-old nerd-girls fighting for survival on Ocracoke Island in North Carolina. Four days that changed us forever. We promised to never lose touch. But promises die.

"I didn't know the FBI had a geology lab in Seattle," she

said.

"They don't." My mind scrambled to catch up, how to set the record straight. After our life-and-death adventure, Lanette and I turned out to be terrible pen pals. I didn't want to write about what was *really* going on in my life, and Lanette's homeschooling mom didn't allow her to have email or a cell phone. Which probably explained the no-phone policy now. "I started with the Bureau as a geologist, in D.C.," I said. "Then I became a special agent. That's how the transfer happened."

"So cool!"

"How about you?" I felt desperate to change the subject. "You go by Lani now?"

She threw her head back and laughed again. *That* was different. As a teenager, she was brilliant but buttoned-up. I couldn't recall ever seeing her laugh, especially like this. "I *hated* the name Lanette. Then I met a guy who started calling me Lani." She smiled. "So I married him. Got a total name change."

"Nice."

There was a scratch at the door. *Madame*. How did I forget her? "Sorry, my dog. Can I get her some water?"

Eleanor took a seat at the small banquette, keeping quiet but smiling like Maggie the Cat caught two mice. Lani filled a bowl with water for Madame and set it on the floor. Madame lapped, and I looked around. I never expected to see this person ever again. Yet here she was, living … I glanced around the small space … living in her own universe. "You live in a trailer," I said.

"I know!" She laughed. "You'd think I'd never want to see another one in my entire life."

Cricket—her homeschooling mom—raised her in a vagabond camper.

"And you still don't have a phone?"

She threw her head, laughing harder. Eleanor clapped her hands. Madame looked up from the water bowl, questioning.

"Life's full of weird surprises," Lani said. "Cricket's indoctrination worked. No phone. And no email. Except through the university."

"I find that oddly impressive."

"Drives people nuts." She smiled, dimples deepening. "Which naturally makes me want to keep doing it."

"Naturally." I lifted the soil samples. "Peter Rosser wanted you to look at some things."

"Rossie. Isn't he great."

Rossie? I made a mental note to tease him and handed Lani the bag of soil from Annicka's grave. "I can't say too much, you know the deal."

She nodded. If she was called on to testify, we needed her to truthfully state that her examination wasn't tainted by any other information given to her. However, I was conveniently not telling her my whole story. Like, that I was here outside the Bureau. "Peter thought you might identify what he can't—"

"Yes!" Lani grabbed the bag.

Oh, I remembered this girl.

"Let's go check it out," she said, her voice full of excitement.

CHAPTER TWENTY-SIX

LANI LED US out of that Airstream and across the seashell-and-stone path, following the strings of lights to another Airstream.

"Why, it's your own little village," Eleanor said.

"Exactly." Lani opened the second silver trailer, looking back at me. "Sorry, no pets allowed. And you both need to put on protective gear."

"More magic!" Eleanor said.

Madame trotted out under the lights, with plenty to investigate, as Eleanor and I stepped inside. This trailer was different. Gone was the music, the painted surfaces. The air in here smelled dry, sterile. Almost acrylic. I recognized the scent. *Laboratory.*

Lani handed us coverings for our hair and shoes, tugged on her own, and walked toward the back. She was no longer host. No longer friend. She had disappeared into the desire to know.

I took a deep breath of the familiar sterile air, letting it out slowly.

At a short stainless steel counter, Lani deposited the soil from the first bag into a glass dish. The grains fell with a sound like rain on a metal roof. She lifted the dish, gazing at it over the rim of her wire-frame glasses.

"Can these trailers be taken out on the open road?" Eleanor asked.

"Yes." Lani opened a cupboard above the stainless steel counter. A shelf slid out. She removed large tweezers from a glass beaker. "But I'm staying in one place. Ask Raleigh. I traveled too much as a kid."

"Yet, you're not living in a house." Eleanor seemed fascinated. "Why is that?"

Lani pinched the soil with the tweezers and lifted a filament so fine I could only see it because of the bright LED lights under the cupboard. "My husband thought a house would be nice. But something about boxes, I can't get comfortable. So he went with the trailers."

Eleanor glanced at me, rhinestones shimmering.

"What," I said.

"Later," she said.

I turned back to Lani. "Married long?"

"Three years. Together for eight." She laid the filament on a sterile glass slide and opened a lower cupboard. The microscope rose, strapped to the shelf, just like it was in Cricket's weird camper-house. "Guess how I met him?"

"He killed someone!" Eleanor said.

"Nope. He's a cop."

"Oh, I love a man in blue."

"He came to a workshop I was giving on how to get out of any knot. Remember the knots, Raleigh?"

I nodded, but she'd already moved on. Sitting at the microscope, she looked fifteen again. And that strange feeling swept over me again. Lanette Yee. Her life had progressed like somebody following footsteps laid out for her. Even the workshop on knots. She'd spent two letters of our correspondence explaining to me how she'd learned to make every nautical knot known to man—including fishing knots that dated back to 5,000 B.C. The third letter contained her instructions on how to get out of a knot, in case I was ever kidnapped. Back then, we were so alike. We had plans. I though my path was laid out, too. Science, crime, lab, everything in order. Then somebody killed my dad.

"Raleigh," Lani said, her gaze still fixed on the scope's lens, "can you give me just the basic location?"

"Eastern side of the Cascades."

"Rural?"

"Not all of it."

"I see why Rossie was baffled." She leaned back, pushing the glasses. "Take a look."

I leaned over the scope's lens. And blinked. "You're still blind as a bat."

"That's a common misconception," she said, while I adjusted the scope's focus. "Most bats have excellent eyesight. Particularly fruit-eating bats. Bats also come equipped with the equivalent of sonar and radar, which is why vision is sometimes—"

"Lanette?"

"I'm doing it, aren't I?"

I nodded. I was so tired. "I just need to know what I'm looking at—hair, right?"

Under her scope, the strand looked like a reddish brown thread. Only with bristles.

Lani walked to the other side of the lab where a bookcase divided the space from the lab's kitchen. She slid out a three-ring binder so large she had to cradle it in both arms, then rested it on the counter.

"I can tell you what it is." She flipped the laminated pages. "But you need to figure out *how* it got there."

She tapped her index finger on a page with a photo at the top. It showed a microscopic view of a hair, similar to what I'd just seen.

"Laxodonta africana," she said.

"Translation?"

"African elephant."

"*What*?"

"Yeah, what I'm saying." She pushed the glasses. "The African elephant isn't a native species to Washington state. So you'll need a good hypothesis for how that elephant hair got in the soil."

Elephant? My mind flashed to that hand, rising above the grave again. How would elephant hair get—*did someone ride one up the mountain?* It was preposterous.

"I once ran away with the circus," Eleanor said.

Lani was already working on the next batch of soil—from Annicka's boots. While we waited, Eleanor described the "grubby existence" with the big top. She stayed with the circus all of one week.

"The stage was calling me," she said.

Lani slipped the boot soil under scope and leaned into the eyepiece. "Okay. It's in here, too."

"Elephant hair?" I asked, incredulous.

She stood, opened a drawer, and up came the printer, strapped like the scope. "I'll make you a copy of this page." She laid the binder on the printer's glass face. "What else?"

I took out the last soil sample. The burnt soil from the church. But I wasn't feeling hopeful. The machine I needed was too big for an Airstream trailer. "You're not hiding a GCMS in here?"

"I wish!" She grabbed the bag. "Same collection site?"

"No." I couldn't say much more. "In this soil, I'm looking for possible flammables. Flame accelerants."

"Arson?"

I didn't respond.

"Seriously," she said, "do you ever wonder what is wrong

with people?" She lifted her small hand. "Don't answer that. You've *always* wondered."

At the other end of the trailer, the door swung open and a voice called out. "Honey? Are you in here?"

"He's here!" She dropped the bag on the counter and raced for the door. He must've been standing on the stairs outside because Lani flew through the opening with a squeal of delight.

I walked over. A stocky man wearing a blue Seattle PD uniform held her in his arms. He was smiling.

"Hey!" Lani pointed at me. "Remember that science contest on Ocracoke Island?"

"When you were a kid?"

"*Yes.*" She nodded so fast her spiked hair raked the night. "Remember Raleigh—my friend?" She squealed again. "That's her. She's *here!*"

"Oh. Wow. Well, hi." He offered me one hand, but didn't let go of his wife. "Mike Margolis. How you doing?"

"She's an FBI agent," Lani said.

Mike Margolis's face changed.

I started to say something, but Lani kept talking, climbing out of his embrace and standing close beside him, stroking his arm. They were one of those synchronized couples. Two people turned into one being. Two people who'd found each other, and were grateful, and knew there would never be another.

When Lani finished talking, an awkward silence fell.

Madame wandered over, sniffing the stone path. I felt an overwhelming urge to leave.

"So, about that GCMS…"

"Right." Lani continued to stroke her husband's arm, absently, like it was her own arm. "I'm teaching at UW tomorrow, so I might be able to sneak it into their lab. But in case I can't, give me a week. Will that work?"

"Yes." I almost sighed with relief. One week was faster than it would get through the state lab. *Redemption.* It was within sight. We would look like heroes. "So I guess I'll drive out in a couple days and check on the status?"

"No." Mike Margolis gave a weary chuckle and reached into his pocket. He took out two cell phones. "Most guys, they just gotta carry their wife's purse around the mall. Me? I carry her phone. Take down this number, it's for insiders only."

I typed the number with the 206 area code into my phone while he typed mine in hers.

"Call that number, leave your message," he explained. "Then I'll give *that* message to Lani, and she'll give me *her* message, then I call *you* back. It's a total pain. And my wife's *never* gonna change." He smiled.

I smiled back at him, but that strange feeling swept over me once more.

"No. Not this time." Lani held out her hand. "Give me the phone."

"What?" Her husband took a step back. "Give *you* the phone?"

"Yes. Give me the phone."

His mouth hung open. But he placed the phone in her open palm. "I can't believe it."

"Believe it." She looked at me, those familiar dimples deep in her cheeks. "If Raleigh's calling, I'll answer the phone."

CHAPTER TWENTY-SEVEN

THE DRIVE HOME felt somber. My mind drifted over all the new developments, all the things I still couldn't put my finger on. But now I had equipment. And Lanette Yee was now Lani Margolis. And African elephant hair was in the soil from Annicka's grave and in her boots.

The elephant hair didn't make sense. But I felt a shred of hope. Clues—even confusing clues—were rising the surface. That was a start.

And yet, deep inside my heart, something still bothered me.

I glanced in the rearview. Madame had fallen asleep on the back ledge. I looked over at Eleanor. She seemed subdued, gazing out the window as if the martinis and the magic had finally worn off.

As The Ghost blew over the bridge that spanned the north end of Lake Union, I glanced down at the water. The houseboats cusped the shore, their cozy lights like salt grains on the rim of a dark glass. Jack was down there, in the place decorated by some woman who was also captivated by those green eyes. That passionate green. My heart skipped. I wanted to reach inside my chest and slap it. *Snap out of it.*

"You still haven't answered my question," Eleanor said.

I looked over. "What question?"

"What's the one thing every woman needs from a man?"

"Oh. That." I stared at the white lines on the freeway. "Actually, I have no idea."

"I'll give you a clue," she said. "Your friend."

"Lanette—Lani?" I looked over again. "What about her?"

"She's found that one thing."

Love?

But that answer was too simplistic for Eleanor. I thought of how the two of them stood together, touching each other like they didn't know, or care, where one person ended and the other began. "It's something beyond romantic love. Isn't it?"

"Correct. I'll give you another clue. I found it with Harry."

I tried to read her face. But even the rhinestones looked demure right now. "Eleanor, I honestly don't know."

"Your first guess was safety," she said. "Then adventure. But this one thing will give a woman both. And more. So much more."

"Okay. So what is it?"

"As is."

"I'm sorry?"

"As-is. Every woman needs a man who loves her as-is. He doesn't want to change anything about her." She sighed. "Oh, no greater safety in this world than that kind of love. And then life turns into the most grand and wonderful adventure."

I waited, expecting her to recite something from Tennessee. Or make a dig about how I blew up my "perfect" engagement to DeMott.

But after several moments of silence, Eleanor only reached out and turned on the radio. She found the oldies station, then sang with the crooning tunes. For once, she sang softly.

But I couldn't listen. Every song was about love. Getting

love, keeping love, cherishing love.

And I knew some woman loved Jack.

Even worse?

He loved her back.

CHAPTER TWENTY-EIGHT

THE NEXT MORNING, after exhausted sleep, I got up before dawn and sped over the Cascade mountains. The sky shifted from obsidian black to gray opals to the pink quartz that makes morning promises.

In the town of Wenatchee, I followed Gunn Road to Euclid Street, then parked outside the main office of the Chelan County Sheriff's Department. Inside, that same bitter scent of cheap coffee stung the air. No receptionist was at the desk. But in the bullpen that spread behind that desk, dispatch radios crackled and in the far back, one man sat at a desk, sipping from a large white mug.

"Detective Culliton?" I asked.

He wore a collared shirt, no tie. As I approached, he rubbed a square hand across his jaw, back and forth, like somebody who had spent last night grinding his teeth.

"Raleigh Harmon?" He stood. He was tall and broad, dwarfing everything around him.

I handed him my card. While he read it, I glanced at his desk. Two binders sat front and center. One lay open. I'd bet four speeding tickets that the binder was labelled *Engels* or *Heller*. "Thanks for meeting me so early," I said.

"Yeah, what else could I do? You call me eleven at night and say you can only meet early in the morning?" He looked at me. His eyes were deep and dark, like the wrong end of a double-barreled shotgun. “You said the family hired you?”

“Yes, sir.”

“How’d you hear about the Heller girl?”

“Her mother.” I wasn’t ratting out Wilcove. And Martha Heller had told me about her daughter. But as I said it, my phone buzzed. I’d turned off the ringtone before leaving Tacoma this morning. But in this empty office, the buzz sounded like a game show contestant giving the wrong answer. The phone buzzed again.

“You gonna get that?” Detective Culliton waited.

“Not right now.”

“Who told you before the mother,” he said.

“Pardon?”

“Before Mrs. Heller.” He gestured to a metal chair waiting next to his desk. “Who told you about her daughter before her?”

“Was I not supposed to know about Esther Heller?”

He sat and placed my card front and center on the desk. His elbows went on top of that open binder, his big arms crossed to prevent me from seeing anything on the open page. “I don’t like outsiders showing up and meddling in local affairs.”

“Even if that outsider is here to help?”

“Too many cooks turn dinner to crap.”

“Unless one of the cooks happens to know *how* to cook.”

One shotgun shell slid into the chamber of his dark eyes. “You telling me you know how to handle this case?”

“Not at all. I’m just reminding you that Peter Rosser’s done great lab work. For just about every sheriff’s department in the state. And Rosser hired me.”

“Only now Rosser’s a free agent.”

“Yes, and?”

"And you ditched the FBI."

No occupational clan was strung tighter than cops. Cops stuck with cops. And Peter and I had left the law enforcement fold. I'd also bet another speeding ticket that Wilcove talked to his brother-in-arms, Seiler or Culliton, maybe to assuage his guilt over giving me Esther's name. And Wilcove would've told them everything about how I left the Bureau by way of mutual agreement.

"That's right, detective, I'm no longer with the Bureau. However, I still consult for them. So I don't see that we have a problem here."

"Bully for you. I still see a problem." He leaned forward, arms still crossed. "You and Rosser are out to make money off people's misery."

My temper crawled from its sour chamber. I shoved it back. "The Engels aren't paying us. They're offering hotel rooms."

"What about the Hellers?"

"What about them."

"They're rich."

"Good for them. But they're not paying us."

"Then why'd you call me about the Heller girl?"

"Because if Esther Heller died six years ago and her murder still hasn't been closed, then she's officially a cold case. Call me crazy, detective, but I thought it might be good to dust off her file and see what we could find."

"Oh, I get it." He smirked. "Then the Hellers will cough up some dough."

"Actually my hope is that Mrs. Heller can one day leave her basement prison."

The eyes chambered another shell. "Did *Mrs. Heller* happen to tell you about the astrologist?"

I felt a chill coming.

"Yeah. That's right. There was also a psychic." Culliton nearly smiled at my discomfort. "The psychic held a séance in their hotel. Total voodoo. He was some 'seer' from Portland. He led us all over the place. And he wasn't the worst. We lost more weeks to other wackos, all hired by Martha Heller. Whoever killed that girl was probably laughing his ass off."

"So he could come back to kill again."

The eyes said *ready, aim.* "You don't know that."

"You don't know otherwise."

I could see *fire* coming next. I needed to block the shot.

"Detective, in all the years Peter Rosser was running the state lab, working on behalf of sheriff's offices like this one, did he ever strike you as a *wacko?*"

He looked at his computer monitor, as if checking to see if an urgent email arrived.

"Do *I* seem like a wacko?"

He kept his gaze on the computer, shifting the mouse as if yet another urgent email was there. I checked my watch—5:53 a.m. I would've liked to be patient. But more shells were chambering in his eyes and the way forward would soon become a literal dead end if I didn't stay alive. So I made the first bid.

"I'm looking at Fritz Engels."

The double barrels swung my way. "The brother?"

I explained my theory. Fritz's deep knowledge of hotel schedules and how housekeeping works. His age. Fritz was old enough that he could've also killed Esther Heller. I watched the detective. Either Culliton was an expert at concealing the truth, or he'd never considered Annicka's brother. "Fritz also seemed really eager to point me toward the boyfriend. But that doesn't add up because if Mason Leming was even close to being guilty, you would've brought him in." I paused. "If Mason's not a suspect, you must've had a good reason to eliminate him from the list."

"How'd you hear about Esther?"

Oh, forget it. Enough with the peace offerings. I loaded my own shotgun.

Glancing around the office, I took in the desks, empty of people yet burdened with paperwork. And Culliton's equally burdened desk. In big cities, police departments give detectives some kind of private space. And they're usually assigned specialties—vice, robbery, homicide. But rural county offices like this were always stretched. Detectives worked everything from drugs and prostitution to kidnapping and murder. The frustration showed on Culliton's large face.

I smiled. "How long have you been with the sheriff's office?"

Culliton returned my smile, but it looked as bitter as the coffee. "Eighteen years."

"Long time."

"Long enough to watch people like you—and all the wacko psychics—show up and leave. It's like I'm sitting next to a revolving door."

"Eighteen years." I nodded. "That's definitely impressive. Eighteen years of a steady paycheck, even when you don't close a murder case. Eighteen years of keeping your job, even if whoever killed Esther Heller never got caught. Even if the killer comes back and strikes again, you're still here getting a paycheck. Do you ever wonder who's really making the money off other people's misery?"

The shotgun racked. The two Cokes I drank for breakfast curdled in my stomach.

"Who the hell." He spoke through his clenched jaw. "Do you think you are?"

"I'm nobody. But I want to find somebody."

"And you expect me to help you?"

"Yes. Because as I told you last night on the phone, we can both win if we work together." I looked at the binders on his desk, covered by his crossed arms. The top page was partially visible. It showed a standard coroner's outline of the human body with horizontal lines radiating outward, with room for handwritten notes. Annicka or Esther, I didn't know who, but the horizontal line extending from the body's neck and clavicle showed extensive notes. "I'd appreciate seeing the autopsies for both girls."

"Just swoop in here like Superwoman and just solve the cases."

"Is that what's bothering you?" My temper jumped up and down, begging me to blurt out the rest—*No wonder Esther turned into a cold case*. "Detective, I'll give you full credit. I just want to find out who killed them."

He glanced at the monitor again. But I heard less of an edge in his voice. "I'll need to run it by the sheriff first."

"Of course."

On the other side of the bullpen, the front door opened. A deputy wearing the same brown uniform as Seiler walked in. He took one look at Culliton, and made a beeline for the coffee machine.

"Anything else?" the detective asked.

"Yes," I said. "Can you tell me where I might find an elephant around here?"

CHAPTER TWENTY-NINE

FOLLOWING THE DETECTIVE'S directions, I drove to the other side of Leavenworth until I found a red-and-white striped awning with the words:

Big Baer's Orchard and Petting Zoo

The place didn't open until nine, so I circled back into town, picked up coffee and schnitzel and sat on a bench in the city park. Another oompah band was setting up, and the early morning light struck the accordion player's buttons, turning them into oyster pearls. My cell phone buzzed.

And buzzed.

When it stopped, I pulled it out. There were now five messages. All from Jack.

I called him back. "Hey," I said.

"Harmon, if we don't leave right now, we'll never make it back to Seattle by noon."

"I'm already here." The tuba player in the park blew a blubbery note. "Hear that? Where else could I listen to an oompah band for breakfast?"

"You *drove* to Leavenworth."

I bit into the schnitzel and tasted nothing.

"Okay." Jack said. The word sounded nothing like that

okay he'd said at night in the boat. "Everything alright?" he asked.

"Yep, everything's great. I'll talk to you later."

I disconnected the call.

The accordion player squeezed his instrument, like my heart was in his hands.

BY FIVE AFTER nine, Big Baer's gravel parking was already filling up. I locked The Ghost and walked along a section of picket fence that contained a petting zoo. White rabbits, black pygmy goats. Brown Shetland ponies with platinum blond bangs hanging in their eyes. I'd felt guilty about leaving Madame home with Eleanor. But now it seemed wise. She chased horses.

A young mother lifted her camera. "Jeremy," she said. "Pet the goat."

The kid looked about four years old, and terrified.

"G'on, pet the goat." Her voice carried that high-pitched tone, like she was trying not to reveal her impatience. "Put your hand out. Pet him."

The boy shook his head.

"He won't hurt you!"

Later, it would all look very different in some scrapbook.

Behind the petting zoo, I found another red-and-white awning. The morning breeze rippled the scalloped edge, and I caught the scent of fruit. Apples. A pretty blond girl was arranging red apples in a pyramid on a display case. Behind her, shoppers pushed carts around a retail area. I stood to her side, waiting for her to finish.

"Crispins," she said, without turning. "Just picked." She stacked another row. "Best Crispin apple you'll ever taste."

"I'll take one."

"One?" She glanced over her shoulder. She was stunningly pretty. "Just one?"

I nodded.

"Nobody's ever bought just one." She handed me the apple in her hand. The skin was red with washes of pale green and gold, like an apple crossbred with a watermelon.

"Go ahead, take a bite," she said, sounding like that mom with the camera. "One bite and you'll see."

The first bite was so juicy it almost choked me. I'd tasted some fine apples in my home state of Virginia, but this one was like a carbonated honey bath of fruit. My tongue wanted to dance. I closed my eyes. My throat hummed.

She laughed. "Right?"

"Oh." I opened my eyes. "Wow."

"Mr. Baer's apples are the best. He breeds them, puts all kinds of science into his orchards. People come from all over to get them." She lifted another Crispin. "So, how many do you want?"

"A dozen."

While she bagged twelve amazing apples, I polished off the ambrosia in my hand and looked around. Apple trees lined the sunny hillside in rows and stretched their limbs to the sun. White ladders leaned against the trunks. Pickers filled bushel baskets and carried them to a large truck.

"Have you worked here long?" I asked.

"I started here the day I could get a job. Ninth grade. That was three years ago."

"Good job, huh?"

"Much better than working in the hotels. Plus Mr. Baer's *super* nice."

She carried my apples under the awning, where two long lines waited for the cash registers. Carts of apples. Crates of apples. Cases of apple cider.

"Busy," I said.

"You're only getting this dozen, so I'll ring you up in back."

She walked me past shelves with jars of apple butter, jars of apple jelly, containers of dried apple rings, and set the paper bags of my Crispins on a back counter.

"One dozen," she said. "That'll be—"

"Did you count this one?" I held up my apple core.

"Samples are on the house." She rung up the sale. "Mr. Baer says samples don't even cost him money, they make him money."

"He's right." I handed her the bills. "By any chance, did you know Annicka Engels?"

The cash drawer had popped open but her young hands froze over it. "Why do you want to know?"

Lying's always an option. But holding this bitten apple in my hand, lying also seemed like my express-lane ticket into Eve's disastrous tribe. "Annicka's family asked me to look into some things."

She placed my twenty-dollar bill in the drawer, carefully. "Annicka was awesome."

"That's what everyone tells me." I took out my card, handed it to her. "I'm trying to find out what happened to her. At the end."

Her cornflower blue eyes widened as she read the card. "Are you, like, those people on TV? Like CSI?"

"Kinda. But kinda not."

"But you do stuff, like find evidence?"

I had no time for show-and-tell—visiting hours at the asylum were ticking toward me like a stopwatch lodged inside my head. "Somebody said there's an elephant around here."

The shift took her a moment. "Buster?"

"Buster—is that the elephant?"

She nodded, looking a bit confused, like she'd missed a step. I stared into her innocent blue eyes, and wondered if I was ever this trusting at her age. *No*. By her age, I was already suspicious of people. Just like Lani had said.

I smiled. "Where would I find Buster?"

Someone called out, "Alma!"

She jumped, and turned. But relaxed when she saw who had called her name. A gray-haired man rolled toward us in a wheelchair.

"Alma," he said, "why are you back here? Mary Catherine's got that long line all to herself."

"I'm sorry, Mr. Baer." She handed him my card. "This lady was asking about Annicka."

He didn't bother looking at my card. I offered my hand. "Raleigh Harmon."

He shook, still not looking at my card. His grip was callused and powerful. "Preston Baer," he said. "How can I help you?"

"I'm working for the Engels. Someone mentioned that Annicka worked here." Culliton, that's who. "And I heard you have an elephant—Buster, is it?"

Preston Baer finally glanced at my card, barely, then tucked it into his shirt pocket. "Alma, please go help Mary Catherine."

"Yes, Mr. Baer."

He grabbed the chair's wheels, pivoting expertly.

"Follow me," he said. "I'll introduce you to Buster."

CHAPTER THIRTY

PRESTON BAER LED me to the back of the retail space where a set of plastic flap doors opened into a warehouse. The chilled air felt icy on my skin. Forklifts crossed the concrete floor, beeping toward a loading dock where white panel trucks waited. The trucks were decorated with a colorful fruit label that read: "BAER NAKED ORGANIC ORCHARDS: We only grow the best."

Baer pushed his wheelchair toward a wooden ramp that led down the loading dock.

"I have a question," he said, braking down the ramp to the paved loading area. "You don't have to answer."

"What's that?"

"I know about Engels' financial situation."

Across the way, the apple orchards stretched up the golden autumn hills, but a small valley spread below them. Wooden ramps crisscrossed the land, connecting several large barns.

"I'm not sure what you mean," I said.

"Your services must be cost a pretty penny. No offense."

"None taken."

He lifted one hand from a wheel and pointed me toward the wooden barns. "I'd like you to give me your bill," he said.

"I'm sorry but—"

"But nothing. The Engels don't need to know." He glanced

at me. His eyes were pale gray and hard as river rock. “They’re proud people, they won’t take charity, even if they need it. You strike me as a clever girl. I’m sure you can find a way to explain coverage of your services. Just don’t take their money. I’ll pay the bill.”

“That’s very generous, but Johann already offered free hotel rooms. In exchange for services.”

“Ah.” Baer nodded, pushing down the wooden walkway to the first barn. “He’ll expect you to take him up on that. But you can still send me the bill.”

“I don’t—”

“Come, come, Miss Harmon.” He stopped, pivoting the chair to face me. “Your work must be quite expensive.”

I said nothing.

“Consider it this way,” he continued. “If I am paying you—beyond free hotel stays—I will feel more certain you’re giving the matter your complete attention.”

“I don’t give anything else.”

He held my gaze a long moment. I willed myself not to blink.

“Yes.” He looked away, with a tense smile. “But let’s make your work official, shall we? That girl never should’ve died that way.”

His chair rolled across the weathered wood with a sound like distant thunder. We passed the first barn, and I glanced inside. More goats. More Shetland ponies, now trotting in launch circles. I saw teenage boys and girls working with the animals, raking sawdust, hauling buckets. We moved past that to the second barn.

I stopped.

A lion cub paced inside a large cage. Across from that, a chimpanzee swung from a wooden dowel, chattering and screeching. Between the cages, a blond woman wearing all-black strolled with a huge leopard that wore some kind of leash. He was longer than the woman was tall and could easily kill her with a quick swipe of his giant paws.

Baer had continued. When he realized I'd stopped, he pivoted the chair to find me.

"Sorry," I said. "I've never seen animals like that."

"Come, then." He gave the chair's wheels a hard push. The ramps between the barns each had another ramp that took him into the barn about ten feet. After that it was sawdust. Baer stopped at the edge and called out. "Susan."

The woman in black turned. "Yes, Pres?"

"Are you done feeding?"

"Almost. Leo's still not well." She had a thick European accent. The word *well* sounded like *vell*. "I've tried everything."

"Perhaps he needs a challenge." Baer tilted his head toward me. "Can she try?"

The woman named Susan could've passed for Alma's mother. Same blond hair, same cornflower-blue eyes, same stunningly pretty features. But unlike Alma, this woman wasn't guileless. I sensed something calculating about her, as if she was a cat herself.

"Please." She walked the leopard to an empty cage and opened its large gate. Without a command, the leopard walked inside. The woman closed the gate and unclipped the leash. The animal almost collapsed to the sawdust floor, as if standing took too much effort.

She motioned me forward. I crept toward the cage, my gaze FBI-tracking the beast inside. I wanted to turn, run away. But I needed Baer's help and he was watching. Was this some kind of a test? I clenched my jaw and stepped to the bars … right behind Susan, using her as a flimsy shield.

"Put these on." She casually turned and handed me a pair

of black silicone gloves. Then she lifted a deep white bucket. "Take a piece. Give it to him."

Inside the bucket, chunks of raw meat swam in a pond of blood. The cloying scent of iron rose, filling my nose. I gagged.

"He won't hurt you," she said.

I still considered backing away, but when I glanced at the leopard, it was staring at me with those kohl-lined eyes. His breathing was labored.

"He can't hurt you." Susan motioned me to get closer. "He is too sick. Just hold the meat for him."

"You mean, throw it."

She laughed, a deep throaty laugh. "But the meat will get dirty and Leo will be sad."

I reached into the bucket. The metallic odor touched the back of my throat. The meat felt spongy with blood.

"Good," Susan said. "Now offer it to Leo."

The leopard got up, with effort, and paced toward me, his front paws crossing over each other like a model on a catwalk. He lowered his head, the gold-and-black fur spiking over his shoulders.

But he looked weak.

"Hey, Leo." I held out the meat and willed myself not to think about how much I prefer dogs to cats. Leo was staring at me like he could read my mind. "Here ya go."

He opened his mouth, slow as a yawn, and sank yellow fangs into meat. Blood dribbled down his whiskery chin. I almost puked.

"Look how sweet he is," Susan cooed. "Such a good kitty."

I slowly, slowly inched backward.

"Good boy," Susan continued to purr. He sank to the ground and licked the meat. But he didn't eat it. Susan turned to me. "He has leukemia."

"Oh." I looked at Leo. "I'm sorry."

Now that I knew how ill he really was, I had to admit, he tugged at my heart. "I'm sorry," I said.

"He is not alone." Susan gestured to the other cages. "They are all sick. People send them. Because Pres has such a big heart."

"No, I don't." Preston Baer had stayed at the edge of the barn, elbows on the armrests of his chair. His hands were clasped tightly across his lap, as if tense about something. Maybe me feeding his leopard.

Susan and I walked through the sawdust to Baer. He reached out, clasping her hand.

"Susan, this is Raleigh Harmon. She's working for the Engels family, investigating what happened to Annicka."

Susan gave the smallest gasp.

"Is something wrong?" I tried to read her expression. Surprise? Or shock? I couldn't be sure.

"Annicka was wonderful," she said, the *w* once more becoming a *v*. "She was the best with the animals. Better than me."

"So she worked here … how long?"

"Several years," Baer replied. "Until she left for college. We still haven't found anyone as good, especially with the animals who are …" He shook his head. "The animals who are close to death."

"Annicka would've been a veterinarian," Susan said.

I nodded, thinking of those YouTube videos on her computer. They were all about caring for exotic animals. Now it made sense. "Her family seems to think her boyfriend was involved in her murder."

The look that passed between them was quick.

"Mason, you mean," Baer said.

"Yes. Mason Leming," I clarified. "You know him?"

"He works here," Baer said. Then, seeing my surprise, he added, "No one told you that?"

I struggled to recover. "Her family didn't mention it."

"Well, considering what's happened to them, they can't be expected to remember everything." He glanced at Susan. "We like Mason."

"*You* like Mason," she said, her accent deepening. "I can't stand that boy."

She was angry. I watched her wrap the leash into a tight coil around her arm. With her sleek build, the smooth blond hair, she was like a German panther. Only she wasn't showing Baer any deference or subservience. I wondered about their relationship. And how much they knew.

"How long has Mason been working here?" I asked.

"Years," Susan said, as if his time was a personal burden.

"Four years," Baer added, softly. "He's a good worker."

"Do you think he was involved in her death?" I asked.

There was a loaded silence.

"Yes," Susan said. "I do."

She looked at Baer. His face revealed no emotion. But Susan seemed to detect something there.

"I'm sorry, Pres," she said, "but I do think he's involved. So I've said it. There. I think Mason was involved."

Baer's face still looked blank to me.

"How do you think he's involved?" I asked.

"I don't know, exactly. But he's acting strange." Once more she looked at Baer.

He turned to me.

"Today's your lucky day," he said. "When you meet Buster, you'll meet Mason, too."

CHAPTER THIRTY-ONE

IN THE NEXT barn, the elephant was trotting in a circle of sawdust. Chubby, jiggly, tooting his trunk. A baby elephant.

And in the center of the ring, a young guy with longish brown hair called out orders. Buster tooted his trunk every time.

"Mason." Baer called from the wooden boardwalk. "Mason!"

Mason Leming jumped. The same way Alma had. He was narrowly built, hips so thin Buster could've wrapped around his trunk around the guy's waist and snapped him like a dry peanut shell.

"I'd like to speak with you," Baer said.

Mason told Buster to stop. The baby elephant gave an earsplitting blast from his trunk, then followed up with another blast when Mason leashed him to an iron ring spiked into the sawdust.

Mason walked toward us but didn't look up.

"Buster's still being difficult?" Baer asked.

"He got that stomach bug and he misses ..." Mason looked at me. His eyes were a muddy hazel, like green leaves mixed with soil.

"This is Raleigh Harmon," Baer said. "The Engels hired her."

I saw some kind of recognition in his hazel eyes. Fear.

No.

Terror.

"She has some questions for you."

"Alright." His voice shook. "But I'm kinda busy."

Baer pivoted his wheelchair, facing me and ignoring Mason. "I'll leave you two alone."

"Thank you," I said.

"No, thank *you.*" He wheeled down the wooden path, out of the barn.

Buster gave another blast.

But Mason's milky gaze stayed on his retreating boss. I've met so many guilty people, both as an agent and as a geologist testifying in court. Some of them could lie about their crimes without one hiccup of conscience. But I'd also interviewed totally innocent people who were so terrified, fear made them seem guilty. Both types had taught me to go for the jugular.

"Did you kill her?" I asked.

"What—?" He staggered back, stumbling in the sawdust. "*What?*"

"Did you kill Annicka?"

"I can't believe you'd—"

"Nobody's asked you that question?"

"I already told the sheriff, he knows what I said."

"What you said might not be the truth." I paused, giving him a moment. "Did you kill her."

"I *loved* her."

"You still haven't answered my question. Did you kill Annicka?"

"*No!* How many times do you want me to say it? I didn't kill Annicka—are you satisfied?"

"No. Why didn't you say it the first time I asked?"

"You—you come in here—with my boss—and you're

working with her family. You don't even say hello. Just—*did you kill her*?!"

His hands shook. When he realized I was seeing that, he made two fists and plunged his hands into the front pockets of his jeans. Sawdust clung to the denim. The knees were brown with dirt.

"Let's start over," I said. "Was Annicka working with Buster?"

He glanced back at the elephant. Buster—gray as granite—grabbed the hasp of a bucket with his trunk and turned it upside down. When he saw the bucket was empty, he threw it, and gave another frustrated blast.

Mason watched the bucket bounce and tumble toward us. "He never did this stuff when she was here."

"He only acts up with you?"

He stared at the ground and shook his head. "What's with you?"

"I don't know, Mason, what's with you? Don't you want to know who killed Annicka?"

"*Yes!*"

"Do you know who killed her?"

"*No!*"

"Are you sure?"

"What is your problem? If I knew who killed her, would I be standing here?"

"I don't know. You keep answering my questions with another question."

"Are you—" He stopped, as if realizing it was another question. "You're some kinda private eye. Like, a detective."

"I'm a forensic geologist."

"What the hell's that?"

I explained the whole concept. How minerals leave evidence in places people never dream of finding it. "You'd be amazed. People have been caught just from the dirt in their shoes. Or from hair and fibers left at the crime scene. Even hair from elephants."

"Okay. So?"

"So let's say elephant hair showed up on Annicka's body. How would you—theoretically, of course—explain the animal hair being there?"

Fear slid over his narrow face. "She worked with Buster."

"According to your boss she hasn't worked here since she left for college. That would be, what, August? Don't you think it would be highly unusual for something as fine as elephant hairs to still be on a person's clothing, months later?"

"You want me to say it again?" His eyes flared. "I did *not* kill her."

"Fritz thinks you did."

"Fritz? Fritz is a freak."

"What's that got to do with anything?"

"He's a loser. He's a loser who hates people who know he's a loser."

"Mason, even you can do better than that."

"His own sister didn't like him."

"Why not?"

"Because he's creepy. He's always hanging around that hotel but does almost nothing the whole time."

"Yeah, that's still not good enough."

"Okay. He assaulted one of the maids. Yeah, that's right." Mason looked triumphant. "That pervert locked one of their maids in a hotel room and tried to rape her. Is that *enough* for you?"

The cold sensation rippled down my back. "When was that?"

"I don't know, like, four or five years ago."

"And what happened?"

"Mrs. Engels paid off the maid. To keep her quiet. Mommy's boy can do no wrong."

"Mrs. Engels paid her off, or Mr. Engels?"

"I never asked." He ran hand through his hair. Switching the focus to Fritz seemed to calm him down. "All I know is that Johann does whatever Helen says. She's the boss. The only time he stood up to her was to protect Annicka."

"Protect her, how?"

He stared down at the sawdust. Wood shavings clung to his black boots. They looked a lot like the boots I found in Annicka's bathroom. Boots whose soles were full of mud, hay. Elephant hair.

"Helen wasn't very nice to Annicka. She always favored Fritz. That's why Annicka worked here instead of the hotel."

His tone was sad, weighted. As if the memory pulled him down.

"Buster's sick?" I asked.

"Stomach." Mason kept his head down. "Some kinda bacteria, I don't know. It's been going on since his mother died."

"His mother died?"

"Last summer. He's an orphan. Mr. Baer took him in, trying to get him healthy."

I thought of what Susan the cat woman said, about Annicka's talent with animals, especially the sick ones. And her email to Mason the day before she died. *Kiss Buster for me*.

"Mason, level with me."

He looked up. On such a narrow face, the tears looked enormous. "Mr. Baer didn't want her coming back after she left for college. He wanted Buster to get attached to somebody else. Because Annicka couldn't be here every day. And Buster wouldn't obey anyone else."

"So?"

"So I snuck her in here." He looked over at the elephant

stomping out a circle in the sawdust. "I thought that was better. She missed him. He was calm with her. But now it's worse. It's like he knows—" He stopped.

I went back to the jugular.

"I heard she didn't want to marry you."

"Oh my God!" The tears were back. "Yeah, she didn't want to marry me. You know why? Because she wanted to wait until I could afford it. Nobody told you that part, huh?"

No, they didn't tell me that part. But at this point, it was Mason Leming's word against the world. Not to mention all the evidence, motive, and opportunity—including elephant hair tying him to the crime scene.

"Mason, why would—"

Buster lifted his trunk and screamed. When he stopped, I heard the distant thunder sound, and turned. Preston Baer rolled across the wooden planks into the barn.

"How are we doing?" he asked.

"I gotta get back to work," Mason said.

He didn't ask for permission. He simply walked away.

"Did you get what you needed?" Preston Baer asked me.

"I think so," I said.

CHAPTER THIRTY-TWO

On my way out of town, I stopped by the Waterhaus and found Johann. He was working in the courtyard beside the pool where stainless steel parts scattered across the browned lawn. A rubber hose snaked among the parts. The pool was still green.

"Johann?" I asked.

He looked up. His white beard was ragged. "You have news?"

"I just learned Annicka worked at the petting zoo."

"Oh, for many years." He took a blue rag from his pocket and wiped grease from his long hands. "Loved animals, especially sick ones."

"Yes, you mentioned her love of animals. But it would've helped if I'd known about her working at the zoo." I tried not to sound annoyed. The man was as undone as the pool's water filter. "I was surprised. Not in a good way."

"But." He picked up a wrench. "She didn't work there. Not anymore."

"It seems she might've been sneaking in. To see the elephant?"

"Her heart." He seemed to want to sigh, only it would require too much effort. "My daughter's heart, it was too big."

"What can you tell me about Preston Baer?"

"What do you need to know?"

"He takes in sick animals?"

Baer used to breed animals, Johann said, for circuses and zoos. He was wealthy and came from a hard-working German family who built their regional apple brand. The special Crispins, I guessed. Although Johann described a man revered by the community, something in his tone sounded tempered.

"As a person, outside of business, what's he like?"

"Wasn't nice. But the accident, it changed him."

"What accident?"

A car accident, he said. Baer was driving his Jaguar over the pass to Seattle when he was struck by a semi truck. "Different man after that."

"In what way?"

Johann reached up, touching neck. "Snapped. Spine. And changed his heart."

After the paralysis, Baer stopped breeding the exotic animals and started taking in circus animals which otherwise would've been euthanized. "That's when he hired Annicka." He gazed at the green pool. "We needed her here. But Annicka begged to work there."

I thought of what Mason said, about Johann fighting for Annicka. I'm sure Helen Engels wanted her daughter working here instead. "Do you think Annicka would still work there, even if Baer didn't know about it?"

"For a sick animal? Yes."

"How about so she could see Mason Leming?"

His fingers tightened around the wrench. "I did not like it."

"The relationship?"

"They ran together."

"You mean *literally* ran?"

He nodded.

I lifted my hand. Clouds had been blowing across the sky,

blocking the sun, but they parted suddenly and the light stabbed the pool, gold turning green to blue. "I heard Fritz assaulted a maid."

In the white beard, his mouth parted.

"Mr. Engels—"

"Johann."

"Johann, I need to know *everything*. I can't stress that enough. Otherwise I can't work for you. Do you understand?"

He wiped the wrench with the blue rag. Something quivered down my spine. He wiped the tool like someone wiping down a murder weapon.

"I need you to tell me the truth about Fritz."

"My son is adopted."

I waited. I was adopted—by David Harmon. "Adoption is no excuse."

He nodded toward the lobby windows. "We could not have children. My wife, her mother was adopted—"

I held up my hand, stopping him. More details that were essential. Especially if DNA was part of the evidence. I tried not to sound frustrated. "You're saying Annicka was adopted?"

"Fritz." He tapped the wrench against his leg. "Only Fritz."

That explained the wide age gap between their two children. Johann said more than a decade passed before "a miracle" happened. I almost winced, imagining how an adopted ten-year-old feels hearing his parents describe his new baby sister as a "miracle." Annicka was the late child, that gift older parents never expected. And then she grew up to be, in the words of Officer Wilcome, "perfect." Was that enough motivation for Fritz to kill her? I was thinking that over as Johann went on a tangent about adoption, why it's so important, why Catholics believe in it, how Mrs. Engel's own mother was adopted as an orphan after WWII.

"Four orphans," he said. "They came from Germany. After the war. Our church did that."

"Yes, I know," I said. "Our Lady of Snows."

His long face filled with even more sadness. "You don't trust me."

"Pardon?"

"You researched my church. Because you don't trust me."

"No, sir." I explained how Father Anthony told me about the adoptions from Nazi Germany. "I'm working on that star burned into the grass. Jack hired me to—"

"My God, what has happened to our town?" His voice sounded metallic. "Hate. It is hate doing this. Why do people hate us? We are simple people. Hard working. Why is all this happening?"

I couldn't answer that. Yet. But my job was to get the truth. I took a deep breath and once more went for the jugular. "Who paid off the maid, you or your wife?"

He drew a quick breath.

"When I said I needed the truth, I meant *all* of the truth."

"Fritz works hard."

"Again, that's not an excuse—"

"It never happened again."

I hated provoking this man, this grieving father. It felt cruel. But my job wasn't to be his friend. Or to trust him. Or to make this go on any longer than it needed to. "I appreciate your talking about it," I said.

He nodded, somberly.

"This morning I left Seattle in a hurry," I said. "Unfortunately I forgot some of my equipment."

"You need something?" he asked. "Anything. What."

"A shovel," I said.

CHAPTER THIRTY-THREE

I DIDN'T BORROW a shovel from Johann.

I borrowed two.

Both were rusted and chipped, and perfect for all the wrong reasons. I carried them to The Ghost and snapped on latex gloves. Using the Ghibli's long door to block any sight of me, I contemplated taking fingerprints from the handles. But I knew any decent defense attorney would just come back with, "Fritz works at the hotel, of course he touched that shovel."

I inspected the metal faces and found enough grains within the rusted divots to put in a baggie. No hair, not that I could see at the moment. But if any of these grains matched the soil from Annicka's grave, I had a forensics' slam dunk.

But there was more to test.

With the shovels riding shotgun, I drove to the Icicle Creek trailhead. Only one other car was in the parking lot, a red Mini Cooper with a white racing stripe. I parked The Ghost directly across from it, hoisted my pack, and carried the shovels down the trail. The first half mile wasn't bad, but after that, I began sweating hard. Maybe it was from the weight of memories. That early morning run with Jack. That perfect moment, when he grabbed me and … now here I was. By myself. Toting shovels for a murder investigation. How quickly things change.

When I reached the cave, two people were sitting by the river. They snuggled side by side on the riverbank, watching the water rush past. The Mini Coopers, I presumed. Two people in love, all the time in the world.

I hefted the shovels over my shoulders and climbed up the boulders. Sweat rolled down my back, making the pack feel even heavier. If Annicka Engels ran this route every Sunday, she was beyond fit. She was a human goat. And that only confirmed my hunch that no stranger killed her. Her murder was calculated, by someone who knew her. And knew her dog, too.

I reached the meadow where wind combed through the brittle grass. Her grave lay open, the yellow police tape already sagging and faded. I set the shovels down and took off my pack. The wind sounded like someone asking for quiet. *Sh-sh-shhh.* As if the open grave was a cradle. I opened my pack. A shadow passed overhead. When I looked up, I saw clouds. Dark, foreboding clouds. Rain was coming. And it would wash away all the evidence.

I laid the shovels perpendicular to the grave's long wall, then lay down across from them on my stomach, staring at the metal edges above the open ground. The soil smelled dry yet rich, that mineral-heavy soil of desert mountains. I closed one eye.

The first shovel's edge was rusted, ragged as a torn fingernail. The second shovel looked newer, in better shape, but it had two indentations at the tapered tip.

I took out my Nikon and shot close-ups both of shovels and their position above the grave's wall. I zoomed in on the horizontal layers of soil, making sure to capture that vertical line that ran through the bands of soil as if drawn by pencil. I stood, brushed the soil from my shirt and jeans, and prayed.

Please.

Picking up the first shovel, I held the rusted spade above the ground just like the person—or persons—who dug this grave. I closed one eye and gazed down the handle to the metal face. But I already suspected this wasn't the right shovel. Its heavily rusted face would've left bits of iron in the soil, and made even more ragged vertical marks. I set it down and picked up the second shovel.

Please?

When I lowered it to the edge of the grave, the dents seemed to match that vertical line. But there was a problem. The shovel face had two dents. It would've left parallel vertical lines. Still, I raised it, lowered it, raised it, as if digging the grave. One word pounded through my head.

Please, please, please.

I kept the digging motion going, but only out of frustration. For one split second, I could see how tempting it was, how easy it was for good cops to go bad. I wanted this shovel to be the right tool, because I suspected Fritz was guilty. My gut sensed it. He wasn't reacting to his sister's murder in a normal way. No signs of grief. Or even sadness. But guilt for a crime and heartless behavior were two different things.

And I wasn't God.

I packed up my equipment, hoisted the pack, and carried the shovels down the mountain. I also checked my watch. I still had four-and-a-half hours to reach Eleanor's and pick up Madame for the visit to Crazyland. I was cutting it close. Maybe now I'd find out if Eleanor was serious about paying my speeding tickets.

As I came to the trail's steepest part above the boulders, I used the now-innocent shovels as walking sticks. I glanced once at the river bank. The Mini Coopers were gone. Probably because the wind was kicking up. The sun was disappearing.

Bad weather coming, soon. I picked up my pace down the trail but stopped to adjust my pack.

He stood in the middle of the river.

Mason.

The river splashed on his bare stomach, his jeans soaked all the way to his skinny waist.

I stepped off the trail. Pine needles crunched under my shoes.

He stretched out his arms and lifted his narrow face to the sky. His eyes were closed. But his lips were moving.

Was he talking? Crying.

Confessing?

I moved down the river bank, using the shovels like staffs because the soil was so dry my shoes were surfing on it. Right before I hit the water, I threw a shovel forward to brace my fall. The iron spade hit granite—TA-*thoing*!—and he turned.

His face seemed whiter than the breaking waves. Panic. Terror. He splashed toward the opposite bank.

"Mason! Stop!"

He stumbled, got up. Looked back. He sloshed forward, kicking at the powerful current.

I tried to gauge the river's speed. Could I make it? And what if I fell, got swept away. Mason wasn't going to come looking for me—or tell anyone what happened.

I looked across the water. He was out, taking the dry slope on all fours. His jeans stuck to him like second skin.

I spun around and zig-zagged my way up the bank, stabbing the shovels like pick axes. At the top, I looked back. Mason, still on all fours, was climbing toward an empty white truck waiting beside the road.

I threw the shovels over my shoulders and took off in a full sprint. When I reached the parking lot, I tossed the shovels into The Ghost and blew gravel peeling out of the parking lot.

I turned left.

Just in time to see Mason going the other way.

Spinning on an Italian dime, I pulled a U-turn and punched the gas pedal. His truck was screeching around a curve. Within twenty seconds, The Ghost was close enough to see his eyes flicking at the rearview mirror.

Terror. That's what I saw in his face. Sheer *terror*.

He hit the brakes.

"Crap!"

I hit my brakes.

The Ghost fishtailed, rubber skidding down the pavement. I slammed the clutch but it was too late. The engine coughed, died. I shoved the gear shift into First and turned the key.

Mason's truck disappeared around the next turn.

I caught him again on the edge of town. Traffic clogged both lanes. I downshifted into First again, and double-footed the gas and brake. Adrenaline hammered my veins.

Mason suddenly took a left. The oncoming vehicle blasted its horn.

The white truck burned rubber up Ski Hill Drive.

"You rat!" I glared at the oncoming traffic. "Come on, come on, come on—"

At the first opening, I swung into traffic and up the hill. The white truck was gone.

I turned down every side street, still riding the brake and gas. All I could see were chalet-style houses and pastures of sheep, goats, and cattle. Fifteen minutes later, I turned back onto Ski Hill Drive and climbed the cresting. Up ahead I could see the six-pointed star burned into the grass. And in the parking lot, the white truck.

"Nice try, jerko."

I parked directly behind the truck. The cab was empty.

I ran for the church's front door.

CHAPTER THIRTY-FOUR

INSIDE OUR LADY of Snows, a woman was vacuuming the crimson-colored carpet. With one hand, she shoved the roaring machine back and forth. With her other hand, she dusted white powder over the carpet. The air smelled like manufactured lilacs.

"Hello?"

She wore ear buds.

I moved closer, glancing left and right for signs of the rat. Whatever music she was listening to, it kept her dancing like a crane, elbows out, forward and back with the machine, up and down with the powder.

I stood beside the front pew and waved my arms.

"Take a seat," she said loudly. "Somebody's already in there."

"Who?"

She yanked out an ear bud. "What?"

"Who's already—"

"I can't tell you! That's *private.*"

I brought out my FBI smile and screwed it onto my face. "I'm looking for someone who just came in here."

"When?"

"Just now."

"Who?"

"Mason Leming."

"Why?"

All she needed to ask was *where* and we'd have all five Ws of good investigating. Except this wasn't good investigating—it was an excruciating exercise in yelling over the vacuum, which she refused to turn off, and breathing air choked with a scent that only a laboratory could describe as floral.

"Is Mason Leming here?"

"What'd he do?" she asked.

The Bureau smile came out again. "That's private."

Everybody knew everybody in this town. And she knew Mason, guaranteed.

Replacing the earbud, she made her way to the other side, crane-dancing across the crimson carpet. When she reached the wooden door in the wall, she popped out the ear bud and leaned into it. She listened for a good fifteen seconds before flicking her thumb on the vacuum's switch, killing the engine. Then she continued to listen on the door.

So much for privacy.

"Father Anthony?" she said, finally rapping a knuckle on the door. She kept her ear to the wood. "Somebody else is here."

The door opened. The priest kept his body in the opening, blocking the view into the room. He peered across the sanctuary, found me, paused thoughtfully, and stepped out holding the door tight to his back until it was completely closed.

The cleaning crane yanked out the other ear bud. "What's goin' on?"

"Nothing, Kayleen. I'll take it from here."

"Hey, you're the padre."

She put one ear bud back in, and flicked the vacuum back

on. The priest made a wide circle around the area, walking only where she hadn't vacuumed.

"Is there something I can help you with?" His tone made it clear. He already knew I wasn't here to talk about the burned grass.

"I'm looking for Mason Leming."

He was so still, he didn't even seem to be breathing. If it wasn't for that white collar, Father Anthony could've won the world championship in poker.

"Father, I know he's here. His truck's parked out front."

He raised an eyebrow, and guilt grabbed me by the throat.

"Okay, I should've said that first. But I really need to talk to him."

Another eyebrow.

"It's for his own good. Really."

"My obligation isn't to law enforcement."

"It is if he knows something about Annicka Engels' murder."

"Maybe he doesn't."

"Maybe your obligation should be to her family."

He glanced at the crane. She was flying over the same patch of carpet, ear buds dangling, with her head cocked this way for better acoustics.

"Wait here," he said.

He didn't come back for quite some time. I checked my watch, felt a stab of panic, and spent several more minutes watching the crane powder the carpet. The smell made my eyes itch.

I stepped into the small foyer by the front door, where I could still see the priest's door but not smell the powder as much. Eight more minutes passed. Nine. My impatient gaze drifted to the pamphlets in the wire rack. Things about drug addiction. Adoption. Counseling. Depression.

The priest stepped out. Alone.

He walked to the foyer. "Mason has nothing to say to you."

"To me," I clarified. "But he had plenty to tell you. After all, it's time for confession."

"I wouldn't tell—"

I pointed to the bulletin board next to the pamphlets. It listed the weekly schedule. Sacrament of Penance, daily 11-1.

"He just made it," I said.

"I hope you have a nice day, Raleigh."

He walked away.

And the vacuum kept sucking.

Just like my entire day.

CHAPTER THIRTY-FIVE

I WALKED OUT of Our Lady of Snows muttering under my breath.

First, because Mason Leming was using the church like it was some type of diplomatic immunity—God's turf, no questions allowed. And second, this horrible little detour cost me valuable time. Now I'd really find out if Eleanor would pay my speeding tickets.

But the reason for muttering was maybe biggest of all.

Now I had to call Jack.

He didn't pick up the first time. I called back.

On the fifth ring, I heard: "Harmon."

"Stephanson," I shot back.

"Where are you?"

"Still in Leavenworth." I walked across the parking lot to The Ghost. Those two shovels were propped up in the passenger seat like crash test dummies who lost their heads. "I'm outside Our Lady of Snowjobs."

"You sound angry."

Digging the car key from my back pocket, I described today's adventures in investigating. I passed Mason's truck and glanced into the cab. A white T-shirt was on the bench seat. Black boots on the floor. So he must've ran into the church barefoot. Empty Sprite cans on the floor. Strands of hay lodged in dirt clumps.

"You're thinking he did it?" Jack asked.

"He's acting guilty." I moved around the truck, checking the tires for soil.

"So what are you going to do?" Jack asked.

I gazed into the truck bed. Blue tarp. Chain saw. Rope. Shovel.

I stopped.

"Harmon?"

The metal face was chipped. Dented.

"I'll call you back."

"Harmo—"

I slid my finger across the screen. My backpack was waiting in The Ghost. I took out latex gloves, snapped them on, and plotted revenge. *Grab the shovel. Take it to the office, run the comparison. Nail this jerk.*

I glanced back at the church. The doors were closed.

But I kept looking. Like something else was there.

Go away.

I yanked Ziploc baggies from the pack and my camera.

Go bother someone with a conscience.

I walked toward Mason's truck, but kept glancing at the church. It was like something was standing at the doors. Invisible, but real.

Leave me alone.

Standing next to Mason's truck, I glared that shovel. I could see the dent in its face. The soil that clung to the edges. I took photos of it, making sure to show the truck, too. With time and date stamped on the image. Authenticated.

I reached over the side. *Take the shovel.* Keep it so Mason can't get rid of it. So you can hike it up the mountain and test it on site.

Right?

I looked back at the church. My personnel file at the Bureau was full of examples. Choices bring consequences. How many times had my ends justified my means.

"*Fine*," I groused to the invisible. "You win."

Lifting my camera, I took three more shots. And left the shovel where it was.

"But, Mason," I said, "you are going down."

THE GHOST HIT 90 on the highway's straight sections. When I crossed the mountain pass, I backed down to 80. Then 70 when I hit the town of Cle Elum. Then 50 in North Bend because rain was pelting the windshield.

By the time I got to Tacoma, traffic ground to a near-halt.

I grabbed my phone and called my aunt. The wipers were going full speed.

"Aunt Charlotte?" I said into the speaker.

"Raleigh! Can I call you back?"

"Sure…"

"I just got a shipment of fire-blood quartz and people are lined up out the door!"

"No problem."

"Are you alright?" she asked.

"Yes," I sighed. "I'm fine."

MADAME AND I arrived at Western State forty-five minutes late. The feudal gang had already left for dinner.

"She's waiting for you," said Sarah the nurse.

"She didn't go to dinner?"

Sarah's smile was just this side of pity. "She wanted to wait for you."

I dipped my face to the shoulder of my shirt, wiping off

the rain and sweat. Madame panted in my arms. My wet shoes squeaked on the white-white-white vinyl flooring. I couldn't feel my feet.

My mom sat on the plastic-covered mattress. She was rocking forward and back. The bed springs laughed. A metallic laughter. *Squee-squah-squee.*

"Mom?"

Her gaze was on the window, out beyond the chicken wire that was embedded in the safety glass. Beyond the iron bars. Beyond the rain that fell in flat gray shavings as though somebody just above us was trying to file away the security bars.

"Mom."

"I saw your car."

I placed Madame on the sterilized white floor. She was shaking but otherwise didn't move. I gave her a soft push forward. She took three steps and circled back to my ankles. I picked her up.

"Sorry we're late." I walked toward the bed. "Traffic was—"

"Where did you get that car?"

"What car?" *No.* That was the wrong answer. I tried again. "Oh, that white car? It belongs to a friend."

"Why do you have it?"

"She's letting me drive it."

"Why?"

"Because I don't have a car."

She looked at me, and narrowed her eyes. "Why don't you have a car?"

Oh, the rotten trade. It was back. I was telling the truth and it drew ten suspicious thoughts into her mind. *Why don't I have a car*? I combed the words, pulling each one from the sentence to examine it. *Why. Because I don't have a car.*

That's why. But why didn't I have any money to buy one. *Why?* Because I changed jobs. *What job.* Why wasn't I living with Aunt Charlotte. *Why, why, why* and even if I told the whole truth and nothing but the truth, my mom's mind would still find something to suspect.

I set Madame next to her on the bed.

"Mom, I—"

"Who are you?"

"Raleigh." I pressed my voice down. "I'm Raleigh. Your daughter."

She stared at me like a stranger. "That car. You were going to take me away in that car."

"What?"

"For a *haircut.*" Her mouth tightened. "There's nothing wrong with my hair."

"We wanted—"

"*We?*"

I hesitated. "Me and Aunt Charlotte."

She laughed, coldly, as if the whole conspiracy was now revealed. "Get out."

"What?"

"Get out, whoever you are."

"But—"

"Get out!"

CHAPTER THIRTY-SIX

I CARRIED MADAME down the stairwell. My hands went numb.

I stopped at the front desk.

"Excuse me," I said. My lips felt swollen.

The receptionist looked up. She was playing a shooting game on her cell phone.

"Is Dr. Norbert here?" I asked.

She looked at me with a blank stare. "You want me to find out?"

"Yes." I licked my swollen lips. "Please?"

She picked up a phone on her desk and swiveled the visitor sign-in sheet to read the last name on the list. "How d'you pronounce it?"

"Raleigh." I took a breath. "Like the city."

"And Dr. Norbert knows—"

"He'll know exactly what this is about."

DR. NORBERT'S OFFICE had the cavernous feel of a wooden skull whose brain had been scooped out for the sake of science.

"Have a seat, Raleigh," he said.

I took my familiar position on the Freudian couch across

from his ergonomic chair.

Right back to square one.

I set Madame at my feet. She sniffed his blue rug, then looked at me.

"I warned you about this weeks ago," he said, throwing Madame a look of disdain. "These visits were highly risky. I told you that missing one visit would destroy any gains—"

"But I haven't missed a day."

He gave me that condescending expression I'd seen too much of during my undercover work for the Bureau. "Today?"

"I was late. I didn't miss it. Not completely."

"Perhaps you've notice that we follow very stringent routines. We don't change our visiting hours from one day to the next. We don't alter meal times. We don't suddenly give meds at a different hour of the day. You see? Structure is crucial, absolutely crucial. Particularly for someone like your mother's who's suffered a highly traumatic psychotic break. We keep life under control. Because she can't."

"Have you been on her ward?"

He leaned back in his ergonomic chair. "Why are you asking?"

"Because they are lunatics."

"This discussion will not continue unless you change your attitude."

I looked away. His office was a shrine to psychology and himself. Books and medical journals and four different degrees from universities and there was nothing to be gained by arguing with this man. "How can I get her trust back?"

"That's up to your mother, frankly." He glanced at Madame and gave a pedantic sniff. "The reports state that your mother enjoys seeing the animal."

I glanced down at Madame, just so he couldn't detect the pain in my eyes.

"I'm fairly certain she will want the animal to continue visiting."

"But not me?" I looked up.

He glanced at his watch, then out his window. More chicken wire and iron bars. How many people wanted to jump out this guy's window? Especially when he left questions hanging in the air like this.

"Okay, look, I'm no longer your patient, I get it. But I'd appreciate some help. Tell me what I should do."

"Don't be late again."

Was he kidding? I waited, even smiling. "Is that a joke?"

"And stop feeling so guilty," he said. "Guilt is a fabrication of the mind."

I waited longer. He had to be kidding. Right?

Wrong.

He checked his watch again. I stood, picked up the dog, and forced myself to sound polite. He was my key back into this crazy kingdom.

"Thank you." I shoved a smile onto my face. "That's terrific advice."

CHAPTER THIRTY-SEVEN

I WASN'T READY for Eleanor.

Or cocktails.

Or Tennessee.

With Madame in the passenger seat, I headed north to Seattle, the car's windshield wipers swiping at the rain and doing almost no good. I parked in a lot across from the Smith Tower and walked with Madame down the sidewalk. No umbrella. No hood. But somehow I couldn't feel the rain. Car wheels hissed past us.

Inside the elegant white building that was named for that "silly gun man," Patterson stood up behind the guard's desk.

"Miss Eleanor with you?" he asked.

"Not tonight." I adjusted the backpack slung over my shoulder.

He walked around the desk, heading for the elevator.

"That's okay," I said. "We'll take the stairs."

"You sure?" he asked.

Very sure.

Madame and I climbed the alabaster steps. Remnants of rain dripped from the ends of my hair, plopping on the stone. By the third floor, my leg muscles burned. I pushed harder, faster, igniting that burn until it became the familiar pain that's always blocked the ache in my heart. My lungs felt seared. I refused to stop.

Panting as I keyed open Harry Anderson's old office, Madame trotted inside. I filled a mug of water for her and set it on the floor, then poured a tall glass of water for myself and guzzled without stopping. Finally, I sat at the desk and plugged in my Nikon to the brand new computer. While the photos transferred, Madame hopped the worn leather couch. She stared at me.

"Alright," I said, picking up the phone. "I'll call her."

Three rings later, Eleanor bellowed, "You're late!"

"Has anyone ever mentioned your resemblance to the White Rabbit?"

"Don't be smart with me, young lady."

"Yes, ma'am."

She was quiet for a moment. I heard music playing in the background. Show tunes.

"What's wrong?" she asked.

"Nothing, I'm fine."

Another pause. "Where are you?" she asked.

"The office." I ran a finger over a keyboard, so new that every letter looked freshly stamped. "By the way, thank you for all of this."

"You already thanked me."

"I can't thank you again?"

"Not if you're doing it because you feel guilty."

I said nothing.

"Raleigh, what is straight?"

"Excuse me?"

"A line can be straight. Or a street," she said.

I swear, I could hear her chin rising.

"But the human heart?" she continued. "Oh, no, it's curved like a road through the mountains."

I tapped the desk. On the window facing north, raindrops

traced the glass, shifting city lights into prismatic neon. “Who said that?” I asked.

“You can come home whenever you’re ready,” she said. “But only when you’re ready.”

She hung up.

CHAPTER THIRTY-EIGHT

WHILE THE NEW printer spit out copies of the photos, I checked my email. There was a note from Lani. I clicked it open.

She still intended to make a cell phone call, she said. But email was one way to work up to it. Her note was long, with many side trips down memory lane. It hurt to read. I closed the note, saving it for later.

I picked up the printed images. On a bare section of the wood floor, I laid the photos in a rough rectangle, recreating the basic shape of Annicka's grave. I lined up the photo showing Mason's shovel head with that vertical stripe cutting through the soil layers. I stepped back.

Madame raised her head. Ears pricked, she gazed at the door. A shadow fell across the pebble glass. She growled.

I stepped to the side.

"Harmon."

Madame growled again.

"Jack?" Before I could out-think myself, I rushed to the door.

His hair was wet. So were his jeans and his wrinkled Hawaiian shirt. He needed a shave.

"Working undercover?" I said.

"How'd you—"

"The shirt." Jack's dubious theory was that wearing crazy-loud Hawaiian shirts while undercover kept people from suspecting he was undercover. "You should stop wearing them."

"You should tell Eleanor to stop calling me Stanley."

"It's a literary reference," I said.

"But I'm not Stanley Kowalski."

I stepped back, inviting him in. He lumbered forward, damp jeans loose around his tight body. Like he'd worn them for days. I stared at the back of his shirt. Really wrinkled.

"Nice digs." He stood at the window that faced Puget Sound. "She really cares about you."

I closed the door. Madame walked back to her couch perch. In another life, I might tell Jack about my bad visit with my mom. Instead, I just stuffed down the feelings. "Eleanor's a generous person."

He continued to stare out the window. I felt another strange mix of emotions. After my day to hell and back, I needed solitude. Including time away from Jack.

"Is there something you need?" I asked. "Right this minute?"

He turned, and reached into his back pocket. "Here. I ran some lists."

I unfolded the pages, trying to not think about how warm the paper felt from being next to his body. Nine pages. I saw names, addresses, and short biographical information. The kind of information that comes from cursory background checks. "Jack—"

"Highlighted names are crossovers," he said. "Those people stayed at both the Waterhaus and the Eiderdown both."

"But—" I flipped the pages, disbelieving, "—this goes back *years*."

"More than twenty years for the Eiderdown. From Esther

Keller's birth year to her death."

"How did you get it?"

"They're good Germans. They keep excellent records. Of everything."

"But you still had to run the names through the system." I scanned the list. At least one dozen names were highlighted in first three pages. "Anything come up with the crossovers?"

"Nearly everyone moved in one direction. They stayed at the Waterhaus, then moved to the Eiderdown."

I felt a stab of pity for the Engels. And something else. But I couldn't look up and say it. "Thank you," I said.

"You're welcome," he said. "Don't you want to know more?"

"You've done enough."

"One of the crossover guests has forty-two unpaid parking tickets. Another just slapped a tax lien on his ex-wife's house because he's bankrupt. Two Starbucks executives are having an affair—both married to other people, who also work at Starbucks, but these two visit Leavenworth monthly and always stay in side-by-side rooms, with a connecting door. You want me to go on?"

I scanned the names, the dates, pulling out the pages. On the last page, Jack had written one name. It wasn't just highlighted, it was circled in red ink. "What about this one—Ezra Sugarman?"

"You'll need to check him out."

I read the name again. Then flipped back through the pages, checking his stays at both places. "The dates…"

"Right. Sugarman is the only guest who stayed at both places, annually. But then he stopped."

I read the dates of his stays. "Couldn't be."

"It is. Sugarman's first stay at the Eiderdown coincides with the birth of Esther Heller. He shows up annually. Five years later, with the birth of Annicka Engels, he starts staying at the Waterhaus. Annually."

"A relative—of both families?"

"He appears every six months. He's the only name with that schedule."

I flipped the pages. "But he stops going to the Eiderdown …"

"Right."

I looked up.

Jack's eyes were green as a forest. "He stopped staying at the Eiderdown after Esther's murder."

I scanned the pages.

"And his last stay at the Waterhaus," Jack answered, before I could even ask. "Was August of this year."

That cold sensation was back. I stared at the man's name. "Nothing came up on his background check?"

"Nothing workable. He's a successful accountant in Los Angeles. Keeps a perfect credit rating. I mean, *perfect.* One wife. Two grown kids, both of whom work in his accounting firm."

"Could he be a hotel accountant?"

"I guess you'll find out."

I nodded. "Thank you for—"

"No big deal." He ran a hand through his damp hair. "I had time to kill, since I wasn't flying to Leavenworth today."

My heart sank. I felt a hot flush of shame rising in my throat. This list just saved me hours upon hours of work. And how did I return the favor? By not showing up for the flight. By ignoring his voice mails. *Real nice.*

"How was your undercover assignment?" I asked, trying to make up for bad behavior.

"Sugarman keeps an apartment in Redmond. Right near Microsoft."

I stared at him. My mouth fell open. "You didn't."

"One bedroom. Nice area."

"Jack, you didn't just—"

"He only stays there twice a year, usually just a couple days. The stays coincide with his trips to Leavenworth."

"Jack—"

He held up a hand, stopping me. I stared at his open palm. The callused fingers. Callused from rowing. And before I could stop it, I saw us that night in the boat. Stroking across the dark water, beads of sweat trickling down his muscular back. "I need to apologize, about this morning."

"Management says Sugarman's the perfect tenant," he said. "So I think he's safe enough for you to take it from here."

A sensation like water washed over me. Water made of wonder, and sadness. I couldn't breathe. "Jack, please let me—"

"What's all this?" He tapped his wet shoe on the floor, next to the picture of the shovel. "Her grave?"

I took a deep breath. He was right; I really didn't want to talk about this morning either.

Setting the guest lists on my desk, I described the elephant hair, about Annicka working at Preston Baer's petting zoo, and how I'd spoken to Mason Leming. And how I found him later at the river. "He took off as soon as he saw me. Drove straight to the church. Father Anthony wouldn't let me near him."

Jack squatted by the recreated scene. He had one of those great guy-squats, one haunch resting on the back of his heel, elbows bent and resting on his knees. At any second he could spring from that position and take off. I swallowed. *Never to be seen again.*

I walked over, slowly, and tried not to stare at the muscles cabling his forearms.

"See this mark?" I knelt beside him and pointed to the vertical line cutting through the soil. "It shows up at regular intervals. Too regular for it to be random. I'm pretty sure it was made by the digging tool. So I took a couple shovels from Johann—"

"*Took?*" He turned toward me. His eyes were blue. "Took, how?"

"I didn't steal the shovels, Jack."

"Good. Continue."

"Those shovels didn't match that mark. But after chasing Mason to Our Lady of Snows, I was passing his truck." I lifted the close-up photo of the shovel's iron face. "That's why I hung up so abruptly."

"Why?"

I laid the photo on top of the photo showing the soil from Annicka's grave. "Look at his shovel. It's got a v-shaped defect. Right there."

I pushed the photos until they were perfectly superimposed.

"Harmon."

I nodded.

He looked at me. Inches from my face, his eyes were green. Alive. Full of passion. "That has to be the shovel that dug her grave."

"I know. Plus, the elephant hair was found in the soil."

"Harmon—you did it." His brilliant green eyes gazed into mine.

His breath smelled of coffee. But it smelled good. Because I knew why he'd had to drink it this late … because he was on surveillance. For *my* case. Watching Ezra Sugarman. My heart turned into a fist. I stood up, controlling my voice.

"Annicka was sneaking into Baer's place to visit the elephant. But her email made it clear that she was going to visit *after* her run. Meanwhile, Mason was taking care of the elephant."

Jack kept looking up at me. He was grinning. Happy. And *proud.*

"Don't get too excited," I said. "When the Heller girl was murdered, Mason Leming would've been about thirteen years old. And the sheriff believes his alibi for when Annicka was killed. He was working—at Baer's place, taking care of the elephant."

"But the shovel," Jack said. "With that tool mark, his alibi doesn't mean as much. Maybe he killed her earlier, or later, or somewhere else."

"Somewhere else is what I'm thinking." I stared at the photos of the soil. "I didn't find blood in that grave. He slit her throat, but not there."

Jack stood, stiffly. It made me wonder if he'd sat in that car all day, running those guest lists and watching Ezra Sugarman.

"I'll check out Sugarman," I said. "Thank you."

"He didn't leave his apartment all day."

I held his gaze. Those eyes. Turquoise. Blue and green and… "Why did you run that list for me?"

"Because you're working on my hate crime."

"Right. The hate crime." I walked over to the desk, trying to disguise my disappointment. *How many signals could I misinterpret—a thousand?* "I've got something for you."

I leaned into the computer and clicked open Lani's email. Jack stood behind me, reading over my shoulder. I wanted to pretend his body heat didn't affect me. But my palm immediately started sweating on the mouse. I scrolled through her long note, skipping right over the part where she suggests a get-together with my *significant other. And if you don't have one, Mike wants to set you up with somebody.*

"What's this?" Jack asked.

"Nothing." I scrolled faster.

Near the bottom, I found an attached copy of her findings. I clicked that open and read over the technical details. Nitrogen spikes. But that was normal because it was in lawn fertilizers. Some other bits of calcium and lime. Lani said the most interesting element was a powerful antibiotic. I read the name out loud, and explained its medical use.

"Why would an antibiotic be there?" he asked.

"Because the flame accelerant," I said, reading over her notes, "is dung."

"Dung," he said. "As in …"

"Crapola." I pointed to the screen, reading Lani's words aloud: " 'I am not yet an expert in wildlife excrement, but it's presence here might also explain the hay which you saw in your cursory soil exam. I suspect this particular dung comes from an ailing animal, because it would explain the presence of the antibiotic. My advice right now is that you find a sick African elephant. Because that animal's excrement is your flame accelerant. Hey, you know what they say, 'dung happens.' "

I turned my head to look him. He was gazing at her note.

"I found hay in Annicka's boots," I said. "And mud. But I'm guessing there's dung, too."

He shifted his gaze, fixing it on me. I felt a flutter of adrenaline. Or hope. Or was it fear. I forced myself back into work mode. "You'll be interested to know that the elephant Mason's taking care of is sick. Stomach problem, he told me."

"You want to fly up there tomorrow?" he asked.

I stepped back and brushed my clammy palms on my jeans. I wondered how ragged I looked right now after hiking the trail, laying in the dirt, running after Mason, driving six hours, and going to the asylum to get my butt kicked. And that wasn't even taking into account my lovely body scent of *eau de loneliness*. "Thanks, but I'll just drive up."

He held my gaze. Then stepped back, nodding as though he'd heard something I didn't say. He walked for the door.

"Jack?"

He stopped, but didn't turn around.

"I want to thank you," I said. "Really. I mean it. I just can't …"

"Harmon." He stayed put, his back to me. "You know what the real problem is?"

"No," I said.

"We're two of a kind," he said.

And left.

CHAPTER THIRTY-NINE

THE NEXT MORNING, I drove away from Eleanor's at 3:00 a.m. Rain was still falling and Madame once again sat in the passenger seat. I wasn't taking any chances, since wet roads slowed me down.

By 5:30 a.m., I was driving up Ski Hill Road. The last fraction of the darkness was breaking and I found Detective Culliton's cruiser parked a hundred yards below Our Lady of Snows. A county cruiser was parked behind him and a vehicle I recognized as the white wagon marked Animal Control. *Seiler?*

I parked behind his wagon, yanked up my rain hood, and told Madame, "I'll be right back."

Rain was falling loud and thunderous, like some spigot had burst wide open in heaven. I was soaked within seconds. I rapped on Culliton's window and jumped inside. His car smelled just like the office: cheap coffee. I yanked back my hood.

"Glad you could make it," he said, with a smirk.

"Glad you got backup. But are we taking Mason into the pound?"

"I didn't get clearance until after midnight. These two were available."

"I understand." Maybe Wilcove would show up. "So you

got the search warrant?"

"Only because of your shovel information. The judge gave us permission to search his truck and his mother's house. But not the church and not the petting zoo."

"It's a start," I said.

"And his mother's threatening to sue us."

"You found something?"

"We took their computer. Some clothing. He kept a handwritten journal. And because you asked, we took his shoes, boots, and sheets from his bed." The detective picked up a folder on the seat between us. "Here's the property list."

Rain pounded the roof as I glanced down at the collection. Culliton had done a thorough job, and I was grateful he had moved so quickly.

"Thanks for telling us about the shovel," he said.

I looked up. The sawed-off shotgun gaze was gone. "Like I said, you can take full credit. I just want to catch the killer."

He took a stainless steel thermos from the cupholder and pointed it toward the white-winged church. "I kept a deputy posted out here all night. Mason's truck hasn't moved. And he never came out. So although the judge refused our search warrant for the church, we do have permission to take Mason into custody."

"Which means we go in." I watched the gray rain pelting Mason's white truck and felt a deep relief for seeing that shovel yesterday. The rain was washing away any soil matches, or elephant hair, but I had photos of the gouges in the shovel's face. That was enough evidence. A match like that was statistically almost as good as DNA. In court, we could bring in hundred shovels and none of them would match that gouge the way Mason's shovel did. I thought again of him standing in the river, arms lifted to the sky like a man begging for forgiveness. Or washing himself of sin.

"You ready?" Culliton held his radio and clicked it.

Two "ready" clicks came back.

I tucked the evidence collection list under my rain jacket and sprinted back to the Ghost.

Madame wagged her tail as I got in.

"Sorry," I told her. "You can't come to this next part either."

CHAPTER FORTY

I'D DONE A lot of things with the Bureau, but busting into a church with guns was a first.

"Probably considered some kind of mortal sin," Culliton said, prying a crowbar between the Our Lady's wood doors. "But that's what confession is for."

The wood splintered, the lock burst, and Culliton yanked the door. The foyer was dark. And smelled of rain.

"Mason," he called out. "We don't want anyone to get hurt."

I followed Culliton, shielded by his size and bulletproof vest.

"Where's the light?" Culliton muttered.

A split second later, the lights flashed on. Culliton and I both turned to see the deputy behind Seiler, standing by the light switch. He was young, blond, and scared. He gave me an almost imperceptible nod.

We moved into the sanctuary. That fake floral scent still hung in the air. Culliton raised one hand and signaled the deputies to split up and comb the pews. Seiler went up one side, weapon poised. The younger deputy took the other side, hand on his gun. I wondered why Culliton had picked him if everybody wanted in on this case.

"He's not here," Seiler said.

Culliton tapped his radio and told Dispatch to renew the APB for Mason Leming. He gave a description of height and weight—*five-eleven, 150, hair color black.*

As he spoke, I moved across the back of the sanctuary. The door that the cleaning crane had knocked was closed. Silently, I pressed my ear against the wood. Silence. I moved to the side of the frame, and tried the door knob. It was unlocked. I held the knob, without opening the door, and signaled to Culliton.

The door burst open.

Five-eleven and one-hundred-and-fifty pounds hit me so hard I flew. Mason jumped right over me. I flipped over. He could run alright. He reached the foyer before I scrambled to my feet. Seiler came running down the far aisle, his body notched low like a defensive tight end.

"Mason!" Culliton yelled. "Freeze!"

Mason cleared the foyer. Seiler passed Culliton.

"Stay on him!" Culliton yelled. "Don't let him go!"

Seiler was out door before Culliton finished his order. I ran into the foyer and saw the busted door *thunk* as Seiler exited behind Mason. The wood shuddered. I pushed it open and the next sound was rain. The sound after that punched my gut.

A gun fired.

And a man screamed.

CHAPTER FORTY-ONE

AT 7:21 A.M. Father Anthony strode into Leavenworth's only emergency room. He wore a flannel pajama top with his jeans, and an expression that said all his work on behalf of God could do nothing for people like us.

"You shot him?" he asked.

Detective Culliton was standing next to me. I waited for him to respond. But when I looked over, he seemed to expect me to say something. *Oh, sure,* now *I'm in charge.*

"Father," I said, "Mason chose to run."

"So you *shot* him?" His raised voice caused everyone in the lobby to turn and stare. Leavenworth's sole medical center, located behind the commercial district, appeared to serve mostly elderly people and tourists who looked like they'd been up all night with alcohol poisoning.

I lowered my voice. "The doctors said he'd make it."

"I was wrong about you," Father Anthony said. "When you came to the church with Jack, you seemed like an honorable person."

A petty piece of my heart demanded to tell the priest *I* didn't shoot Mason. Deputy Seiler shot Mason—after Culliton had given several warnings. Mason Leming was a murder suspect. And a fugitive. He was dangerous.

But all of that sounded defensive, like we'd done something wrong. I was convinced we didn't. Mason was guilty. His shovel proved it.

"Speaking of Jack," I said, "I've got the results on that six-pointed star burned into your grass. We know the accelerant. Would you like to hear it?"

"Oh, switching subjects." Father Anthony shook his head in disgust. "How mature."

"We're still on the same subject, Father."

"How so?"

"The fire on your lawn was fueled by animal dung. More than likely elephant dung." I thought of Lani's report. Finding that antibiotic remnant was pure gold. Buster with his stomach ailment. "You do know where Mason works, don't you?"

I watched the fog clear. Just as it had cleared for me more times than I wanted to admit. I'd climbed onto the high horse before, only to realize I facing the animal's rear end.

"Not Mason." The priest glanced at the detective. "Mason?"

Culliton's sigh sounded as sibilant as tires in the rain. "There's even more, Father. I can't explain everything to you right now. But trust me. We got the right guy."

The priest reached up, absently touching the collar of his flannel pajamas. I watched another fog evaporate, as another realization swept over him. It made me wonder what Mason had confessed. And what Mason would confess to us. Father Anthony's face softened.

"You understand my position?" he asked.

I nodded, and marveled at how quickly a situation can turn for the better when someone's humble. "I do. And I respect it. But we might need your help."

"Now?"

"The doc sedated him," Culliton said. "Could be a couple hours before he's awake. And then you'll have to stand in line—no offense, Father."

"No offense taken." He looked slightly shaken. "I think it would help if I stay."

"Why?" Culliton asked.

"His mother's on her way."

Culliton gave another sigh. I looked over, questioning.

"Edwina Leming," the detective said, "doesn't exactly run our fan club."

EDWINA LEMING TURNED out to be a tall, frazzled, energetic woman—on a good day.

Today was not a good day.

Soaked with rain, she came through the medical clinic's automatic doors looking like a feral cat that somebody tried to bathe. And now they would pay for their mistake.

"He was working that day!" she screamed at Culliton. "I told you!"

"Edwina, we have evidence that—"

"Evidence? You don't have *evidence*. All you've got is a badge and a murder you can't solve. So you make my kid the target." She pointed a finger at him. "Hear me, Louie, and hear me good. When I finish exposing you pigs for what you really are, you'll be lucky to get job picking up litter."

"I wouldn't be making threats," Culliton said.

"It's not a threat. It's a promise."

Culliton's shotgun-gaze fired on her. Edwina never felt the blow.

"*And* I got a medical waiver," she added, "so shove your idea about my pot growing. I'm free and clear." She glanced around the clinic, her face pinched with annoyance. "Where's my kid?"

"Ma'am." A male nurse in yellow scrubs rushed toward

us. "You need to keep it down, we have patients who—"

"Any of them shot?"

The nurse looked around, as though his question might be legitimate. "No, none of them were shot but—"

"My kid was *shot*. So don't tell me to shut up."

"I didn't—"

"Yeah, you did." Edwina turned back to Culliton. "And I'm gonna sue your department for every last cent."

"Best of luck," the detective said.

"I don't need luck. I got you dopes."

She stormed off, trailed by the male nurse still asking her to keep it down.

"I can stay," he said to me. "If you've got other things to do."

Now we're pals. Amazing what a little success does for a person.

"I do need to follow-up with a few people," I said.

"Go ahead," Culliton said. "Just make sure you come by the department before you head back to Seattle. I've got something for you."

CHAPTER FORTY-TWO

SMALL TOWNS TURNED everyone into gossips.

I had just parked The Ghost outside the Waterhaus, holding open the passenger door for Madame, urging her to hurry up because rain was pouring from the sky, when the hotel's front door opened and Johann stepped out. He walked through the rain—no coat, no hat, no umbrella—with his arms outstretched. The mournful blue eyes held glistening pools of tears.

"God bless you, Raleigh."

He wrapped his arms around me.

I closed my eyes.

His scent was grief and turpentine. And relief. It seemed to pour out of him like the rain falling on this drought-stricken land. And I knew when the water that pooled in his eyes broke. His body shook.

"Thank you," he said into the rain. "Thank you, thank you."

I wanted to say it, too. But the words hurt too much. I pressed the tip of my tongue against the back of my teeth and swallowed my gratitude. Thanks for having confidence in me. Thanks for believing I could do this job. Thanks for reminding me just how much these awful burdens are part of me.

It matters to this one.

"They sedated him," I managed to say, breaking from his embrace. "So we won't know all the details for a while."

Johann wiped his eyes with the flats of his long hands. Grief had many stages. But stoic grief's layers ran as deep as the Grand Canyon. Now that this first torrent had broken inside him, I knew he would be very, very tired. Maybe he would even sleep.

"I cannot believe it," he said.

"That we found him?"

"That it was Mason."

I waited a moment. "But you suspected Mason."

"Fritz, he convinced me." Johann wiped his eyes again. "I knew Mason, he loved Annicka. It was hard to believe he … but now? I wonder, what kind of love was it?"

"Self-love," I said. "The opposite of true love."

His tears appeared again. But they didn't fall. "You are wise, Raleigh."

Wise in pain, maybe. Wise in grief. But not in relationships. Or making choices that helped my mom get better. That kind of wisdom seemed to elude me.

"Take care of yourself," I said. "It's going to be a long process."

He nodded. "And you will do me another favor?"

"Of course."

He lowered his face, until the white beard touched his chest. "Please give Jack my thanks, too."

"Oh, absolutely." I patted my leg, calling Madame back to the car. Her black fur was slick with rain.

"Raleigh."

I looked up. Johann's mournful blue eyes matched the feeling in my heart.

"The cup of joy can refill itself," he said.

I nodded, to make him feel better. Because I knew the cup

of pain refills itself, too.

But there was no point in saying that. This man already knew it.

CHAPTER FORTY-THREE

THE EARLY MORNING rain did nothing to keep shoppers from Preston Baer's apples. I parked in the almost-full lot, yanked up my hood once more, and apologized to Madame.

Rain was sluicing off the scalloped edge of the red-and-white awning, draining it onto the spot where I'd met the blond girl named Alma. For a moment, I thought I saw her in the back area. But I was wrong. Every girl working Preston Baer's retail area was a beautiful blond. Like Annicka. I passed through them, and wondered about her final Sunday run on that scenic mountain trail. What had she felt when she saw Mason there—and realized he came to kill her?

I stood in line and waited for one of the young blonds to finish ringing up the customers.

"Is Mr. Baer here?" I asked.

The girl picked up the phone by a register and tapped two numbers. "That CSI lady is here," she said.

Yep, everybody knew everybody in this town.

"Okay," she said, and hung up. "Mr. Baer will be right out."

I wandered over to the merchandise. Apple butters. Apple honeys. Apple tartlets, caramel apple spread for ice cream. And every Baer Naked label screamed: "100 percent pure. We breed only the best!"

I picked up a jar of apple butter and read about the Baer family's years perfecting its orchards. Cross-pollinating, eliminating imperfections—

"You caught him."

Preston Baer wheeled to a stop beside me.

I put the apple butter back on the shelf. "How did you hear?"

"Johann. He just called. I think his next phone call is the Vatican. He'll nominate you for sainthood."

"That would be a big mistake. Do you have a moment for some follow-up questions?"

"Of course." He spun ninety degrees. "Let's go to my office."

I followed him across the retail area and through the plastic flaps that kept the cold inside the warehouse. On the metal roof, rain drummed its fingers. The chilly air seemed to rise from the concrete. More blond teenagers worked at the loading dock, shipping pallets of boxed apples. But now I saw their faces. Several of them had broad-pan faces with small eyes and flattened noses. I recognized the features. They came from chromosome mutation of Down's Syndrome.

Baer turned left, away from the loading dock.

His office was at the back of the building. It was a square room that looked somewhat ordinary, except for the furnishings. His burled wood desk faced crimson leather chairs with ball-and-claw feet.

"Have a seat," he said.

When I sat down, the chair felt like a throne, like some historic antique rescued from the Lusitania.

"Something wrong?" he asked.

I gestured to the furniture. "I never realized apples were such a lucrative business."

"Hard work." He smiled, briefly. "That's what's lucrative." He rolled to the desk and pointed to the framed photos on the wall behind it. "My great-grandparents came here from Hamburg. They had nothing but the clothes on their backs. That's the work ethic I'm trying to instill in all these kids."

"Including kids with Down's Syndrome."

"Yes." He hesitated. "I think we have an obligation, to help people who can't help themselves." He changed the topic. "You have some questions for me?"

I pulled out one of my photographs and slid it across the desk.

"This shovel was in the back of Mason's truck. Do you know whether it belongs to you or to him?"

Preston Baer studied the photo.

"Is something wrong?" I asked.

"Very."

I stepped behind his chair so I could look at the photo with him. But I still didn't see the problem. "What is it?"

"Annicka should've never been murdered. It's evil." He shook his head grimly and looked back at the photo. "You believe this shovel was used to kill her?"

"I can't say, without compromising the case. But I'd like to know whether Mason keeps this shovel in his truck."

"Or whether he took it from here," Baer said.

"His mother claims he was working that Sunday morning. I assume she means here. He didn't have another job?"

"Not that I know of." Baer set the photo on the antique desk, then backed his chair away, as if needing more perspective. "It's hard for me to know about the shovel. I'm no longer doing the manual labor around here. So I don't know whose shovel it is."

"Do you still believe Mason was working here that Sunday morning?"

"I'll tell you exactly what I told the police. Sundays were

among my most lucrative days. But I had a change of heart, after my accident." He indicated the wheelchair. "Now we're closed on Sundays, but the animals still need tending."

"Yes, but Mason—"

"Mason *insisted* on working Sundays. These animals require daily care, feeding, water. My wife Susan was doing that work—you met her. You can see how dedicated she is. But with Mason taking over, my wife got a day off. So Mason works here on Sundays."

"Alone?"

"Alone."

"Do you have timecards, schedules, anything that can corroborate that?"

"Sunday's are …" Baer hesitated, with a sigh. "I pay him for Sundays off the books. Cash. I'd prefer that didn't come out. I don't need the IRS after me, too."

"Did anyone see Mason here that Sunday?"

"Nobody comes in that day. As I said, Mason works alone."

"You've never doubted his story?"

"Not for one second."

"Really?"

"Really," Baer said. "Mason Leming's one of my best workers. There was no way I would believe he killed Annicka. But now …" He reached for the photo, taking in the visual with a deep breath. "Now we know otherwise. Would you like me to ask around, about the shovel?"

"Yes, sir."

"*Sir?*" He smiled, briefly again. "Where are you from?"

"Virginia."

"Ah, yes. I detected a southern accent. What's your stock?"

"Pardon?"

"Ancestry. Lineage. German, by any chance?"

"English." *I think.* My mom never mentions my birth father. "And some Irish."

"Well, the Celts have a strong heritage, too." He tapped the photo. "I'll make this a priority. You'll have an answer by day's end. Will that work?"

CHAPTER FORTY-FOUR

AFTER BUYING SOME more Crispins and an apple biscuit for Madame, I headed west. The rain was falling even heavier when Culliton called my cell phone to say he had to leave the hospital.

"You want me to stay?" I asked.

"No, Mason's not awake. And Edwina's not leaving. I'll come back later."

"Okay."

"You're still coming by the department, right?" he asked.

I had forgotten about that, so I swung by the Sheriff's department before heading toward the mountain pass. County cruisers filled the parking lot. I decided everyone was here to find out how Culliton apprehended Mason Leming. I didn't want any part of that, but didn't want to risk losing Culliton's help.

In the bullpen area, the sheriff stood at the front of the room facing a herd of deputies wearing brown rain jackets. In yellow lettering, the word SHERIFF'S DEPT was printed on the back of their jackets. The sheriff himself—still looking as short and angry as the day I interviewed him—was issuing orders. Nobody noticed my entrance.

"—on all main roads," he was saying. "Caution. That's our word of the day. Safety. Don't take any chances. Is that understood?"

Nods all around.

"And don't allow anyone through. Especially the Oktoberfest folks. They're going to demand to leave. Half of 'em will be inebriated, so keep the breathalyzers ready. The situation is likely to get worse."

I glanced around the room. What *situation*?

"Don't hesitate to call dispatch. I've got it triple-manned today. Now go out there and save lives."

The herd of brown uniforms headed for the door. I stepped aside and saw Seiler walked among them. He gave me a nod. He didn't look so cocky anymore. We both knew he'd be under investigation for shooting Mason, even if it was a valid decision based on Culliton's orders.

The detective stood at his desk, shoving his big arms into one of the brown rain jackets.

"What's going on?" I asked.

"Oh, hey." He actually smiled. "Good to see you."

Nothing changes a girl's social status like collaring a killer. "You had something for me?"

He reached for a stack of binders next to his computer monitor and handed me two. "Everything's in there. Autopsies, interviews, status updates. Maybe you'll catch something I missed."

"Thanks. I'll look at them tonight." I glanced back at the force, walking out the door and climbing into the cruisers. "What happened?"

"We've got flash flooding, landslides. They just shut down the passes."

"What?"

"The roads are a mess. You got some place to stay tonight?"

"What?" I couldn't breathe.

"You'll probably only have to stay one night. DOT's trying to get one lane clear by tomorrow." He zipped the jacket. "But you better hurry. Rooms will go fast.

"Okay." A sharp claw raked across my heart. "But there's got to be another road out of here."

"Not unless you're Maria von Trapp. The only other way out is to walk over the mountains."

"But …there must be …?"

"Sorry." He picked up a brown rain hat from his chair. "But try to enjoy your stay."

IN THE PARKING lot, I sat inside The Ghost and listened to the rain pound the roof. Madame sat up with anticipation, but laid back down when I didn't turn the key for several minutes. Resting her black head between her paws, she sighed.

Through the fogging windshield, I watched the rain wash down the brown hillsides. The water carved gullies and spread sediment across the pavement. When soil was this dry, it couldn't absorb water.

Madame sighed again.

"I hear you."

I pulled out my phone, and swallowed my pride.

"Jack?" I said.

"Harmon, where are you?"

"Purgatory."

"I hear the food sucks."

"Yeah."

"Did you get the guy?" he asked.

"Uh-huh."

"Any problems?"

"Plenty."

"Such as?"

"I'll tell you later. Right now, both passes are closed."

"Oh."

"Yesterday I was late getting back. Remember, the whole chasing the guy from the river to the church?"

"Yes …"

"So I was late. Really late. And if I don't show up today …"

The rain sounded like it wanted to burst through the roof.

"Harmon," he said it, slowly, as if words were being pressed through a sieve. "If I could get you back here, I'd fire up the plane right now. But the only planes getting through that weather run on jet fuel. There's even a snow advisory for the higher elevations."

"Are you saying there's no way you—"

"None."

My throat tightened.

"You collared the guy," he said. "That's huge. Think about that."

"Yes, but we now have a complication. Remember that county deputy, the one who ragged on me about Madame?"

"Animal control."

"Right," I said. "We were moving so fast on the church that we didn't get great backup. He shot the guy."

"What—fatal?"

"No. But now Mason will hire lawyers."

"But *you* did good, Harmon. Really good."

I looked out the fogged windshield. All I could think about was my mom waiting for Madame, sitting on that single bed with its plastic cover. And no dog showing up.

"You remember how to get to my cabin?" Jack asked.

I nodded.

"Good," he said, as if he could see my nod. "There's a key above the back door. Make a fire, settle in the the night."

I nodded.

"Is the mutt with you?" he asked.

"Why?"

"Because if she's at Eleanor's, I'll take her to your mom."

Rain smeared the glass. But something else was blurring the landscape. I opened my mouth, and hoped that everything wouldn't spill out.

"Harmon, it's going to be okay. The roads'll probably be clear by tomorrow."

"Jack, I—"

"Don't have to say anything," he said. "I already told you. We're two of a kind."

CHAPTER FORTY-FIVE

WITH RAIN PELTING, the lake looked like hammered steel. I found the cabin key and opened the door. Madame raced inside. I dropped my pack near the door, then took out my phone and called Aunt Charlotte.

"Seattle Stones," she answered. Her voice was full of robust cheer. "Where Mother Nature heals all wounds."

Right.

"Aunt Charlotte, it's me, Raleigh."

"Oh, no—I didn't call you back, did I?"

"That's okay. Could you possibly visit Mom today?"

"Today?"

I explained yesterday's less-than-ideal series of event. "Now I'm stuck in Leavenworth. Landslides closed both passes."

"Oh, honey, don't you worry, I'll call Claire right now. She can watch the store."

Claire. The "clairvoyant" friend. At least she wasn't going to the asylum with my aunt.

"Thank you, Aunt Charlotte."

"I'll bring turquoise," she said. "It's heals painful emotions."

I said the only thing possible: "I love you, Aunt Charlotte."

"Love you, too, honey."

I FOUND FIREWOOD in the shed and made five trips, stocking the living room's pot-bellied stove.

In the kitchen, where red gingham curtains covered the cabinets, I found jelly jar drinking glasses, white Correll plates, and a cookbook from the 1950s that was a fundraiser for Our Lady of Snows. I stared at the hand-drawn cover. It showed a child and a quote from the Book of James: "True religion is this, to care for widows and orphans in their distress."

Something about the image gripped my heart. Maybe the word *distress*, and thinking of Annicka. I thumbed the pages. Veal bratwurst. Sauerkraut. Kugel.

I found canned chili, and a can opener. The oven range was gas-fired but no pilot light was on. And no smell of gas, so the service must've been cut off. I poured the chili into a saucepan and placed it on top of the woodstove. As it heated, I pulled a rocking chair over so I could sit by the fire and still look out the front window to the lake.

I tried to say grace. But my mind kept filling with that image of my mother, all alone. So lonely, yet she didn't want to see me. That was probably why the quote from James struck a chord. My mother was a widow, in distress. And I couldn't be there. *Help her. Because I blew it. Again.*

I checked the chili. It was warm enough, but my appetite was gone. I placed the sauce pan on the stone hearth and called Madame. Her tail wagged happily as she dove into the chili. I sat down again, staring into the amber flames. When my phone rang, the Tijuana Brass suddenly sounded like a funeral march.

I walked over to where my rain jacket hung on a peg by

the door. The sleeves dripped water on the slate floor. I dug the phone from the pocket. The screen read, *unknown caller*.

Jack.

I slid my finger over the screen. "I'm fine."

"I am glad to hear that."

Not Jack.

"I'm sorry—who—"

"Johann."

"Oh. I thought you were Jack."

"Ah, yes. He would call you." He paused. Then: "We have a room. For free."

"Thank you, that's very generous. But I'm already at Jack's cabin."

"Good, good." He sounded pleased. Or relieved. My free room probably bothered Helen Engels right now. "You call me," he said, "if you need anything."

I thanked him, disconnected the call, and dug the battery charger from my pack. All the while I couldn't stop thinking about the Engels. What strong people. To keep working despite their child's murder, this investigation. Keeping their hotel open and taking in guests, yet still thinking of me. Preston Baer was right. Hard-working Germans. Good people.

My own self-pity disgusted me.

Reaching into my pack, I pulled out the binders Culliton gave me and carried them to the rocking chair. Madame lifted her head from the pot of chili, licking her whiskers.

"I'm glad you're here," I told her.

She wagged her tail and went back to her meal.

Sitting beside the fire, I opened the first binder, but started reading from the back.

The initial report about Esther Heller's murder showed that on the cusp of turning eighteen and heading for art school in Seattle, she was found in room 412. In the white-tiled bathroom by her mother. Her skull had been shattered, her throat slit, and her body then bled out in the same bathtub she'd just cleaned.

I checked the report. Culliton had been at the scene. He was the officer writing up this initial dispatch. He noted that the water flowing from the shower head was hot. As it rained on the dead girl's body, the warm water quickened her blood loss. The water also washed away evidence.

In fact, the crime scene was so clean that only two sources provided trace evidence: Esther and her mother, who had climbed into the tub.

Culliton had written, "When officers arrived, Mrs. Heller was in the tub rocking her deceased child and weeping."

My eyes burned. I held my breath for a count of five before checking the crime photos. The images had an unusually stark appearance, probably from the camera's flash on the bathroom's white tile. I let my eyes roam the terrible truth. What struck me was there was no blood spatter. No mess. The killer—or killers—had taken her life with almost laser precision. Who does that?

I read through the rest of Culliton's investigative notes. He had locked down the hotel and interviewed every guest along with the staff. No one appeared to be a viable suspect. Also, Esther Heller had no boyfriend, no enemies, and no life outside of school and work at the hotel. I also saw that Cullton pursued any lead that arose, including the séance in the hotel's lobby.

In his recent notes, he acknowledged the possible connection between Esther and Annicka's deaths. I thought of his shotgun gaze, and how it fired when I accused him of getting a paycheck no matter what happened with the case. No wonder he was angry. Six years after Esther died, he was still thinking of her.

I closed the binder, and watched Madame lick the pot clean. Then she lay down beside the rocking chair.

The second murder book was thinner, but its details were just as gruesome.

"Partially masticated right hand," Culliton wrote, "protruding from the ground."

Like Esther, Annicka's skull had been shattered and her throat slit. The neck wound was so clean that the detective speculated on the knife. It had to be extremely sharp, and the killer had to be an expert with it.

The coroner's report offered all the medical-legal terminology that I could translate from my time in the Bureau's Materials Analysis Unit. *Hypovolemia.* Blood volume loss. Her jugular vein opened in one smooth movement of the knife. *Intracranial contusion*s. Traumatic brain bruising from the shattered skull.

The shovel?

I tried to picture Mason swinging that tool. If he hit Annicka's head with the metal face, he could knock her out. That would leave her unable to fight.

But the coroner's notes on the skull injury said the initial blow struck Annicka's forehead. And the impact created a *concave* bone injury. Most likely the object was round, "with an approximate three-inch radius." The blow cracked her skull and created "a pattern of fractures radiating from the point of impact." A kill-shot.

I tried to think how Mason could accomplish that with the shovel. The only way was if he struck Annicka's forehead with the *tip* of the shovel's handle. Not an easy move. Especially if the other person was moving.

Either Mason was stronger than he looked, or Annicka was already neutralized before he drove the handle into her head.

I opened Esther's file again. Her head injury was eerily

similar. Round object, three-inch radius, similar fractures that spidered out from the point of impact.

Three inches?

Most shovel handles were two inches, at most. Mason's shovel included.

Culliton had circled the words *postmorten lividity* in Annicka's file. That's where the blood pools in the body's lowest parts, drawn by gravity. Lividity gave the skin a bluish color. The coroner noted it in Annicka's hands, arms, and legs. Even with the blood loss from a slit throat. Perhaps because she was running. Her skin was already flushed from exertion.

I stared at the first photo. It showed Annicka in her shallow grave. She laid face-up, with grains of soil embedded in her delicate eye lashes. Her right arm was extended in that rigored wave, and her long legs were tucked beneath her. I pulled the photo closer.

That bluish lividity ran down her thighs. The tops of her arms. I'd used these same discolorations to reconstruct a dead body's original position. But if Annicka lay face up in the grave, her lividity should've run down the *back* of her body. Gravity would ensure that. There were only two explanations for lividity showing up on the front of her body. One, the weight of the soil bruising the skin. Or two, she died in a different position.

I read the coroner's notes again. He detailed the lividity, remarking on the same questions I had. He also noted *maceration*. Or excess moisture in her skin. I picked up another photo and examined her left hand. It had stayed buried. Her fingertips showed the rippled texture of raisins. Like skin kept in water too long.

But there was no water where Annicka was buried. None.

Except the river. I thought of Mason standing in the water, arms raised in some kind of penitence.

I went back to Esther's file and checked the coroner's report. There it was. *Macerated dermis.* Waterlogged skin, from the shower raining water on her body.

I set the binders on the floor, side by side, and opened my notebook.

I made two columns and lined up the similarities.

Same head injury, I wrote.

Slit throat.

Waterlogged skin.

I watched the flames flicker through the stove's iron slats.

Turning eighteen.

Moving to Seattle.

Parents own hotel.

I drew a line horizontally, then made another two columns. Under Annicka's name I wrote, *Mason Leming.*

But for Esther's column, Mason was highly questionable. Barely thirteen when she died. And the photos all pointed to a professional crime scene. I wrote down, *Mason helped someone kill Esther?*

Or, another idea. Everybody knew everybody. What if Mason heard about Esther's murder, knew the details. He could kill Annicka the same way, and throw even an experienced investigator like Culliton off his track.

Was Mason that smart?

I picked up the photo of Annicka in her grave. Her face was barely recognizable. Bruised, swollen, bloated. Forehead dented by the blow to the skull.

A crime of passion?

Mason.

Mason, who Preston Baer never suspected. Who Johann didn't suspect—until Fritz convinced him otherwise.

Fritz.

I wrote his name under Esther's column. And under Annicka's.

I stood, paced the room, and threw another log into the stove. When I walked over to my phone, it was fully charged. I called Culliton.

"Yeah?" His voice was raised, almost yelling. In the background I could hear something like static. Rain. Heavy rain. And cars hissing past.

"I was just wondering if you had time to check on Mason," I said.

"No. I'm still on road duty. It's a mess out here. But I've got somebody stationed outside his room."

A car honked. Culliton muttered something.

"Roads are really bad?" I asked.

"Yeah. Where're you?"

"At a cabin. On Lake Wenatchee."

"Too bad," he said. "Edwina's going to have him lawyered up before he blinks one eye."

"I can get there."

"Don't risk it."

"From here to Leavenworth, is the road clear?"

I couldn't tell if I heard more hissing cars, or a sigh. "The road's clear but—"

"On my way."

I disconnected the call and picked up Madame's licked-clean pot. I set it in the sink, and was passing the refrigerator when the white piece of paper caught my eye. Held to the fridge with a blue magnet advertising Lake Wenatchee.

The handwriting. That same girlish penmanship. I told myself to keep walking.

I grabbed my coat, pack, and car keys. I called to Madame.

But my voice sounded choked. Because the words on that note were now etched into my mind. They would never leave.

Jack,
I waited here all day.
Where are you?
Love you with all my heart,
—M.

CHAPTER FORTY-SIX

IT TOOK ME twice as long to reach town, but maybe it only felt that way. My heart weighed a thousand pounds.

Madame sat rigid on the passenger seat, staring through the rapid beat of the windshield wipers. At the medical center's entrance, two ambulances were parked, red lights flashing.

"Wait here," I said.

Inside, I found Mason Leming's room, guarded by a large man wearing a dark blue private security uniform.

"Hi." I smiled. "Here to see Mason Leming."

"Family?"

"No." I reached into my wallet and took out my business card.

He read it. Nothing registered.

"You can call Detective Culliton, he'll vouch for me."

I waited while he called and they chatted about the roads. My mind was racing—how did all of these pieces fit together?

"Louie says you can go in." He holstered the cell phone.

"Thank you."

I parted the white curtain around the hospital bed. Edwina Leming was sprawled in a reclining chair beside the bed. Her thin mouth was parted, the frizzy-haired head tilted to the side, like someone had pulled the plug on her electrified personality. In the hospital bed, Mason lay tubed up, eyes closed. But water leaked from under his dark lashes. The tears streamed down pale unshaven cheeks.

I started counting. *One one-thousand.*

Two one-thousand …

At *nineteen one-thousand*, I decided it was true what they say. People can feel a person staring at them, even under a glaze of narcotics.

He recognized me and quickly wiped the tears from his face with the hand tubed to an IV. Then he glanced at his mother.

I walked to the other side, opposite Edwina, so I could keep an eye on her, too.

"How're you feeling?" I whispered.

He took another glance at his mother. One loud word, he could wake her.

But he whispered, "What d'you want?"

"I want to know why you ran. Twice."

"You were chasing me," he hissed.

We both looked at Edwina. She seemed far more narcotized than her son. But she could instantly wake up screaming.

"Did anyone advise you of your rights?" I asked.

"Sure." Another hiss. "In the ambulance. Nice cops."

I gave Culliton points. He wasted no time.

"Why don't you and I start over?" I opened my notebook. "Did you carry the shovel up there, or stash it there ahead of time?"

More water filled his milky eyes. But I saw despair behind it. And something else.

"Mason," I said his name softly. "You'll gain nothing by lying."

"I didn't kill her."

"Except right now there's enough evidence to convict you.

And not circumstantial evidence. Forensic proof. Do you know the difference?"

He wiped his eyes.

"If you want any sort of deal, anything that's better than life behind bars, you better start telling me exactly what happened."

"I was *shot*," he hissed. "Does that mean anything to you?"

"Yes. But I just looked at the crime scene photos. I'm not interested in making you feel better about yourself."

He looked away and placed a hand over his mouth, muffling his sobs. The IV tubes in his arm shook. Remorse. It was always a good sign. But sometimes remorse was about getting caught. Not about doing the deed.

"Tell me, Mason. *Now.*"

He whipped his hand away. The tubes slapped the bed rail. "I didn't kill her!"

We both looked at Edwina. She shifted her position. The frizzy hair created a penumbra around her frazzled face. She didn't wake up. But time was short. I tried a different track.

"Who told you about Esther Heller?"

"*What?*"

"Esther Heller." I had a sinking feeling as I repeated her name. His reaction wasn't right. "Her family runs the Eiderdown."

"So?" He scowled.

"Their daughter died, six years ago."

"Six years ago? I wasn't even living here." He shifted his eyes toward his mother. "Wake her up. Ask her. We lived in Seattle."

No wonder Culliton didn't suspect him. The sinking feeling gained momentum.

Mason shifted in the bed, wincing.

"You alright?" I asked.

The tears were back. "Why did he shoot me?"

"You ran."

"Because you were chasing me!"

Another glance at his mother. We waited. But the only sound came from down the hall, the distant call for Dr. Mueller.

"Tell me about Annicka."

"Like, what?"

"Like what happened the day she died, Mason."

"I—"

"The truth," I said.

"If I tell you, will you help me?"

"Yes."

"I found her."

It took me a moment. "You found her?"

"She didn't come see Buster that morning. It already was past ten. Annika was always there by nine. I drove by the Waterhaus. Fritz said she went running."

"Fritz. He was at the Inn?"

"He's always there. But he was acting weird. All sweaty and stuff. Johann and Helen were at church. I knew Annicka ran the Icicle trail on Sundays, so I drove out there." He squeezed the white sheet between his fingers. "Kaffee was running down the road."

"Her dog."

He nodded. "The leash was chewed off. And his eyes … bulging. Scared. I've never seen him like that. I stopped and picked him up. He was shaking. I couldn't figure out why he wasn't with Annicka—he always stayed with her. And he knows that trail, so he wouldn't get lost. But …"

"But, what?"

His whisper was urgent, panicked. "When I parked at the

trail, Kaffee jumped out of my truck and took off. I ran after him but I couldn't keep up. Until he stopped."

My pen hovered over the page. "The dog stopped, where?"

"The cave." Mason stared at the wall across from his bed, a distant expression in his glazed eyes. "Kaffee was standing there. Howling." He reached up, pressing his palms against his ears. "God, that howl."

I wrote down the information and waited for him to calm himself. He kept his hands on his ears, but I figured he could hear me. "Was Annicka in the cave?"

He nodded. "In the water."

That familiar chill went down my arms. "What water."

He lowered his hands but stared at his fingers.

"Mason, what water?"

"A pond. In the cave." He looked like he might vomit. "So much blood."

Pieces fell into place. Annicka didn't have stress fractures—she took her run and made it all the way to the bottom, only to find her killer waiting. "What did you do next?"

He didn't say anything.

"Mason."

"I carried her—up the trail." His voice was dull. "Got the shovel."

His description of her death matched the coroner's report. Annicka didn't die in that grave. But was Mason clever enough to throw false clues? "You didn't tell this to the police."

"And if I did, they'd believe me?" He pointed to his side. "Look what just happened. I'm the number one suspect."

"Not telling them made it worse."

He held my gaze.

I felt inclined to believe him. For one thing, he couldn't have killed Esther, too. And he didn't seem incapable of delivering a perfect kill shot to a forehead with the thin end of a shovel. And the water, that was another item. Nobody had mentioned water. But it explained what coroner noticed about her skin. And finally, the lividity. That bruising showed Annicka died face down, not face up.

Mason Leming looked at me, almost pleading.

"If you want anyone else to believe you," I said, "you better start telling me everything. And I mean *everything.*"

CHAPTER FORTY-SEVEN

STANDING IN THE rain outside the hospital's entrance, I called Culliton.

"We need to talk," I said. "In person."

He gave me directions. It took forty-three minutes to drive seven miles. The wet roads were choked with commercial trucks, RVs, and infuriated Oktoberfesters who couldn't party in the open air beer gardens but couldn't go home either.

On the north end of Blewitt Pass, I found Culliton directing traffic. In head-to-toe rain gear, he stood in front of a jackknifed semi. The empty cab was tipped into a culvert of rushing water. An EMT truck was parked beside it.

When Culliton saw The Ghost, he gave me one of those hand signals that stewardesses use to indicate the location of emergency exits. I parked behind one of two county cruisers. A deputy got out of the first cruiser and replaced Culliton's position. The detective jogged for the other cruiser.

I grabbed the two binders, tucked them under my jacket, yanked up my hood, and told Madame I'd be right back.

"Promise," I said.

Rain fell in thunderous applause. In just twelve feet from my car to the cruiser, I was soaked. I jumped in, yanked back the wet hood, and said, "We've got a serious problem."

"Lawyered up, did he?" Water dripped from the brim of

his hat. "I knew it, Edwina—"

"Mason didn't kill her."

Culliton stared at me. The dark eyes were almost shotgun. "What'd you expect him to do, confess?"

"Oh, he confessed. He confessed to burying her body. But he says he didn't kill her. And I believe him."

Culliton looked like he suddenly doubted my sanity. I pulled my notebook from my jacket, my damp fingers sticking to the cottony paper. I read Mason's statement. When I finished, the windshield was fogged.

"And you believe him?" Culliton asked.

"I don't *want* to believe him. But what he's saying matches the autopsy." I lifted the binder with Annicka's name on it. "Her skin. It's waterlogged. *Macerated,* as the coroner called it. And Mason said there's water inside that cave on the trail. Probably a water table fed by the river."

"So what?"

"So Mason claims he found Annicka's body submerged in that water. She was already dead."

Culliton moved his jaw side-to-side. "He killed her there. Then moved her up the trail."

"That's possible. But you were there when they recovered her body?"

He nodded, grimly.

"Was she face up or face down?"

"Up."

"Okay, look." I flipped through the binder to the post-mortem photo. "Look at the lividity on her legs."

He stared down at the photo.

I said, "We both know that kind of blood pooling means she died face down. Mason told me he thought she'd drowned. Because she was face down in the water. He thought she'd hit her head and drowned. When he rolled her over, he saw her throat was slit." I paused. "He retched when he told me that part."

Culliton's voice boomed through the car. "Why the hell didn't he tell us!"

"Because he knew he'd be the prime suspect. He's no idiot. Would you have believed this story?"

"I'm not sure I do now." Culliton wiped impatiently at the condensation on the windshield. "And I don't suppose he's got any suspects for us to look at?"

"Random killer, he said. Or Fritz."

"Right."

"And he knew nothing about Esther Heller. He claims he didn't live here then."

Culliton's sigh obliterated the windshield's clear spot. He looked over, shotgun shells ready to fire. "I am not cutting him loose."

"I don't expect you to."

"He *knew* it was a murder."

"Absolutely."

"He should've told us."

"Absolutely."

"He's an accessory after the fact."

"Absolutely."

"Are you going to do anything—besides say *absolutely*?"

"Yes."

"What?"

"What I always do." I watched the clouded windshield.

"Which is?" he asked.

"Keep looking until I get the answer."

CHAPTER FORTY-EIGHT

THE NEXT MORNING, I tidied up the Stephanson's cabin, washed the pot, and ignored the note on the refrigerator.

At the edge of Leavenworth's commercial district, I found a Safeway. The exterior was designed to look like an Austrian lodge. I bought two cans of Coke, one bag of dog treats, and stood in the check-out line, tapping my cell phone for the Washington Department of Transportation website.

"One lane, that's what I heard," the checkout girl said to the man in line ahead of me.

"I heard it's real slow over Steven's Pass." The man slid a bank card through the payment machine. "But it's moving."

I glanced at the DOT webpage.

One lane open over Steven's Pass, the advisory read. *Expect delays.*

Small towns.

Where news travels faster than WiFi.

SIX HOURS LATER, I pulled into Eleanor's driveway. She wasn't there. I took a shower, changed clothes, and left her a note. Madame ate real dog food.

Back in the car, we arrived at Western State five minutes before visiting hours began. I signed the visitor's sheet and carried the dog up the empty stairwell. Her small heart thudded against my fingertips. When the door opened at the top of the stairs, the nurse named Sarah poked her head out.

"I'm sorry, Raleigh," she said. "She only wants to see the dog."

I handed Madame to her. The dog gave me a pleading gaze.

"Also," Sarah whispered, "Doctor Norbert says he can see you now."

"See me, for what?"

She gave that sympathetic smile. "To help you."

"Right."

Wrong.

I WALKED OUT the front door. When I glanced back at the hospital, the gray stones seemed to melt into the dreary October sky. This sad place. This holding pen for tortured souls, built decades before Washington even became a state.

Because crazy's always been with us.

I circled the campus and found a familiar narrow path that led to a small building with peeling beige paint. The front door was unlocked. I stepped inside, listening. The air was stale and bitter. A small appliance rattled in the makeshift kitchen to my right.

The brown carpet was worn to burlap threads. I followed it to the main room where taupe-colored curtains covered the four walls. The piano waited to one side, smothered with dust. On the other side, a cardboard box spilled identical pamphlets, the bright headlines asking, *Are You Depressed? Thoughts of Suicide?*

Twelve folding chairs formed a circle in the middle of the room. Two paperback copies of the *Big Book for Alcoholics*

Anonymous sat on one of the chairs. The pages were dog-eared.

I sat on the dusty piano bench and listened. The refrigerator sounded like it was dying. Outside, a car passed by slowly. I thought about what the nurse Sarah said. Dr. Norbert wanted to help me.

But I'd already heard Freud's great remedy.

Stop feeling guilty.

Really great advice. Super. Thanks, doc.

Just one problem.

Sometimes we deserved our guilt. Sometimes we earned it. *Stop feeling guilty*?

It didn't work like that.

I stood and pulled back the curtain. Dust flamed the air. I closed my eyes, coughed, waved my hands, and when I looked up, it was still here.

Here in this little building that once was the chapel, the wooden cross waited. I lowered myself beneath it and leaned forward, listening.

Another car passed. The refrigerator rattled.

And then, silence.

When the invisible found me, it came like water. Water that flowed over my sadness and my pain. Water that spread over the barren landscape of my heart and flooded the rocky remains. Deep called to deep, and water turned into a river, wave rushing upon wave, sweeping away what I couldn't remove from my soul. I saw the river crash over the rocks and the waves break gray and their sound became a song. Only this song had no words, only melody. A tune that harmonized with the water, the deep, the invisible.

I knew this song by heart.

It was called Forgiveness.

CHAPTER FORTY-NINE

I LEFT THE chapel feeling twenty pounds lighter.

Until my cell phone rang.

I checked the screen. *Unidentified Caller.*

Maybe Johann, wondering if I got out.

"Hello?"

"Harmon."

"Jack."

"Which side of the world are you on?"

"The downside."

"At least you have momentum."

"Picking up speed even as we speak."

I was crossing the campus, when the hospital's main door opened. Dr. Norbert stepped out. I spun an about-face and hid behind an oak tree. When I peeked from behind the trunk, Freud was walking toward the parked cars. He wore a tidy brown sports coat, dark slacks, and polished black shoes. His gait was clipped, tight. My diagnosis? Anal retentive.

"You need a ride to Leavenworth tomorrow?" Jack asked.

"I don't know."

Freud climbed into a two-door Toyota sedan that was the same dreary gray as the hospital.

"Harmon?"

I watched him drive away. *Bon Voyage, Freud.*

"I don't know if I need a ride because my murder suspect is no longer a murder suspect."

"What? What about the shovel?"

"Oh, he's guilty—of burying her body. But I don't think he killed her." I described Mason's confession. "The coroner's report described a really precise blow to the head. *Then* her throat was slashed. *Then* she was laid in water. The boyfriend found her in water, already dead."

"That doesn't entirely rule out the boyfriend."

"No. Anyone can do anything."

"Harmon, you know what I mean."

"This boyfriend's an impulsive type. Nervous. Emotional. Whoever murdered Annicka Engels was cold and calculating. Same with Esther Heller."

"You're sure?"

"I'm never sure." I leaned against the tree. "Apparently there's a pond in the cave."

"The cave you wanted to explore."

I recalled that day, the horrible stench leaking from that cave. I'd told Jack that all caves smelled bad. Now my stomach knotted. "I'm hoping to check it out tomorrow."

"So you need a ride," he said.

The tree bark scratched my spine. "No, that's okay. I've got it covered."

He said nothing.

"But you could help me out another way," I said. "Remember that list?"

"The list."

"The list with names of the guests who stayed at both hotels."

"I gave you a copy, Harmon. Where is it?"

"Not on me." It was in my office at the Smith Tower. After this morning's long drive, I didn't want to motor into the city to get it. “You must’ve made a copy.”

“You think I’ve got it just sitting here,” he said, “waiting for you to ask me for it?”

“No, I think you’ve got *two* copies sitting there.” Because every piece paper in the Bureau got copied in triplicate. “Since you gave me one copy, that means you’ve got two—”

“Ezra Sugarman.”

“So the list was right there.”

“Right,” he said. “Just waiting for you to call.”

He hung up.

CHAPTER FIFTY

MADAME AND I got back on the road just in time for rush hour. The slow crawl of traffic gave me time to watch her. She was panting. Her fur was falling out.

Crazyland.

"I'm so sorry." I scooped her into my lap. "So very sorry."

Nearly an hour later, I caught the 405 heading northeast. Traffic wasn't much better, but The Ghost growled to the city of Redmond where I found the address for Ezra Sugarman. It was a quarter mile past Microsoft's main campus, in a conglomeration of condominium and apartment buildings that looked so identical they could've been built by an erector set on autopilot.

"You deserve a break," I told the dog. "I'll be right back."

I opened the glove compartment. Back when I left the Bureau, Jack loaned me a Sig Sauer. I didn't carry the gun often, because my concealed-carry permit was still awaiting approval. But sometimes a girl had to risk jail in order to avoid nasty surprises. Although Jack hadn't turned up anything on Ezra Sugarman, that didn't mean the guy was entirely safe.

I tucked the gun into the back of my jeans and headed for the apartment buildings. Night had fallen and it turned out apartment 37F was located in the complex's farthest corner. Outdoor stairwells zigged up the building and linked to open hallways that zagged across back. I walked down the third floor hall. Kids were yelling behind one door. Someone else was cooking dinner that smelled of curry and onions. I walked to the end of the hall. 37F.

I listened. The window to my left was covered with slatted blinds but I could hear water was running, maybe in a sink. I knocked. The water stopped.

After a notable pause, a man's voice asked, "Who's there?"

"I'm looking for Ezra Sugarman." I looked up, into the door's peephole. "Is he here?"

"What do you want?" The voice was now right behind the door.

"My name's Raleigh Harmon." I smiled into the peephole. "I'm with the Leavenworth Hotel Association."

Not a *total* lie. The Engels ran a hotel. So did the Hellers. In Leavenworth. And we were associated. *Right?*

I looked up again, feeling his gaze. "Could I speak to Mr. Sugarman?"

The door opened. The short man standing there wore a black apron that said SHMUTZ HAPPENS.

"You're with the Leavenworth hotel association?" he asked.

"Yes, sir. Are you Ezra Sugarman?"

He had dark eyes and wild black hair, parted down the left side and slicked into place. Like a burnt marshmallow was secured to his head.

"Do you have a card?" he asked.

"Oh, no. I left them in my car. And it's parked way over there." I pointed down the long hallway. "Are you Ezra Sugarman?"

He glanced past me, checking the hallway, the ground below, even the next building. He eyed me as though expecting an accomplice.

"I parked on the wrong side of the building," I said. "I'm not really familiar with this area."

His eyes were sharp, intelligent. The glance came fast—I lunged, catching the door as he swung it shut. I shoved my foot against the bottom, both hands gripping the edge of the door. He pushed. I pushed.

"I'm calling the police," he said.

"You do that." I pushed harder. "Tell them why you made all those trips to the Eiderdown and Waterhaus."

His startled gaze was inches from my face. I felt the door give a fraction of an inch.

"I did nothing wrong!" He leaned his body into the door. "Why are you here?"

"You really want to do this out here—so all your neighbors can hear?"

The door relented another inch. "I need to see your identification."

Keeping one hand on the door, I reached back and yanked out my cell phone. "Call the FBI. Or better yet, the Chelan sheriff."

His furry head shifted. "You're with the police?"

"And we know all about your stays."

Inside the apartment, a timer dinged. And dinged. And dinged.

Neither of us let go of the door.

"Sounds like dinner's ready," I said.

"I'm going to call someone." He lifted one hand from the door, holding it up in a gesture of good will. "But I want to use my phone. Is that alright?"

"Sure." I reached back, pocketing my cell phone and lifting the stippled gun butt from my waistband. But I held the gun behind my leg. "You want the number for the sheriff?"

"No. What's your name again?"

"Raleigh Harmon and I—"

His gun came up. But I was fast, too.

We stood, barrel to barrel, with the door between us.

"Mr. Sugarman, you do not want to shoot me."

He narrowed his dark eyes to slits. "Hotel *association?*"

"Yes."

"It's called *Hotelvereinigung*."

"That just confuses people."

He shifted the barrel. I shifted mine, matching his position.

"Who are you?" he said. "I want the truth."

"My name really is Raleigh Harmon. The FBI knows I'm here."

"You're with the FBI?"

I hesitated.

"*What?*"

"I'm a consultant."

One dark eyebrow lifted. "Like you're a consultant for the hotel *association*?"

"Look, Mr. Sugarman, we have records of all your stays in Leavenworth." I took a quick glance at his gun. Smith & Wesson. Pristine condition. "What's your business in Leavenworth?"

"No. You give *me* the truth."

One more glance. The thumb safety was still on. I felt my whole body relax. "The Engels hired me."

"*Hired* you? They don't have money."

"We worked something out."

The dinging timer kept going. And now I could smell the food. Roasting chicken. Salt. I licked my lips.

"Don't move." He kept the pistol pointed at me but he was holding it the way someone holds a flashlight. I doubted he even knew about the safety. "Don't make one move," he said, holding up his cell phone. He thumbed the screen and tapped another button. It was on speaker phone because I could hear the ringing.

Then: "Welcommen to Das Waterhaus!"

"Helen?" He stared into my eyes. "This is Ezra Sugarman."

"Ezra! Are you coming back, so soon?"

"No, I had a question for you. Do you know a Raleigh Harmon?"

"Yes. Johann hired her."

"To do what, exactly?"

"I didn't want her to do anything. At first. But she just found …" She hesitated. "She found out who killed Annicka."

I watched as Ezra Sugarman's entire expression changed.

"Thank you, Helen," he said. "I'm sorry to bother you."

"Is there a problem?"

"No. No problem. Everything's fine."

"How do you know Raleigh?"

"I have to go, Helen. We can talk another time."

"Alright," she said, uncertain. "You're sure everything is alright?"

He hesitated. "Yes."

He lowered the gun and disconnected the call.

"Well," he said. "I guess you're staying for dinner, Raleigh Harmon."

CHAPTER FIFTY-ONE

IN THE KITCHEN, Ezra Sugarman set the pistol on a black granite countertop.

"My bubbie used to say, *Worries go down better with soup*. So we eat first, then we talk."

He turned off the timer and removed a casserole from the oven. I stared at the bread crumb topping. It had browned around the edges of the glass dish, while cream sauce bubbled through the center. My mouth watered.

"Hungry?" he asked.

"Always."

From a cabinet, he took out two white dishes, but from separate sections. One section was marked K. I recognized the symbol. Kosher. He handed me the non-kosher plate and spooned a hefty serving of the casserole. I couldn't stop staring at the food. My childhood was spent eating truly awful casseroles baked my mother in some delusional psychosis that she was Betty Crocker. This casserole? It was from another universe. I took a deep breath. My salivary glands were in overdrive.

Ezra Sugarman held the kosher plate. "Are you waiting for something?" he asked.

I opened my mouth.

"Is it grace?" he said. "Do you say grace?"

I nodded.

He set his plate of food on the counter, and wiped his hands on the Schmutz Happens apron. "My people say grace *after* we eat. But my bubbie also said, *You don't bend, you break*. Okay?"

He closed his eyes and murmured words in a language I didn't recognize. But I understood what he was saying. Prayers of gratitude—genuine gratitude—have their own four-part harmony. One part remorse for who we are. One part amazement that such goodness comes to the undeserving. And two parts joy in the receiving.

"Now." Sugarman picked up his fork. "We eat."

There was no table. No chairs at the granite counter. We stood in the kitchen and ate. After the first bite, my taste buds went into shock. The chicken was roasted so carefully the flavor seemed nurtured from the meat. The cream sauce was luscious as summer clouds while tarragon and salt danced through it all. My throat hummed.

Neither one of us spoke, strangers with guns savoring every bite. It was warm food in a cold place in an otherwise empty kitchen. And when we finished, Sugarman set our plates in the sink and turned to face me. His eyes filled with agony.

"I failed them."

"Excuse me?"

"Esther. Annicka." He shook his furry head. "I failed them."

My right hand hitched back on my hip. Near my gun. "I'm not sure I understand."

"They don't know."

"Who?"

"Helen. Johann. The Hellers."

My palm wrapped around the gun. "You just called Helen."

"Oh, they know *me*. I'm their very regular guest, as you apparently know. I'm the guest who tips at hundred percent. Of course they know *me*." He leaned forward. My fingers closed around the gun. "But they don't know *why* I'm there."

"Why are you there?"

He sighed and looked around the empty room. "I never thought I'd need seating in here."

"Mr. Sugarman—"

"Ezra. Please. Call me Ezra. Do you trust me enough to go into the living room? There's carpet. Much better for the tuches."

Tuches. I knew that too. Yiddish for *rear end.*

He left the Smith & Wesson on the counter. But I still made sure he walked in front of me. And I kept one hand on my gun. The living room was small. Green drapes covered what looked like a sliding glass door. Sugarman walked to a desk in the corner, and flicked on the light. He sat on spotless white carpet.

"You know much history?" he asked.

I sat down across from him, with my back to the wall. "I grew up in the South."

"Ah, yes, history." He tucked his stocky legs into a cross-legged position. "But you're aware of the Holocaust?"

"Of course."

"Concentration camps?"

I nodded.

"Jewish children survived those camps—as orphans. Did you know that?"

I shook my head, trying to follow him.

"It was tragedy upon tragedy," he said. "And after the war, poverty gripped all of Germany. The degradation, it was unspeakable. Butchers sold rats—*rats!* For people to eat!"

"I can't imagine."

"No, you can't. I can't. But as my bubbie used to say, *If charity cost nothing, the world would be full of philanthropists.*"

"You had a wise grandmother." I shifted, stealing a glance at my watch. Madame was in the car. And maybe, just maybe, this guy was nuts. "Mr. Sugarman—"

"Ezra."

"Ezra, I'm here because—"

"I'm getting to it," he said, irritably. "You *must* know the facts. After the war, immigration wasn't like today. And Israel wasn't recognized as a country for another three years." He held up a hand. "Patience. It's good for the digestion. So listen to me. There was a group of American Catholics. They came to Germany, late 1945. All of them former Germans. They offered to adopt the orphans who survived the camps. You can imagine, not everyone was pleased. *Are you meshuggina?* Send God's Chosen to those people who follow the Pope? *Oy, gevalt*!" He lifted his hands, palms up. "But who else? Germans couldn't feed their own kids, let alone a bunch of starving Jewish orphans. Better that these children live, than die. In the end, thirty-four orphans went to America. All got adopted. It was a great *mitzvah*. That means—"

"Good deed."

"You knew *bubbie,* too."

"And *tuches.*"

He smiled. "How does a nice southern girl know Yiddish?"

"My best friend was Jewish."

"*Mazeltov*. Now, back to the orphans. One was named Saul Sugarman. My grandfather. Eleven years old in 1946, the oldest of the orphans. Saul had survived Dachau by working for those *dreck* Nazis." His eyes narrowed. "You know *dreck*?"

I nodded. Not a word that should be repeated. But in this case, it fit.

"Saul was my grandfather. Are you following me?"

"Yes."

"He comes to America old enough to know he's Jewish. The Catholic family who adopted him didn't try to convert him—another *mitzvah.* They lived in California. German immigrants. Hard-working. Nice people. But when my grandfather left for college, he joined a temple in Los Angeles. He told us that he prayed every day for these Catholics who saved his life. And he prayed for the other thirty-three orphans who came to America. You understand?"

"Yes but …"

"These Catholics, they were special."

"Yes, but—"

"And these orphans, they were special."

"Yes, but how does—"

"You knock at my door." His eyes seemed black as anthracite. "You lie to me. You threaten me with the police. You point a gun at my head. *And* you eat my food—but you won't let me tell the story? What's the matter with you?"

"Sorry." My face flushed with heat. "I'm just anxious to get some answers. For the Engels. And the Hellers."

"Desperation." He shook his furry head. "It's the devil's workshop."

"Please, continue."

"That's better." He adjusted his position. "My grandfather worked hard. Very hard. He became a wealthy man. A manufacturer of industrialized plastics—don't knock it. Finally, he was rich enough that he didn't need to work every day. So he decided to find out what happened to the other orphans from the camps who came to America. He named them 'the chosen among The Chosen.' You understand?"

"Yes."

"Good. He found about half of them. But never contacted them." Sugarman wagged his finger. "*Never.* He did not want *anything* from these people. Not even their memories. Some of them were Catholic now." He sighed, heavily. "But they were alive, some not so well. My grandfather started making donations to them. To their families. But never, *ever* letting them know where the money came from. Always anonymous. When he died, his will left orders for us to keep taking care of these special children. We were to take care of them to the third generation. It goes back to the Torah. In the Bible it says—"

"Blessings and curses continue to the third generation. Sorry, I interrupted."

He studied me. "Christian?"

"Yes."

"We can get along," he said. "Because now we get to Leavenworth. And you look ready to *plotz.*" He smiled. Impishly. But quickly it changed to sorrow. "Four Leavenworth families adopted orphans like my grandfather. They belong to a church called—"

"Our Lady of Snows."

"*Oy!* The impatience."

"I'm sorry." I explained what Father Anthony told me about the church's missions. And that I'd seen the orphan fundraising cookbook in the Stephanson's cabin. And while Ezra Sugarman kvetched about the church's name, the cold sensation went down my arms. Johann told me Fritz was adopted. He said adoption was important to his wife. Helen. Helen with those burning dark eyes. I stared at the man in front of me. His dark gaze. I waited for him to pause.

"Mrs. Engels," I said.

"Yes, you understand now. Her mother." Ezra Sugarman bowed his head. "And Mrs. Heller's mother."

"That's two. You said four orphans went to Leavenworth."

"One boy died of polio. More tragedy." He sighed. "Can you see why grandfather wanted to help? These precious children. And the females."

"What about the females?"

"It's rabbinical law. The Jewish line carries through women."

"Even if they become Catholic?"

"God's law. Not mine."

"So Esther, Annicka ..." That chill went through me again. "They're considered Jewish, from their grandmothers?"

He sighed, wagging his head. "I tried to protect them—"

"Who else knows?"

"About?"

"What you're doing?"

"No one! My grandfather's will *swore* us to secrecy. He believed real charity was anonymous."

"But you're telling me."

"*Oy gevalt!*" He raised his open palms again. "You suspected me—when my job was to protect them."

The FBI's computers were faster than the state or local authorities. But it was only a matter of time before more law enforcement zeroed in on Sugarman's name. "No one else has contacted you?"

"Listen to me. Nothing can be known. The money, it gets to these families. But it has no connection me, or my family. It *must* stay that way."

"But—"

"But nothing. The Kellers, they need little now. But the Engels? You saw. That Annicka, she was *very* bright. She wanted to be a veterinarian. She should go to college, get a good education."

"And she won a scholarship."

Sugarman made a see-saw motion with his hands.

"What?" I couldn't contain my fury. Something here felt like betrayal. "She didn't earn that scholarship?"

"Never—*never!*—tell that family. I want your word. Right now."

I gave him my word. "What happened?"

"An anonymous donation was made to the University of Washington. An athletic scholarship. We made sure the language was so specific that the money could only go to one particular applicant. Female, cross-country runner, from rural Washington state. Not yet eighteen, and would major in pre-veterinary medicine. You see?" He smiled, but it disappeared again. "That scholarship was tailored for that beautiful, chosen child."

I stared at him. My emotions rioted. "And Esther?"

"You're angry," he said. "Why?"

"Because when Esther was killed, you didn't come forward."

"Esther? She was killed. My heart broke. But all these orphans, their children, their grandchildren—they suffer. Leukemia. Car wrecks. Freak accidents." He lifted his hands, pleading. "God's choices are not my choices."

"But you can do something."

"Yes."

"And you did nothing."

"What should I do?"

"Their murders are connected."

"By location."

I watched him. I wanted to trust him. I thought of Jack's background check. Helen Engels' voice when she heard it was him. And I needed to know. "You must know how Esther died."

"Her throat—what, no, are you saying Annicka?" His whole body tensed. "No. Not Annicka."

I knew Ezra Sugarman could keep secrets. But it was still a risk. "Give me your word. Nothing said tonight is ever repeated."

"You have my word." He nodded, his eyes glistening.

"The way Esther died. Did it mean anything to you?"

"Shechitah." He whispered the word.

"What?"

"Sheh-HEE-tah." He wiped his eyes and drew a ragged breath. "*Shechitah.* It's a Jewish ritual. For kosher."

Jewish law prohibited the ingestion of blood from slaughtered animals. So the butcher sliced the throat, bleeding out the animal.

"Martha Keller told me how Esther died," he said. "Someone had killed that precious girl like she was nothing but an animal marked for slaughter."

"You didn't tell the police." My voice almost growled.

"What was I to tell them? That two generations ago, her grandmother was a German Jew who survived a concentration camp?" He stood up, abruptly, and grabbed a handful of paper from the desk. He shook it at me. "I come here to honor my grandfather. I promise silence. Who are you, telling me different?"

I looked away. This barren room. It was depressing. And yet somehow noble. "And now that they're dead, you just leave? That's it?"

His shoulders sagged. He set the paper back on the desk, smoothing out the wrinkles. "Four orphans went to Leavenworth."

That chill went down my back again. "Where's the fourth orphan?"

Sugarman shook his head.

"What?" I felt a bolt of adrenaline. "Don't tell me that one's dead, too."

"Not yet," he said. "But she's close."

CHAPTER FIFTY-TWO

I LET MADAME out of the car. While she sniffed the grass around the apartment complex and emptied her bladder, I checked road conditions through an app on my phone.

By the time I parked in Eleanor's driveway, it was just past 9:00 o'clock. I felt weary from so much driving in one day, and from listening to Ezra Sugarman's *only-in-America* tale. There other part of the fatigue was sleeping in Jack's cabin, tossing and turning all night, and trying not to think about those love notes from the woman *M.*

In Eleanor's kitchen, I picked up Madame's water bowl. But it was already filled. So was her food dish. I could hear a low murmur of voices coming from the living room. Eleanor had company.

And I had no energy for anyone right now.

I tiptoed past the doorway and saw Eleanor. She was stretched out on the velvet couch, eyes closed, ringed fingers folded over her chest. I listened and realized the voices were coming from speakers. And one voice sounded very familiar. No mistaking her trumpeting tone.

I walked over. Someone was remarking that silence only magnifies a thing. I turned down the volume. Eleanor's eyes opened.

"Hope you didn't wait up for me," I said.

"Of course I did. You're grown woman with a grudge and a gun."

"I should've called. I got stuck in Leavenworth."

She took her glasses from the side table and put them on. The rhinestones sparked. "Were you alone?"

"Madame was with me."

Eleanor glanced at the dog, now trotting into the room, licking her whiskers. "I will never repeat this … but I also missed that dog."

"She's like that."

Eleanor pushed herself to a sitting position. "How long were you stuck in the boondocks?"

"Much too long." I looked away.

"Don't tell me. You missed visiting hours?"

I could only nod.

"Raleigh, what are we?"

"Pardon?"

"We are human," she said. "We break things. No matter how careful we are."

I was too exhausted to play the game, but in some strange way, I still wanted her to ask. "Aren't you going to ask me, *Who said that*?"

"You're tired."

"Go ahead, ask."

She pushed herself up further. "Who said that?"

"You did."

"Correct. I said that."

"Now you're patronizing me."

"My dear, I only patronize the arts." She reached out and took hold of my hand. "All of us break things. We're nothing but bulls in the china shop of life."

"Tennessee?"

"Me."

"It sounds like something from one of his plays."

"Yes." She squeezed my hand. "Because art gets all its meaning from life. And life hurts." Her rings dug into my skin. "And broken things can be fixed."

I wanted to say something about that. But the words refused to come.

ELEANOR WENT TO sleep in her room. Madame curled into a ball on my bed. And I stuffed fresh clothes into my backpack. The dog's keen eyes tracked my movements.

"I'll be back tomorrow," I said.

Her ears pricked forward.

"Remember what the playwright said." I zipped my pack. "Time is the longest distance between two places."

AN HOUR AND a half past midnight I pulled into the parking lot for the Chelan County Sheriff department. A black truck was parked near the entrance, directly under a security light. Dispatch, I figured.

I drove to the lot's far corner, closed down the Ghost's pop-up headlights and shut my eyes, waiting for dawn.

FIVE HOURS LATER, I sat across from Detective Culliton at his desk, wiping sleep from my eyes. We both drank the cheap coffee. It tasted like a brutal cure for cholesterol, where every sip could scrub your arteries. Culliton gulped it.

"I think there's a third girl in danger," I said. He looked at me with utter skepticism. "Kimberly Kegelman. Do you know her?"

He put down the mug of drain cleaner. "Yeah." He typed on his keyboard. "She's a runaway."

"My source says she's still in the area."

Culliton's eyes bore into me. "Who's your source?"

"Can't say. But I've got some addresses. Apparently she moved around this summer, last seen at the following address." I shoved a piece of paper toward him.

When Sugarman came to Leavenworth this year for his bi-annual checkup, Annicka Engels was still alive, having won that scholarship to University of Washington. Sugarman gave his 100-percent tip at the Waterhaus, then stopped by the Eiderdown to check on Mrs. Heller in her bunker-basement. But he couldn't find Kimberly Kegelman, so he paid a Seattle private eye to track her. It took three PIs to pinpoint her locations.

"Your source some kind of drug dealer?" Culliton asked.

I didn't answer.

"These addresses you got—they've gotta be dope dealers. Those people move around like gypsies."

"My source is not a drug dealer," I said.

"Your source tell you about Kimberly's situation?"

I knew this tactic. Whatever I said, Culliton would gather clues about my source. I gave Sugarman my word. "Not really."

According to Sugarman, the Kegelmans were devoted to a highly conservative strain of Catholicism. It involved daily Mass, near-constant confession, and isolated homeschooling. The family's only girl, Kimberly, was banned from wearing pants or riding a bike or having friends. At seventeen, she ran away with a migrant farm worker. Sugarman made the difficult decision to stop all financial help. "The money will be waiting," he told me last night. "But right now, she's not ready."

"I don't get it." Culliton continued to stare at me. "How's Kimberly connected to Esther and Annicka?"

"I'll explain on the way over."

"Over where?"

"To pick her up."

"*Now*?"

"I didn't sleep in my car for the fun of it."

"You should've called me." He pinched his shirt. "See what I'm wearing?"

Checked shirt. Jeans. Tennis shoes. "Yeah, so?"

"So I've been waiting for this day. We finally figured out who's running the prostitution ring in the hotels. I've got three deputies waiting—"

"Can't you wait?" I felt a sinking sensation. "Go later today?"

"Later, we lose the element of surprise. Later, they get away." Culliton watched me. "If you'll wait just a couple hours, I can send—"

I shook my head.

"What's your hurry," he said. "That girl's been gone for months."

"She turns eighteen next week."

CHAPTER FIFTY-THREE

THE ADDRESS SUGARMAN gave me was all the way across Leavenworth, way past Preston Baer's busy petting zoo, and far down a two-lane road that snaked for miles through apple and pear orchards. But with each mile, the rolling hills turned into craggy cliffs and the soil became a deeper shade of rust. The fruit warehouses that lined the road looked abandoned, their roofs sagging. The road was empty.

I pulled out my phone and called Jack.

"You want me to fly?" he asked.

"I'm already here. Heading for the town of Pehashtin."

"What for?"

I gave him a quick summary of last night. I could feel him listening carefully. "I'll explain more later. I was just calling to see if you're serious."

The phone was silent. The road sliced through a narrow gap of weathered basalt, so I thought the signal got dropped.

"Jack?"

"I'm here," he said. "Serious, about what?"

"Taking Madame. To Western State."

"Oh," he said.

"If I can't get back in time."

"Right."

"I'm hoping to make it back, but just in case, it'd be nice

to have backup. And I promise, I'll pay you back."

"You bet you—"

He didn't finish.

"Jack?"

Silence.

I looked at the screen. *Call ended.*

I hit redial.

No signal available.

"Terrific." I pulled to the side of the road, because I'd also lost my GPS. Inside my notebook, I found the address, and I remembered that the GPS showed the destination was about two miles ahead.

But with each quarter mile, I doubted. Weeds grew around abandoned fruit warehouses. Orchards disappeared and mounds of copper-colored soil smeared the pavement, mudslides left behind by that sudden rain. The Ghost climbed over them, slowly.

When the road shifted downhill, I checked my odometer. It was close to two miles since I stopped. At the bottom of the hill, I drove another quarter mile. Three fruit warehouses were clustered by the side of the road, with some low cinderblock buildings in back. Behind them, the hills held fruit trees so dry their limbs looked like desperate figures waving for help.

I checked the address, and got out of the Ghost.

The morning air smelled sweet, and wrong. Rotting apples. Grass grew through the cracked blacktop. Flies buzzed my head.

I reached back into the car, and took out the Sig Sauer, stuffing it into the waist of my jeans and yanking my shirt over it. I walked around the warehouses. The odor shifted to something rank, foul. The corrugated metal buildings were rusting. I decided the smell was urine.

I found an old Datsun behind the first cinderblock building. It had one flat tire. The building had signs in Spanish, something about hours. And the word *prohibo.* The first window was blown out. I glanced inside. Trash scattered across a dirt floor. One sink, brown. One toilet, nearly black inside.

I walked the length of the building. It was some kind of abandoned dormitory, probably for migrant fruit pickers. At the third building, another old car waited. Its windshield was covered with road dust, except where the wipers had brushed it away. I wrote down the license plate and heard something like high wind. But when I glanced at the long grass pushing through the pavement, the blades were still. The sound continued. I walked around the edge of the building. And heard it again.

Singing.

It came in rasps and pauses. Like lone notes searching for harmony.

I moved to another broken window and looked over the sill.

A girl sat on a soiled mattress. It was pushed up against the wall, as if thrown there. She wore denim shorts and a tank top and no bra. Her clothes were filthy. Her fingers were playing with her bare toes. Each time she touched a toe, she sang a new note.

"Kimberly?" I said.

She stopped singing. But she didn't look up.

"Kimberly Kegelman?"

Her face lifted toward the busted window, slowly, like a helium balloon caught on a soft breeze. "I know," she sang.

"Are you Kimberly Kegelman?"

Her glazed brown eyes stared at the wall across from her. A moment later her gaze found the window. I tried to smile. But she scared me. Not just the vacant eyes, or the skin that was the shade of white before death. It was the blood, dried under her nose. It was the color of the mudslides in the road.

"You're Kimberly?"

She opened her mouth. Her lips were dry, crusted. "Kim—"

"Yo!"

Her head snapped toward the voice. I pulled back from the window and dropped to a squat.

CHAPTER FIFTY-FOUR

"GET UP." HIS voice sounded rough, disgusted. "Shanae needs you."

I heard some movement in the room. Then a pause.

The voice roared. "I said, *Get up.*"

She whimpered.

I stood, leaning against the building, and glanced into the room. His back was to me. Gripping her arm, he dragged her limp body across the dirt floor. I lost sight as they left the room.

I walked the length of the building, following his harsh voice. He was yelling something about Shanae, and someone named Hector. Sunlight burst through holes in the building's roof, the light flickering across my path. I stopped at what looked like an old entrance. The door hung drunkenly from its hinges.

"You tie it real tight," he was saying.

I pulled the gun and stepped around the door. The single hallway split the building in half. I looked both ways. More filth on the floor. The man's voice was coming from my left. I kept one shoulder against the cinderblock wall, and moved in that direction.

"Tight, you hear me?"

I dropped to another squat just outside the room. He was

berating her for leaving Shanae like this. I shifted, glancing quickly.

A brown-skinned girl lay on another slumped mattress. Long black hair fell over her face. Next to her, the girl I suspected was Kimberly Kegelmen sat swaying, like she might pass out. In her mouth, she bit a rubber hose. Her hand gripped the other end, wrapping it around the brown woman's arm, just above the elbow.

The man reached down. He swatted her hands. "Not there, stupid."

The hose fell on the dirt floor.

"Hector don't like seeing marks on her arms."

Kimberly leaned forward to pick up the hose, but lost her balance. Her body pitched into the mattress. The man lifted her by her brown hair.

"Get with it, Kim."

She fumbled for the woman's twitching leg. After two tries, she finally wrapped the hose around the woman's ankle. The man handed her something.

"Between the toes," he said. "And don't screw it up. I'm coming back. Hear me?"

I moved into the next open room, crossing the threshold as his shadow fell in the hallway.

I counted to ten, then looked down the hall. It was empty.

I could hear the singing again.

"…yes … I know …"

I stepped into the room. The brown girl was no longer twitching. Kimberly was tugging off the rubber hose, petting the woman's foot.

"This … I know." She raised a syringe. A quarter inch of clear fluid remained in the plunger.

"Don't—"

She stabbed the needle into her lower lip, pushing the

plunger. A moment later she pulled the needle out. A drop of blood glistened on the tip. She licked her lips.

"Kim." I whispered, "Wanna go for a ride?"

She reached over, petting the girl on the mattress.

"Let's take a ride," I whispered.

"Can't leave. Lily."

I glanced at the girl. Her body was still. Her head turned toward Kimberly.

"That's her name," I asked. "Lily?"

"My friend."

I kneeled beside them. The man called her Shanae. Another runaway, guaranteed.

The mattress smelled foul. "Lily?"

Her head rolled toward my voice.

"Lily, we're going to take a ride."

She gave a hazy nod. Kimberly pushed herself up, swaying. I reached under Lily's arm. She was dead weight. I got her propped against the wall, but her head slumped forward. Lifting her chin, I gently slapped her cheek. Her face felt rough, dry.

"Lily, look at me. I need you to stand up."

I glanced back at the door. When was he coming back, when Hector got here? I wondered what drugs he gave them, heroin? Or something even stronger. The girl was looking at me like she might be hallucinating. "Lily, can you understand me?"

She rolled her head.

I glanced back.

Kimberly was gone.

Crap.

I looked back at Lily's dark eyes. Both of these girls had dark eyes. Sugarman never gave me a description of Kimberly. Both young enough to be teen runaways. Which one was—

?

I stopped.

It matters to this one.

I lifted the girl, feeling a twinge of pain in the small of my back. I laid one of her arms over my shoulder and hoisted her to my hip. I took three steps. She dragged the injected foot.

"Yo!"

The guy. Yelling. Down the hall.

"Hey—man—you can't—"

The gunfire sounded like a bomb going off.

I dragged Lily to the the hall. But it was empty. I could hear the guy was yelling again, but farther away.

Another shot fired.

I placed Lily against the wall. Her hands plopped into her lap. I pulled out the Sig.

The guy was yelling but now it sounded more like frustration. When I glanced into the hall, I saw him pacing the dirty floor. His hands were balled into fists, punching the air. When he spun my way, I raised the gun and stepped into the hall.

"Freeze."

He froze.

"Hands above your head."

He lifted both hands, palms open.

"Where's Kimberly?" I asked.

"I dunno."

"You want me to shoot?"

"That cop just took her."

"What cop?"

"Dude in brown."

In the room behind me, Lily was hiccupping. My mind pinged. Culliton, he sent a deputy. True to his word. But the deputy wouldn't know I was here, because The Ghost was parked on the other side of the warehouses. Kimberly was the priority. *Good.* She was safe. But.

It matters to this one.

"Face down on the floor," I told him. "Keep those hands above your head where I can see them."

He dropped to his knees. His eyes were mean, haunted. I could see the deception playing in them, the habit of evil.

"Hey, we can work this out—"

"Twitch one muscle, I'll shoot you."

"Hey, baby—"

"I'll shoot you where you can never wipe your own butt again. You got it?"

He laid his greasy head on the dirt floor.

I kept the gun trained on him and reached back with my left hand, grabbing Lily's elbow. I hoisted her up. She could stand on that foot now, which meant less dead weight for me. I carried her down the hall. As we passed the guy on the floor, I saw a cell phone sticking out of his back pocket.

I pressed the gun's barrel into the back of his head. "Move and you're dead."

I set Lily against the wall, and took the phone from his pocket. The screen said, *Missed call. Hector.*

Lily hiccuped.

I pocketed the phone. It would help Culliton.

I moved her toward the door.

"You're going to count to 500," I told him. "Then you're going to count to another 500. If you move before 1,000, I'm going to shoot you. Got it?"

He nodded, face in the dirt.

"Start counting. Out loud."

The morning sun was behind the building. I dragged Lily through the shadows, swiveling my head for threats. She kept hiccuping about every third second and each time my heart jumped. A barren breeze blew through the abandoned buildings. This place felt like the end of the earth. As we passed the dusty car, I shot out the tires.

I opened The Ghost and laid Lily in the passenger seat, clipped on her seatbelt, and hopped in. I roared high speed down the two-lane road. Each time it twisted, Lily's head rolled. I barely braked for the berms of dried mud and kept the gun in my lap. I grabbed my phone. If Hector's call got through, there was some signal out here. I called Culliton. He didn't pick up. Which didn't surprise me because of his prostitution bust.

"Thank you for sending a deputy," I told his voice mail. "He didn't see me. But I've got another girl." I glanced over and gave him a description. "Check the list of runaways, first name might be Lily. She's in the car with me, I'm heading for the medical clinic. Call me ASAP."

I disconnected the call and braked for a hard turn. My memory said the big hill was just ahead. The hill that took us out of this God-forsaken valley. I shifted gears, pushing the engine.

When I came out of the turn, a white truck was in my lane.

I braked, hard.

Lily's head rocked forward. She moaned, "Uh-nnn."

"Sorry," I said.

The white vehicle wasn't a truck. It was a wagon of some kind. The black lettering on the back read, *Chelan County Sheriff's Department.*

The deputy. He had Kimberly. Excellent.

But my mind stuttered. The other words on the vehicle were *Animal Control.*

The wagon. I'd seen it before. And Culliton told me to wait. Deputies needed in town. This was a remote area … but Animal Control. It could be here. Animal Control went everywhere.

Right?

The road straightened and the white wagon picked up speed. I stepped on the gas, keeping The Ghost close enough to see the driver's face in the side mirror.

The driver glanced left.

Seiler.

CHAPTER FIFTY-FIVE

I STARED AT the white wagon, and Ezra Sugarman's words rang in my head.

Someone killed that precious girl like she was nothing but an animal marked for slaughter.

And I knew.

Animal control.

I slapped my hand across the console, searching for my phone. I tapped the screen. No signal.

"Crap!"

"Huhn," Lily said.

The road curved left, cutting between the basalt mountains. Seiler barreled over the dried mudslide. The Ghost hit the berm hard, undercarriage scraping.

I grit my teeth. "What are you doing, Seiler?"

We started up the hill. I thought about passing him, forcing him off the road. But the wagon took a sudden right. This was not the route back to town. I followed and hit a gravel road. The rocks hammered The Ghost. The washboard surface bounced Lily. Her teeth clacked.

"Lily?" I called out.

Her hands were on her stomach. Like she might puke.

"Hang on," I told her.

I grabbed the phone again, tapping the screen. The signal

came back. I found Jack's number in recent calls, and hit redial.

"Jack—"

"Don't worry, I'm going to get the dog."

"Listen to me—contact the Chelan sheriff. The detective named Culliton. He—"

"Harmon, what's wrong?"

I gripped the steering wheel with one hand. Seiler was speeding up.

"Remember the animal control deputy who met us on the trail?"

"Yeah."

"Jack, he's totally rogue. I think he's killing these girls. He just kidnapped the third one and—"

"Where are you?"

I glanced out the window. Pine trees. Grainy hillsides. "I'm on a gravel road. Somewhere near Pehashtin." I leaned forward, looking up at the sky. "The sun's behind me so I'm heading west but I can't see—"

"Harmon?"

"What?"

"Harmon? Are you there?"

"Jack!"

"If you can hear me, call back. Your voice is breaking up."

"Jack?"

"—hear me? Oh. Man. You're gone."

I slid my thumb over the screen, glanced up, and slammed my foot into the brake pedal.

The white wagon had stopped in the middle of the road.

The Ghost scudded sideways over the gravel. Lily slumped against the door. The engine coughed. And died.

I peered through clouds of road dust. I sat crossways, facing the forest on the side of the road. Lily's passenger window faced the wagon's back doors. I stomped the clutch into the floorboard, shifted the gear into first, and turned the key. I tried again. The acrid odor of gasoline filled the air. I turned the key off. And waited. The engine was flooded.

The wagon didn't move. And nobody got out.

I pulled the emergency brake. Sig in hand, I stepped out but stayed behind The Ghost's long door. Another twenty seconds passed. I leaned over to see the wagon's side mirror. It looked empty. Slowly, I moved around my door and crept toward the wagon. I pointed the gun at the driver's window.

"Freeze."

I leaned forward. The cab was empty. I glanced across the bench seat and saw something on the floor. Blue nylon bag. Yellow rope. Metal. Tools. Sunlight glinting off chrome curves.

"Looking for something?" he asked.

I felt the gun jab behind my left ear.

"My dog," I said. "She ran away."

"Again?"

"That's what dogs do."

"Right," he said. "Drop your weapon."

I lifted my right arm but kept my index finger alongside the trigger. My mind scrambled for escapes. Spin. Shoot. Hit—

He slammed me into the truck. Pain fired into my wrist, radiating up my arm. I felt every inch of him pressing against my back. Something sharp bit into my left shoulder. His badge.

"Think you're real clever, don't you." He breathed into my hair. "I'm gonna fix that."

He threw me to the ground. One shot. That's all he needed. I closed my eyes. Prayed. Road dust coated my tongue. *Lily.* She was sitting in the car, right next to my cell phone. *Pick up the phone. Press 9-1-1.*

He twisted my wrists behind me. My skin burned. Rope. He was tying my wrists. I pulled them apart as he bound them, and wondered why he didn't use handcuffs. When he was done, he kicked his boot into my right side.

I gasped.

"Stand up."

I twisted sideways, rolled onto my knees. Gravel dug into my kneecaps. I staggered into a stand.

"Walk to the back."

I glanced at The Ghost. Lily was gazing through the windshield like somebody watching a movie that made no sense. *Pick up the phone. The phone, the phone …*

Seiler shoved the gun into my back and snapped open the wagon doors.

Inside, Kimberly sat curled inside one of the metal cages. Her skin looked slick from sweat. Her hands were cuffed in front of her. Her body shook.

"Get in," Seiler said.

"What about the other girl?" I tried to glance over my shoulder. "You can't leave her out here."

"Sure I can." He gave me another stab with the gun. "They'll find that fancy car of yours and they'll know *you* abandoned her. Now get in."

I kneeled on the wagon's bumper. My mind kept flashing scenarios. *Mule-kick.* Knock the gun from his hand. Every superhero maneuver that got you killed early.

"The cage." He shoved me forward. "Next to hers."

The cage door was open. I shifted, making sure I backed into the small space. Seiler stood at the open doors, wearing a cold smile. Now I saw the gun. It was a .38 revolver. A gun for putting down animals. The air stunk of fear fear fear—

"This." Kimberly sang. Her voice shook with her body.

"This … I know."

Seiler shoved me into the cage and clipped the door shut, making sure no animal escaped.

CHAPTER FIFTY-SIX

WHATEVER SHOT SHE took earlier, it wasn't enough. Kimberly was coming down. She was shaking. Her sweat smelled rancid.

Seiler started the engine. The muffler rumbled beneath us.

"Sing me your song," I said.

"I … know …" She was breathing oddly, as if suffocating between words. "This."

She sang those same three words, over and over. *I know this.*

I kept track of the seconds, counting from the moment Seiler stepped on the gas.

One one-thousand.

I stared out the small porthole window.

Two one-thousand.

Pine trees passed. Blue sky.

Three one-thousand, four one-thousand, five …

When I reached *sixty one-thousand*, I curled one finger. One minute had passed. At five minutes, I made one fist. Ten minutes, two fists, then started over, and pressed my tongue into the farthest tooth in the back in my mouth. Another ten minutes, my tongue moved forward one tooth.

Kimberly was dry heaving, her face pushed against the cage. The metal cage left indentations across her cheeks.

Twenty-eight minutes later, the wagon stopped. I could see black asphalt shingles through the porthole window. A roof. Gray smoke curled into the blue sky.

The wagon's back door opened. A bald man stood next to Seiler. The blue tattoos on his flabby neck made the skin look bruised.

"You said one," the bald man said.

"There is only one. But she—" he pointed the .38 at me—"found the Jew. So now we gotta get rid of her too."

The bald guy stared at me. His eyes were full of certainty and wrong answers. "We?" he said.

"Me," Seiler said.

"What if somebody comes looking for her?"

"Nobody will," Seiler said.

"Family? Husband?"

"She doesn't have anybody," Seiler said.

They pulled us out of the wagon. I scanned the area. The asphalt shingles belonged to a roof on a log cabin. It was large, crudely built, and shaped like an L. Trees had been cleared for other buildings. In the center of the clearing, a large fire burned below a dead animal rotating on a spit.

I glanced into the pine trees. The forest was too thick. I couldn't read the landscape. The sun's position said it was still morning, I knew that, but I tried to recall the geological maps of this area. Seiler had driven about thirty minutes. But which direction? Pehashtin was south of the Cascade mountain range. Further south was Blewitt Pass. The roads ran mostly east-west. But that wasn't enough information. If Seiler drove west, then we were … where?

I glanced at Seiler. He held Kimberly's arm like she was roadkill. Animal Control, he knew this county. He probably drove back roads to get here. Which meant I really had no idea where we were. Except this was real purgatory. Where the food sucks and—

Jack.

I didn't call him back. Would he realize something was wrong? No. Because sometimes I didn't call back. *Pride.* I kicked myself. My stupid pride.

The bald guy held my elbow. He asked Seiler. "Now, or later?"

"Now. But I gotta figure out who's going first."

"You need help?"

"Better not. Anything happens, you can say you didn't know. And nobody can beat it out of you."

Kimberly's body twitched like an electrocuted rag doll. Seiler dragged her across the open area. People were stepping out of the cabin. Men. Women in dirty dresses. Ragged children. Nobody said a word.

Seiler glanced over at Kimberly. He was evaluating her. "You got anything to give her? I don't want her puking on me."

"Waste good drugs on a *Jew?*" the bald guy said. "Get real."

"You got a point." Seiler drew back his free hand and punched the side of Kimberly's head. She dropped like kindling.

He shook out his fingers. "Get the boys."

The bald man whistled. Two boys came running from a low wooden building beside the log cabin. They looked about twelve years old, with heads shaved like Marines.

"Pick it up," Seiler said.

One boy took Kimberly's bare feet. The other boy took her shoulders from behind her head. Her cuffed hands flopped on her concave stomach. The boys followed Seiler.

When I looked back, one of the woman was turning a metal crank over the fire. Fat dripped from the animal, sizzling in the flames. I made eye contact with the woman. She looked away.

The bald man slapped the back of my head. "Face forward."

Seiler was leading us toward a barn. In the field behind it, horses roamed. Pigs rooted an area beside it. And cows grazed beside the barn. In the distance, I heard metal clanging. Metal on metal. Like a blacksmith. But my senses were so piqued, I could hear the horses ripping grass from the soil.

The soil.

I looked down, and pretended to trip. I dragged the toe of my shoe deep into the dirt. It was that russet red color. Heavy with iron. Basalt, not granite. That most likely meant we were east of Leavenworth. I raised my face to the blue sky again. *Help me.* The bald guy smacked my head once more. My ears rang.

At the barn, Seiler stopped and pulled a key ring from his utility belt. He keyed open the lock in the galvanized plate and slid back the door.

Sunlight cut between the weathered boards. The sharp beams threw spotlights on the dirt floor. One ladder led to a loft. I could smell the dry hay. And something else. Something bad.

The boys carried Kimberly inside.

"Where you want 'er?" asked the boy holding her feet.

"Where I don't got to move her again," Seiler said. "Put her in the chamber. And don't come back. Tell the rest of them kids, too."

The boys carried Kimberly to a wooden box under the hayloft. The box had three sides. On the open side, a leather strap dangled from the rafter. I could see sunlight tracing the small door in the barn wall, behind the box. The fields were beyond that. The animals. Behind that door. And I knew what the three-sided box was used for. Slaughter.

I pulled at the rope around my wrists. My skin burned.

"She'll have to be second." Seiler grabbed me and yanked down that leather strap attached to the rafter. He pushed my head into the noose.

"Hang tight," he told me.

They laughed, and left.

CHAPTER FIFTY-SEVEN

IN THE HAZY light of the barn, I listened to Kimberly's labored breathing. She lay behind me in the slaughter box, and her wet snoring that told me blood filled her nose.

I stood on my tiptoes to keep the noose from tightening around my neck. My calf muscles burned, but my eyes were adjusting to the dark. On the opposite wall, I could see farm tools. A rusted scythe. Two winnowing forks. Baling hooks shaped like question marks. My fingers worked at the rope around my wrists. Long ago, when I was a teenager who believed my life would turn out differently, someone taught me about knots. Lanette. Now Lani Margolis. As Seiler tied my wrists, I'd pulled them apart to create some slack. My thumb worked between the knots. My fingernail caught on a strand, tore. I grit my teeth, twisting my index finger into another turn in the rope.

"Most people think knots are knots," Lanette had written, way back when. "But they're not."

I'd written back—telling her to get a life. Now my eyes burned. My shoes slipped on the dirt floor. The leather strap garroted my windpipe.

"I . . . know . . ."

I turned my head. Kimberly's dirty bare feet hung over the edge of the slaughter box. Her toes moved with her song, her voice wet and snurgly. And sad. On the third time she started it, I realized what tune she was singing. That old Sunday school song. But her drug-addled mind had reversed the words. *I know this,* she sang.

This I know. Jesus loves me, this I know.

"Kimberly?" I perched on my cramping toes. "Are you with me?"

"Uh-nn."

"Can you stand up?" I worked my index finger into the knot. The rope gave a little. "I need you to do something."

She was whimpering. The drugs, wearing off.

"You feel lousy," I said, rasping against the leather strap. "We need to get out of here. Right. Now."

She seemed to be rocking back and forth. Trying to stand up? But I heard the sound. Vomiting. I turned away.

When she stopped, I said, "Kimberly, stand up." My fingernails were torn. "*Please.*"

She moved. All I could see was her bare heel.

"I'm begging you," I rasped.

The heel dropped against the box's slatted side.

"You can do this." I gave her directions. Hold the sides. Push up.

She swung one leg over the box's wall.

"That's it."

Across the barn, the metal bolt slid back. My heart sank.

"—and then get back to work," Seiler was saying to somebody out of view. He spoke over his shoulder. "They'll be finishing that sting operation, wondering where I am."

He stepped into the barn, and stopped. Kimberly stood beside me, swaying, her cuffed hands gripping the edge of the slaughter box.

"Look who's up," he said.

I heard no surprise in his voice. And no worries. Because

where would we go—where could we run?

Nowhere.

I swallowed. My windpipe ached against the leather. Sweat traced down my back, as slow as a painful death.

Seiler walked to the opposite wall. He passed through columns of sunlight, blinking at the bright pieces of sun. The tools waited on the wall. He examined them idly, like a businessman deciding which tie to wear. He took two tools from their hooks and turned. Sunlight glinted on a blade in his right hand.

"Why—" I choked. "Why are you doing this?"

"You want to know why?" He seemed almost glad. Like he'd been waiting for someone to ask. "Purity. That's why."

"What purity?"

"German." He looked surprised. "We're tainted by the Jew blood."

I searched his face for the dutiful deputy who came to help. That man was gone. "You killed Annicka."

"Now. Come on." He gave me a patronizing smile. "Were you hoping for a confession?"

"Esther—did you kill her too?"

He started walking toward Kimberly.

"You couldn't have killed Esther," I said.

He stopped. His mouth tightened.

"I read the autopsy. You couldn't have been old enough. Someone else did it."

"No!"

Pride. There was the avenue. "You're lying," I said. "You couldn't do it."

"It was me—all me." He lifted the knife. "And this is all me."

"Annicka, maybe." I drove my fingers into the knots, fingernails ripping. "But Esther? No. I don't believe you."

He glanced at Kimberly. She'd dropped back down into the box, whimpering. Defeated. The white-death skin of her face glistened with cold sweat.

"Just tell me," I said. "You're going to kill us. So just tell me."

He smiled. "Preston Baer."

"That's impossi—"

"Not then. Back then he was a real man. He taught me about pure blood. Untainted lines. Breeding."

I remembered Baer in his office. He'd asked about my heritage. It mattered to him. "Aryan."

"Damn straight." Seiler sneered. "But then Baer became a gimp and went soft. The weak, they always pull down the strong. And now he's surrounding himself with those freak kids who should all be euthanized. Those dying animals. He even refused to kill another Jew."

"Annicka."

"She had the Jew blood." He waved the knife. "Baer knew it. He showed me the records."

My sweaty fingers slipped over the knots.

"Then he *hired* her." Seiler gripped the tools in his hands. "Said it was time to stop purging. Start forgiving."

"But you didn't."

"Jews marry. Jews have children. They've already infected our line here. We have to stop them from breeding."

No wonder. Realization flooded me. I pulled at the knots. No wonder Baer never suspected Mason—he already knew who really killed Annicka. The very same person who helped him kill Esther.

But Baer couldn't name Seiler, because Seiler would turn around and name him for Esther's murder. And the whole repulsive house of hate would collapse around the king of *100 percent pure*.

I glanced at Kimberly. Broken. Damaged by drugs. Ruined by the greasy creep who pimped her out. Death might feel like relief.

"I'm purifying my town," Seiler walked toward the slaughter box. "The last Jew girl. We'll be all German again."

"But there's another one."

He stopped, turning toward me. "Another … what?"

"Another Jewish orphan." My fingers felt raw.

"That's not possible."

"Really? You're sure?"

The knife dangled in his hand. He held a different tool in his other hand, but I couldn't see it.

"I knew where to find Kimberly," I said.

He glanced at the barn door. It was partially open, a piece of blue sky above it.

"I saw the records, too." I wedged my thumb, and wondered if someone was coming. "Four Jewish orphans came to Leavenworth."

"Where did you see the records?"

"I can show you."

"You're lying." He lifted the knife.

"Baer didn't tell you about the fourth orphan?" I was losing my footing. "I know all about it. Which means killing this girl won't purify the blood. You'll need that last orphan."

"I don't believe you." He lifted the tool in his other hand. It was chrome, round. Shaped like something between a gun and a notary's stamp …*Oh. God.* It was a stun gun. To knock out animals. The circular blow to the head. No struggle. Then slit the throat and bleed them out. Animals, led to slaughter.

"I can find that other Jew." He squeezed the stun gun. *Ka-pow!* I jumped. "I'll get it out of that Jew-loving priest." He turned toward Kimberly. She'd lifted her face. Her eyes looked haunted. Like she knew. Even in her destroyed state, she knew something bad was about to happen.

"This …" The word floated from her dry mouth. "I know …"

"Oh my God!" I rasped.

Seiler spun toward me. I kicked the dirt floor, sending up a spray of soil. When his hands flew up, I kicked again and yanked my wrists out of the rope. He dropped the knife, clutching his left eye. My fingers ripped the leather off my neck. I lunged for him.

He shifted out of my grasp. His open right eye was tracking me, blinking and watering. He lifted the stun gun.

I darted right. He swung the stun gun. I felt my left arm go limp. My right flew roundhouse into his good eye.

He stumbled sideways. I shoved his body toward the slaughter box, reaching for that stun gun.

Kimberly cowered in the box. But when he hit the side, she pulled the chain against his head. Seiler lifted the stun gun. My right foot came up, connecting with his spine. He fell forward, and dropped the gun.

I grabbed it, and held it to his head.

"Hey, Al, everything alright?"

I looked back at the door. Somebody was standing outside.

"Al, you still in there?"

I pressed the round metal into his temple and whispered in his ear. "Say, I'm fine."

His face mouth twisted.

"Say it." My lips touched his red ear. "Or I'll kill you with one shot."

"I'm fine!" His voice sounded high.

"Now say, Don't come in."

"Don't come in!"

"You're almost done."

"—almost done!"

I stared at the door. Sunlight and shadow and dust motes shimmered in the air. Blood pumped my eardrums. I pressed the stun gun to Seiler's head. After a minute of silence, I tried to pat him down. Something was broken in my left hand. The pain was so sharp I felt nauseous. I pressed the round kill-shot into his temple.

"Unbuckle the holster," I said.

I had him place the .38 on the ground, then pushed it across the floor.

"Now it's checkout time." I slammed the stun gun into the side of his head, the same way he'd punched Kimberly. I hit him again. And a third time, until blood dribbled from his ear and his eyes fell shut. My heart banged inside my chest like a snare drum. Seiler didn't move.

I patted him down once more and found the key ring attached to his utility belt. I unlocked the cuffs on Kimberly, and secured them to Seiler's wrists. He didn't move.

I found the key to his wagon, stamped with the sheriff's gold star, and glanced at the open door. Kimberly was singing again, soft as a breeze. I told her to be quiet. Her pants were wet.

"Can you walk?" I asked.

She stared at me, blank as white paper.

I helped guide her out of the box, then leaned her against the small door that opened to the field of livestock, ready for slaughter.

"Don't move." I made sure she was steady.

I crept through the sunlight and shadows and stood beside the larger door. I could see the woman by the fire. The bald man with the neck tattoos stood on the other side of the clearing. He was talking to three skinheads. One glanced back at the barn. My heart kicked.

I looked at Kimberly. Two of us, and all of them.

No. One of us.

I put down the stun gun and picked up Seiler's revolver. It was a standard .38. But no gun shot like any other, and I hadn't fired a revolver in a long time. The white wagon was on the other side of the sprawling compound. We'd have to cross that clearing, stumbling like dead ducks in a shooting gallery. And who would ever find our bodies, here in the middle of nowhere.

Seiler said it. We had nobody.

I stepped away from the door. Blood was pumping so hard against my ears, I couldn't hear. But somebody yelled.

No, screamed. A woman.

I ran to the door. The air shook. I heard the staccato roar of gunfire.

"Get down!" I pulled Kimberly to the floor.

More gunfire. But maybe it was the blood inside my head. It pounded against my skull, so angry and loud and I couldn't think, couldn't move, couldn't decide what to—

The barn door shift. Dust swirled into the barn. I covered Kimberly's face and raised the gun. But I could see nothing. Dirt filled the air. The barn door blew open, banging against the wall. I crouched, blinking into the sand clouds, and got to the door.

Figures ran through the swirling dust. I heard more gunfire. The furious wind shoved me back. I leaned forward, blinking as the helicopter came into view. Three white letters on its side.

FBI.

Lifting my arms to block the sand pulsating from under the rotating blades, I saw the cargo door was open. Four feet off the ground, men in black jumped out and scattered across the compound, semi-automatics lifted.

SWAT.

I watched the black figures disappear into the trees. When the rotor blades slowed, I lowered my arms.

The pilot's door swung open. My heart jumped inside my chest.

"Harmon!" he yelled. "You alright?"

His name was a hoarse whisper in my gritty mouth.

CHAPTER FIFTY-EIGHT

KIMBERLY RODE IN the back bay on a stretcher. As the chopper went up, she was coming down down *down*. One of the SWAT guys trained in medical care hovered over her. The same guy who'd already splinted my left wrist.

I sat in the passenger seat.

Below, through the fish-eye windshield, I saw the sweep of autumn golds and burnt reds. Those fierce evergreens stood among them, refusing to change. Steadfast trees. Jack lifted his hand and pointed. We wore wired headsets. His voice sounded like it was inside my head.

"Look," he said into the mic. "Your car."

I leaned forward. The Ghost was coming down that dirt road. But it was on the bed of a tow truck. I pushed the button on my headset. "What about the girl?"

"Culliton has her. Wanted to tell you thanks. Family's been frantic. She's been missing for more than a year."

"And the guy at the fruit warehouse?"

Jack grinned. I couldn't read his eyes because of those aviator shades, but his smile was wide and white and rakish.

"Culliton's throwing you a party," Jack said. "The guy in the warehouse helps run a prostitution ring in town." Jack raised his index finger. "That's one." He raised another finger. "Two, you found the missing girls. And three—" another finger—"you just blew my case wide open."

"Your case." I pushed the button again. "You mean, the church fire?"

He looked away, banking the chopper to the left. He seemed to be following a road out of town. "You thought it was pot farming," he said. "Remember the star? It had six points. Two intersecting triangles. Star of David. I suspected neo-Nazis, and found them squatting up here on federal land. But it wasn't enough to bring them in."

"Wait." I held up my hand. "The elephant dung. How—"

"Animal Control." Jack shook his head. "He was trying to frame Mason. He lit that star the night before Annicka died. Seller's been around enough police work. He knows the accelerant would be traced, and come back to Mason."

"Or Preston Baer," I said.

"What?"

I shook my head. "I'll tell you later. But be prepared for the paperwork."

He looked over. "Harmon, you did it. You broke three cases." He wasn't grinning now. "Now you see why I brought you up here to consult?"

"Anybody could've run that soil."

"Yeah. But you needed to remember who you are."

He looked out the windshield again. I pressed the button on my mic.

But he beat me to it.

"You can't live without this work, Harmon. Neither can I. This is how we're built. How we function in a really screwed up world."

I looked away. Down below, the cars seemed like nothing more than Hot Wheels on a gray track.

"You've got obligations," Jack said. "I get that. But without this work, you'll die inside."

I watched the landscape change from single roads in dry mountain deserts to forested mountains to the wide open green valley of western Washington. The city of Snoqualmie laid out its emerald welcome mat. Rain was here. Wet and dreary and so beautiful.

I touched my mic. “What time is it?”

“Stop worrying,” he said. “You’ll make it, even if I have to *fly* you to Eleanor’s to get that mutt.”

CHAPTER FIFTY-NINE

WE ARRIVED IN time that day.

And the next day, even after Eleanor made me go to the doctor and get my arm X-rayed. Bones were broken. The doctor covered them with a cast that stretched from my elbow to the tip of my fingers. And itched.

The Ghost was towed from Leavenworth to Tacoma. Eleanor didn't say one word about the cost. Or the scratches to the classic car's white paint. She only said this: "We're all guinea pigs in the laboratory of God."

Camino Real.

On the third day, the FBI sent two agents to Eleanor's house. I knew them because they were with the Office of Professional Management. OPM was, unfortunately, a part of my life inside the Bureau. Because I bent rules.

Now they wanted to know about Jack's case. Had he revealed privileged information. Were we working together on the case, illegally? I answered every one of their questions with monosyllabic responses. Because that's how this interview would get written up on the FD302. *Just the facts, ma'am.* I left out all my wonderings. All my questions. All my hunches. I left out everything I felt, especially what I felt when that helicopter door opened and I saw Jack.

I hadn't seen him since we landed in Seattle that day.

The agents stayed three hours. When they seemed almost satisfied by my answers, I walked them across Eleanor's living room to the front door. I shook their hands with my good hand, and watched them drive away. It was a green Mustang that I was certain came through confiscation of some drug runner.

But even after the car was gone, I watched the street. I was thinking about all the interviews I'd done, how I'd typed them up and copied them into triplicate. Always trying to be the good girl, the best agent. I really did love that job.

Behind me, I heard the clicking sound on the wood floor. Madame's claws.

"Alright," I said. "We'll go for a walk—and don't give me any looks, I am not pining for my old job."

"You sure?"

I turned.

Jack stood in foyer. "Hi," he said.

Behind him, in the doorway to the kitchen, Eleanor waited.

"She's realized I'm not Stanley Kowalski," he said.

"Have you been listening this whole time?" I asked.

"Of course."

"Jack—."

"Harmon, you and the FBI are like oil and water. It never mixes right."

"Did you hear me say anything wrong?"

"*Wrong*? That depends."

I closed the door. "On what?"

"On whether the Bureau will give you credit for cracking this case after they fired—"

"I resigned."

"See?" He turned toward Eleanor. "That's exactly what I'm talking about."

"I know." Eleanor nodded. "But would you want to change

anything about her?"

"Change her?" he asked. "Why would I want to change her?"

Eleanor shifted her gaze, catching my eye. The rhinestones glinted. "If you'll excuse me, I need to see a man about a horse. Or maybe I'll need to see a horse about a man."

Jack looked confused.

Eleanor lifted her chin. "All you need to know is that sometimes—there's God—so quickly."

She left without asking, *Who said that*?

Madame laid down on the floor, sighing.

Jack looked at me. "Raleigh."

Raleigh? I tried to think of the last time Jack called me by my first name. But he kept talking.

"You remember that first day we went to Leavenworth?" he asked.

"Yes, I remember it."

"And if we hadn't gone running," he said, "another girl would be dead."

"And your case wouldn't be heading to federal court."

"True." He nodded. "But the run. You remember that run?"

Like it was this morning. Like I could still taste that autumn air. Touch the golden sunlight that poured over granite peaks. See Jack glancing over his shoulder, telling me to speed up. "Yeah, I remember that run."

"We started running back, because you said the race was round trip."

"The race *was* round-trip."

"But I started to ask you a question."

"And Madame barked."

"Right." He looked down at the dog. Then up at me. His eyes seemed as green as the steadfast trees. "Did you wonder what I was going to ask?"

Every second of every minute of every day. "Sometimes."

He reached out. Madame lifted her head, but she didn't growl as he took my hand. "This is what I wanted to ask you. Can we agree not to see other people?"

"What?"

"Just us." He pulled me close, his voice husky. "You and me, nobody else. Can we agree?"

"*That's* what you were going to ask me?"

"Yes."

I opened my mouth. But the words refused to come. We stood in silence, my heart beating too fast, the dog staring up at me. "Jack, I—"

"Okay." He dropped my hand, letting me go. "I thought maybe—"

"The notes."

"What?"

"The notes." My heart pounded. "Jack, I saw those notes, on the refrigerators? This woman, she can't live without you. She *waits* for you. Tell me. I want the truth. Who is *M?*"

"M?" He looked confused. "Are you talking about Mary?"

"Mary. That's her name."

"Yeah, Mary. My sister."

"Your … sister."

He ran a hand through his hair. "It's a long story, Harmon. Mary's got problems."

My heart hiccuped. "What kind of problems?"

"She's an addict, for one thing. And I tried to tell you about her."

"When?"

"Every single time I said we were two of a kind."

I thought my heart couldn't beat any harder. But it could. *It could. It could. It could.* His sister. He takes care of his sister.

He smiled. “You thought Mary was my girlfriend?”

My face flushed.

I looked away, ashamed. But he reached out again, pulling me into himself. I dropped my head, resting my face on his chest. His arms wrapped around me. I could hear his heart beating, beating so fast, beating like mine, beating a million miles a minute just so we could meet each other in the middle.

“So.” His voice felt hot on my ear. “Do we have a deal. Just you and me?”

“Yes,” I whispered. “It’s a deal.”

I closed my eyes and breathed in his scent. With every breath, something burned behind my eyelids. A moment later, I felt a tear, slowly tracing its way down my cheek. I tried to breathe in again, but there was no room left inside my chest.

All my life I’d run from love. Run fast, run hard, run away.

But now?

Now, I would run to it.

ACKNOLWEDGMENTS

Every Raleigh Harmon book creates another adventure in writing. She remains as surprising to me now as she did at the beginning of this series. Rest assured, many more Raleigh Harmon mysteries are coming—soon.

But since Raleigh constantly catches me off-guard, these books only get written with help from other people. Too many people to list. But here are a few.

My editor, Lora Doncea. She offers nothing but support, yet holds me accountable and laughs with me when life spins out of control. Her sister Pamela Nastase—genius reader, aficiando of backyard fowl—provides still more insights and encouragements. I can't thank these two sisters enough.

As for the vast puzzle of forensic geology, it comes together in these mysteries only because of the smart people who are doing the real-life work. All mistakes are mine. Two of the world's best forensic geologists have generously answered my many questions: William Schneck and Raymond Murray. If you'd like to learn more about forensic geology itself, check out Murray's marvelous book, *Evidence from the Earth.*

For police matters (again, all mistakes mine), I am indebted to former Navy SEAL and former Washington State Trooper, Joe Ulicny. This wonderful guy has been helping me since *The Rivers Run Dry.* Thank you, Joe.

And readers, thank you for the wonderful emails and notes. I adore hearing from you, please don't stop writing. Thank you for reading. Thank you for appreciating books. And thank you for being YOU.

Last but never least, my family. They keep me in check—and stitches. Three amazing, amusing, and wonderful men populate my immediate universe: My sons, Daniel and Nico, and my husband, Joe. Thank you for all the times you pranked me while I stressed about deadlines. Thank you for dealing so generously with my absent-mindedness. And thank you for eating pizza whenever I fell behind schedule. For all that, I will never name a villain after you. Yes, that's right. I love you *that* much.

—Sibella

Sign up for Sibella's newsletter to learn about upcoming Raleigh Harmon releases and other books. You'll also receive a **free** Raleigh Harmon short story, "Hers." Go to www.sibellawrites.
com.

Raleigh Harmon's career as an FBI agent began in *The Stones Cry Out*, which is available.

There's also a young adult mystery series featuring Raleigh Harmon as teenager, solving crime and trying to survive high school. In these books, her dad is still alive—but her mom's still crazy.

Stone and Spark

Stone and Snow

Stone and Sunset

ABOUT THE AUTHOR

Sibella Giorello is the fourth generation of her family to grow up in Alaska. After riding a motorcycle across the country, she wrote feature stories for the *Richmond Times-Dispatch*. Her stories won state and national awards, including two nominations for the Pulitzer Prize. She now lives in Washington state with her husband, sons, a large dog, a sweet parakeet, and a Russian tortoise that could've worked for the KGB.

Made in the USA
San Bernardino, CA
14 October 2016